DAWN TO DUSK

Dawn to Dusk

Folk Tales from Benin

IRO EWEKA

FRANK CASS
LONDON • PORTLAND, OR

First Published in 1998 in Great Britain by
FRANK CASS PUBLISHERS
2 Park Square, Milton Park,
Abingdon, Oxon, OX14 4RN

and in the United States of America by
FRANK CASS PUBLISHERS
270 Madison Ave,
New York NY 10016

Transferred to Digital Printing 2005

Website http://www.frankcass.com

British Library Cataloguing in Publication Data

Eweka, Iro
Dawn to dusk: folk tales from Benin
1. Tales – Benin   2. Bini (African people)
I. Title
398.2'096683

ISBN 0-7146-4811-6 (cloth)
ISBN 0-7146-4362-9 (paper)

Library of Congress Cataloging-in-Publication Data

Eweka, Iro.
Dawn to dusk: folk tales from Benin / Iro Eweka.
p.   cm.
Includes bibliographical references and index.
ISBN 0-7146-4811-6 (cloth). – ISBN 0-7146-4362-9 (pbk.)
1. Tales–Benin. 2. Folklore–Benin. 3. Bini (African people)–
Folklore.   I. Title.
GR351.4.E9   1998
398.2'096683–dc21   97-44834

Typeset by Regent Typesetting, London

Cover photograph: Reproduced with the kind
permission of cathy Midwinter/Development
Education Project, Manchester

Contents

PART TWO

Dedicated to my precious four

Eghe Ruth, Arit Oku, Atu and Tracy

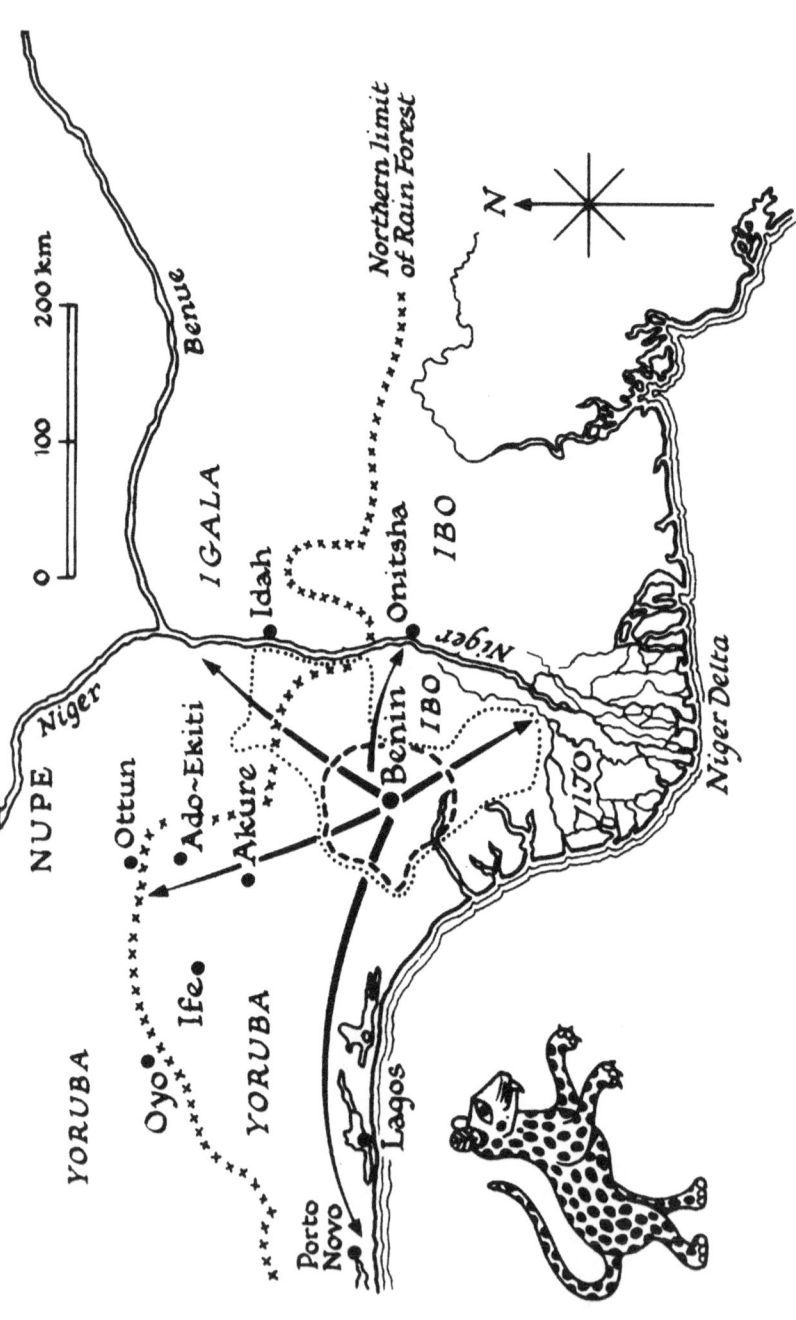

Map reproduced from Cathy Midwinter, *Benin: An African Kingdom*, WWF UK, 1994, with permission from WWF UK and Peter McClure.

Foreword

Myth, though essentially a coding of basic ideas which may
justify existing social systems, is also a lasting record of the
origin and development of traditional custom and belief.

(Lyall Watson, *The Nature of Things*, 1991, p. 75.)

THE EXHIBITION of African art held at the Royal Academy
in 1995 was a reminder of the unique cultural wealth of the
Èdó people as manifested in the wonderful pieces fashioned in
bronze, ivory and wood. No less striking, though less familiar to
outsiders, is the story of a people that has been passed through
the generations by those whose office or talent it was to bring
the past to life, in the form of narrated chronicle or folk tale, for
the instruction and entertainment of an audience.

With the Èdó, as with all peoples, the boundary between
history and myth was never sharply defined. How important a
part oral tradition plays in the understanding of Èdó (or Benin,
as it is more commonly known) history became evident to me
when I embarked on a study of that history with the late Dr R.
E. Bradbury some forty years ago. Benin tradition was then
enshrined in the works of Chief Jacob Egharevba, works justly
renowned for their thoroughness and authority. Most of Chief
Egharevba's writing,[1] notably his *A Short History of Benin*, is
concerned with the record of history; only very occasionally, as
in *Some Stories of Ancient Benin* and *The Murder of Imaguero*,
did he put into print any of the great store of Èdó folk tales.
Some folk tales had earlier been published by N. W. Thomas, a

---

[1] Chief Jacob Egharevba, *A Short History of Benin* (1936), *Some Stories of Ancient Benin* (1938), *The Murder of Imaguero* (1940).

colonial official, in an article entitled 'Thirty-two folk tales of the Ẹ̀dó-speaking peoples of Nigeria'.[2] More recently, Joseph Sidahome made a significant contribution to preserving this vital part of the Ẹ̀dó cultural heritage with *Stories of the Benin Empire*[3] which, despite its title, draws its material exclusively from the author's native province of Esan (Ishan). Since then silence has fallen.

Memory in a society is as fragile a faculty as it is with an individual: against the relentless erosion of time, only a written record or diligent cultivation will prevail. In Benin the impact of the outside world during the twentieth century has inevitably fractured many of the links which formerly ensured the transmission of its traditions, and the passing of generations makes it ever more difficult to restore them. It is therefore of the utmost importance to establish a permanent record of what remains while authentic voices are still to be heard.

The court of the Ọba, the dynastic ruler of Benin, has always been a focus of historical and cultural record. Among its officials were those specifically charged with the duty of preserving that record; these were the priests of the royal ancestors who, as part of their ceremonial function, would recite the chronology of rulers. Also within the palace there existed a complex structure of chiefs and retainers, organised into associations with specific household and state functions; like the monarchy itself, each group cherished its ancient traditions. In moments of relaxation, entertainers amused and instructed the court with songs and tales, many of which evoked the past of the ruler and his people. I use the past tense to describe these features of the Ọba's court because, in addition to feeling the impact of alien influences with the rest of Ẹ̀dó society, its very existence was called into question when the British exiled Ọba Ovọnramwẹn in 1897. Although both monarcy and court reappeared with the installation of Ovọnramwẹn's son as Ẹ́wẹ́ká II in 1914, they never regained their former power and glory,

---

[2] N. W. Thomas, 'Thirty-two tales of the Ẹ̀dó-speaking peoples of Nigeria', Folklore, vol. 31, pp. 210–30.

[3] Joseph Sidahome, *Stories of Benin Empire* (Oxford: Oxford University Press, 1964).

either during British colonial rule or under the independent Republic of Nigeria.

Dr Iro Eweka belongs to the last generation of the Èdó royal family to have spent its childhood among members of the court formed by and familiar with the traditional culture. As he explains in his Preface, along with other children of the royal family, he was regularly entertained by relatives and retainers, whose recital of the old folk tales made a profound and lasting impression upon his imagination. A psychologist, a poet and an Èdó patriot, Dr Eweka has been inspired to record the stories he heard in his youth in the conviction that they merit preservation among the universal store of folk memory. Even the most casual reader will be struck by the occurrence of so many themes common to all human myth. The author also cherishes the hope that, in preserving these tales and proverbs, he will sow seeds that may awaken in future generations of his people a renewed pride in the culture of their homeland. Others will assuredly be charmed by the lively invention and language of these narratives, with their colourful cast of gods, humans, animals (especially the inimitable Tortoise) and denizens of the vegetable kingdom. In the proverbs they will find, along with universal values and attitudes, numerous shrewd insights into the particular mentality of the Èdó people. By rescuing from oblivion this chronicle of a passage from dawn to dusk, Dr Eweka has ensured that night does not irrevocably fall upon the world it portrays.

Professor Alan Ryder
Bristol 1996

Preface

Now do not dream
Good patient friend
That you have seen
This search's end

That's beyond me
That's out ahead!
By you

To be continued . . .

(Basil Davidson, Africa Revisited, 1992.)

MANY YEARS AGO, when I was a post-doctoral researcher in the USA, I met an American gentleman in Washington, DC. Probably in his mid-fifties, he was a professor at the Catholic University of America, and he was kind and generous and extremely jovial. He invited me to his office in the city where we talked for several hours and where I discovered that, in addition to being a university professor, he was also a reputable publisher. At the end of our talk he suggested that I should write my own personal history of Benin.

Fifteen years have passed since I accepted that challenge, and *Dawn to Dusk* is my belated response to it. I make no apology for the delay, however. For, as an *Èdó* proverb would have it, *Eno ke'dinran, ma gia deghe'no k'odo* (That which is near prevents one from seeing that which is further away).

Dawn to Dusk is a collection of *Èdó* folk tales. In fact, when I first began to write it, I thought it would be called 'Stories My Elders Told Me'. The tales in it were all told me either by my mother or my older brothers or by professional story-tellers who were often brought home to entertain my family. I have never in my whole life been more fascinated by anything than by these stories. I have written them here just as I remember them, without any adornment. They belong to what is generally called 'oral history'. But for me, they are the foundation of Èdó culture and tradition, which I prefer to call the *real* history of my people.

The first story in the book tells of how the world was created. To some it may sound childish, to others it may seem bizarre, while to yet others it may appear mere fantasy. But to me, it is the true story of how ancient Èdó conceived of the world and how they attempted both to explain the origin of human existence on earth and to interpret their environment.

In a revealing passage, Immanuel Velikovsky wrote that the human being 'does not know what life is or how it came to be and whether it originated from inorganic matter'.[1] That situation is not peculiar to Èdó people. Indeed, it is fascinating that there is a great deal common to the Èdó version of creation narrated in this book and other versions to be found in other cultures around the globe.

In his controversial book, Velikovsky reported numerous examples of far-flung cultural traditions in which the world was created out of a massive flood. Indeed the story of Noah's flood is repeated with numerous variations all over the world and the Èdó version is just one of many. Caius Julius Solinus, according to Velikovsky, wrote that 'following the deluge which is reported to have occurred in the days of Ogyges, a heavy night spread over the globe'. It was out of that 'night' that the creator-king of this book arose to create the world.

But no less universal is the story of the sky (the *Iso* in this book) which, at one time, was so low that human hands could touch it. From China to Brazil, from Australia to Canada, from East to West and North and South, the low sky features in stories about the earliest earth. As Velikovsky puts it,

> Because the same elements can be recognised in very different settings, we can affirm that there was no

[1] Immanuel Velikovsky, *Worlds in Collision* (Sphere Books, 1950).

borrowing from one people by another. A common experience created the stories, so dissimilar at first, but so much alike on second thought.

In other words, although there are common elements in the various stories, they are all of independent origin. Thus the reductionist attitude of the academic historian is a handicap to the understanding of a people's history. Velikovsky wrote – and I couldn't agree more,

> The scholars who dedicate their efforts to gathering and investigating the folklore of peoples are constantly aware that folk tales require interpretation, for, in their opinion, these tales are not innocent and unambiguous products of the imagination, but veil some inner and more significant meaning.

That 'inner and more significant meaning' is the 'meaning of life' in each culture.

Comparisons, they say, are odious even though historians frequently indulge in them in their frenetic search for 'points of reference'. They feel more comfortable when they are able to put a finger on some resemblance, however flimsy it may be. Thus, according to Carsun Chang, Tang Chun-I, Mou Tsung-San and Hsu Fo-Kuan in 'A Neo-Confucian Manifesto', 'Western civilization was moulded by rationalistic Hellenism, legalistic Hebraism, and jurisprudential Romanticism'.[2] In other words, without Hellenism, Hebraism and Romanticism, there can be nothing original in Western civilisation. Such reductionism is unfortunate, especially when it is applied in the process of comparing the recorded history of Benin with that, say, of the British. It is usually claimed that the 'younger' or 'newer' culture has 'borrowed' this, that and the other from an 'older' culture. If that were true, then British culture would owe part at least of its origins to Èdó culture, particularly in those areas in which there happen to be similarities and resemblances in their folk

---

[2] 'A Neo-Confucian Manifesto', in Jaroslav Pelikan (ed.), *The World Treasury of Modern Religious Thought* (Toronto: Little, Brown, 1990), p. 368.

tales. For Èdó culture, regardless of claims to racial or cultural superiority, is 'older' than its British counterpart.

In 1485, when the English were fighting at Bosworth Field, an Èdó king was establishing diplomatic and trading relationships with Portugal. That was the year in which Joao Affonso d'Aveiro first made contact with the Benin kingdom which, in the Portuguese's estimation, compared quite favourably with his own in terms of 'civilisation'. By that date, the Èdó king, Ozolua, had already extended the boundaries of the Èdó kingdom by one of the greatest margins in the history of Benin. Further back in time, in 1300, when Mansa Kankan Musa reigned in what is now known as West Africa, the Èdó king and people were already well known, feared and respected as far away as the present Mali. It is possible that Benin was one of those 'great forest kingdoms' about which Ibn Batuta 'heard' during his travels in 1325.[3]

Dawn to Dusk attempts to reveal the cultural background to all of that distant past. It has not been written to exalt or condemn, to praise or dispraise, to claim superiority or inferiority. Its main aim is to show the beginnings of a culture to which one should be proud to belong. Unfortunately – and this is the part that hurts most of all – when the light went out over the kingdom in 1897, its language, traditions and everything else of cultural significance seemed to have gone up in the smoke of the fire that burned down the city. And so today the language is all but dead, the traditions are all but disowned. To find a name for their children, Èdó parents now turn to the British; to find the way to their families' doors, Èdó youths now turn to the Americans; to decide what is the best thing to wear, the Èdó now turn to the French. They have abandoned what were once their guiding principles in life in pursuit of what they can neither get nor keep. It is, as Ovonramwen lamented on his way to exile in 1897, 'merciless and wicked' to abandon a culture so.

Whether such abandonment is the result of wickedness or stupidity is a moot point. More importantly, whether or not anything can be retrieved and whether or not any attempt

[3] Ibn Batuta was an Arab traveller who wrote about his travels in North and West Africa in 1325.

should be made to do so are questions indirectly posed in *Dawn to Dusk*.

The book is full of *Èdó* words, spelt in the most accurate way, in the faint hope that their appearance in this form will help to rekindle some interest in the language. Part Two contains a selection of old *Èdó* proverbs which point to the origins of much of the culture, traditions and customs that have now all but vanished. The serial numbering of the proverbs in Part Two does not correspond to the original numbering as arranged by the compilers named below. In making the present selection, I have arranged the proverbs so as to illustrate specific themes in *Èdó* life. The numbering goes through from 1 to 136 for the convenience of the reader.

Perhaps the biggest single advantage of what we call 'oral history' is its lack of dates. That makes it easier for the stories to be told fluently without the encumbrance of 'accuracy'. Dating events – history is nothing but a record, oral or written, of events – is detrimental to the integrity of the stories and exposes the story to unanswerable questions and debates, out of which no one emerges the wiser. That, in part at least, is why no one has been able to fault Immanuel Velikosky in his claim that the Oedipus of ancient Greek legend is the same person as Akhnaton of ancient Egyptian legend.

In any case, the dating system employed by European historians is only one of many such systems employed through-out the world and is in no way superior or more accurate than any of the others. And the Foreword in this book may help to tempt into some semblance of humility those who claim that Benin has an 'eight-hundred-year history', lasting 'from its development in the eleventh and twelfth centuries', etc., etc., etc. Perhaps they will learn to say that the little they know about Benin dates back 800 years and to leave matters at that. It is particularly important that they realise that the history which informs them about Benin has been written strictly by the victors of the conflict of February 1897.

Here, however, I must pause and pay a highly deserved tribute to the young men who undertook the difficult task of collecting the proverbs from which those in this book have been selected. They collected over 500 of these sayings in 1985–6 and my promise to them was that their magnificent effort would be rewarded in print. I hope they have not waited in vain and my thanks are due to them. They are S. Omo Ogbebo(r), J. U. Ekhato(r), A. O. Uwagie-Ẹro, J. N. Tubonimi, B. C. Nwosu, D. E. Ogunmola and E. U. Aihevba. They were all members of the Intellect Society, based at the College of Education, Iya-Ẹro, Benin City, where they were all employees. It is rather sad, on reflection, that all their first names have been drawn from foreign (mostly British) sources. Thus where there is an initial 'J', it stands for 'John', followed, only sometimes, by the initial which has been drawn from an Ẹ̀dó source. For who, in his right mind, wants to be called 'Emmanuel' if his culture has given him the name 'Idemudia'? The latter has a meaning in the Ẹ̀dó language which the former does not possess.

Finally, my heart-felt gratitude goes to the well-known and well-beloved expert on Ẹ̀dó History, Professor Alan Ryder who, except for my daughter, Eghenayarhiorhe-orowie, was my inspiration in the writing of this book through his enthusiasm and intellectual guidance. Whatever fault may be in it is entirely and exclusively mine.

Iro Eweka
Bristol, 1996

PART ONE

1

Dawn

The highest intellects, like the tops of mountains are the first to catch and to reflect the dawn.

(Lord Macaulay, Sir James Mackintosh, July 1875)

LONG AGO, before *Time* began and when neither *Name* nor *Counting* was known, a figure lay prone on the surface of still waters. Eyes shut, there was silence all around.

The figure lay perfectly still, barely breathing, on the surface of the still waters. There was no telling when or how the figure came to be where it was or for how long it had floated face-up. It was the figure of a *Man*. In him were no desires because he was the *Desire*. In him were no hopes, since he was the *Hope*. There were no names, for he was *Naming*. And, since he was the *Arrival*, he had arrived from nowhere.

Then, from nowhere a voice opened his hearing. The voice was everywhere, like the waters. The voice and the waters were one – inseparable. And the voice was neither soft nor hard, loud nor quiet. It was all-embracing, a wilful, commanding pleader.

'Open your eyes,' said the voice.

His eyes snapped open. He did not move a muscle. The waters remained still and unruffled. There was neither urgency nor delay in the eye-opening. There was no rush but neither was there a lingering. Events, if any, occurred only as and when they must – mere acts of compulsive *Will*. With no *before* or *after* with which to reckon, events were not events until they occurred; and they occurred only because they wanted to do so.

The voice was heard externally only that once. Then it took abode inside the man and the lone hearer became the heard.

'It is dawn,' said the voice, and, at his own will, the man rose slowly to a sitting position. He looked one way and then another. Nothing was visible but a simple stillness on the silvery surface of the still waters. It was neither dark nor light – just a simple nothingness that heralded portents without rousing anxiety.

He looked down and saw floating beside him, a whip. He reached for it and picked it up. It was a long, slender white stick, tapering to a rope at one end to which was knotted in place the red tail feather of an absent parrot. He held the whip in one hand and with the other hand he picked up the snail shell that floated beside him on the other side. He turned the shell mouth-down and a chain of fine, brown grains drained out of it on to the surface of the still waters. Each grain in the chain was a complete universe. And each universe was a complete man – the man himself. The man and the universe were faithful reflections of each other. But as the grains fell on to the still surface of the waters, the waters receded and a dry, solid surface appeared. It was earth, as it was later to be named. As the waters withdrew in all directions at once, more solid surface emerged and spread out all around him. Slowly and deliberately, he rose to his feet.

The waters in the distance began to rise, too, rising into the soft, grey haze that hung within arm's length above his head. He swayed a little, the solid earth firm beneath his feet and the fluffy haze hovering over him. He raised the whip and struck the dry earth with the rope-ended stick. Not a word was spoken because words had not yet been born. The action was the word and the word was the instant fulfilment of the destined response. As the rope-ended stick struck, a point appeared in the distance beyond the haze. It spanned itself out from a yellowish circular core and stood still, glowing. From it, flooding everywhere, issued the heat of light. It lifted the pervasive gloom that had heralded the causeless portents. And, in the new heat of light, he looked with unspoken approval all about him. The risen waters had now settled into a solid mass of eternal whiteness. The solid brown hardness beneath his feet remained bare. Carrying the whip in one hand and the snail shell in the other, he surveyed the scene with contentment. Ahead was the round-faced glow and behind, had he looked over his shoulder, lay a long shadow keeping him company and stretching darkly away into the distance.

He took his first step, walking in a slow, deliberate measure towards the source of the heat of light. He stopped, turned and walked back, slowly and deliberately, following rather than being followed by his long dark shadow. He stopped again and changed direction. He walked one way and then back the opposite way. Beneath him the earth remained solid and as naked as a new-born baby. The four-sided movement made it all square. Thenceforward, said the voice, there would be no movement except forward, backward and to one side and then the other. With this birth of movement was *Counting* first born. And with the birth of counting, *Time* began. And with the birth of *Time* came the birth of *Knowing*.

He raised the whip and struck the hard, bare surface that supported him. Vegetation sprang up all around him. Trees and glades and shrubs and grass and herbs of all and every description appeared instantly. The round-faced glow began to turn red-hot. Surrounded by blooming vegetation, the only clearing was where he stood.

Unhurried, deliberate, contented, he surveyed the fresh vegetation. But again he raised the whip and struck. The jungle sprang to life with wild and varied noises and cries. Four-footed inhabitants and crawlers and winged lives hailed his presence. As he looked with contentment, the new inhabitants approached him gleefully.

'My name is *Ubidon*,' proudly announced the leopard, graceful, spotless, brave and agile. The red eyes smiling, the leopard continued, 'I'm the younger sibling of the fearsome tiger. I salute you, my king.'

He nodded acceptance as the leopard danced away into the shades.

'I am *Erhue*,' claimed the deer, hopping forward in nervous agitation. 'I am notoriously paranoid, my lord king and I feed nervously on evergreens wherever I can find them. That's the way you made me, my creator-king.' On that last note, the deer leapt away into the undergrowth.

3

'I am *Ivbiekpo*, my loving creator-king,' intoned the deadly adder. Without hands or feet, the new speaker crawled forward on its belly. 'I am the most poisonous snake around. I swallow what I can find and kill only when carelessly trampled upon. I worship you, my creator-king.'

He nodded and the adder crawled silently away.

'My name is *Ahua*, your mighty majesty,' announced the hawk. With powerful talons and glossy wings, neatly folded backwards, the speaker's strong sharp beak touched the earth as he paid his homage. 'I feed on weaker birds, just as your majesty has ordered my nature to be. I respond to my nature as destined.' The hawk soared up into the hazy firmament.

And so it went on until all the inhabitants of the newly created jungle had paid homage to their creator-king, in the same manner in which the plants had earlier performed their own self-naming introductions. Every tree and every shrub and every grass had named itself and bowed to the creator-king and had turned away to the business that defined its own specific nature. Both the animals and the plants spoke the same language. By the end of the animals' introductions, the heat-of-light glow had shifted position higher above and stood at the zenith from where all shadows were ordered to stay directly beneath those who had cast them.

The creator-king struck the earth again with his whip and all at once row upon row of impressive dwellings sprang up in the clearing where he had been standing. A fresh burst of sounds arose all around him. They came from the voices which were later to be recognised as *human*; but the spoken language remained that previously heard from the other created beings, animate as well as inanimate.

'I am *Okpia*,' announced the first voice, deep, resonant and firm. Stepping forward and kneeling before the creator-king, the voice continued, 'As a *Man*, I worship you, my lord, with the strength of my body and my soul. I am yours to command.'

He stepped aside and another creature, resembling the man but gentler in looks, less bold in carriage, approached the king.

'I am *Okhuo*,' it said in a prayerful manner, 'and as a

Woman, all my loyalty to your majesty is through my man, my husband.' She rose from her knees and stepped aside.

A third figure appeared, diminutive although bearing all the features of the first two. There was trust but no sign of fear in the demeanour.

'I am *Omo*, my friend, and as a *Child*, I worship you with my joyous innocence.' The figure moved away to join the previous two.

The entire clearing, filled with dwellings and swarming with active, busy life, warmed the heart of the creator-king. At the far end from where he stood, there was the largest dwelling of all. It spanned the entire width of the clearing and was an enormous, awe-inspiring abode, totally unlike the others either in shape or in dimensions. From it and all around it swarmed a hive of men and women, all dutifully and happily awaiting an arrival. The creator-king walked slowly and deliberately towards the large dwelling, stick in one hand and the empty snail shell in the other. Adoring crowds parted to let him through. He felt no doubt that he was honoured. Head held high and gaze fixed on the distant yet immediate horizon, he walked straight into the pre-ordained large dwelling for a pre-ordained final welcome.

The cry of 'Welcome home, Lord from the Sky' greeted him from all sides. He looked this way and that and nodded his acknowledgement. His eyes surveyed his domain, not from the outside as he had done hitherto, but from within.

'So,' he reflected, 'I am the Lord from the Sky. The Lord of all this creation. My orders are obeyed by all. I am ruler of Man, Woman, Beasts and Plants.' Pausing in his reflection but still surveying his abode with keen eyes and keen interest, he selected a few from among the crowd and called them forth to stand beside him. They ranged themselves with eagerness of body and soul beside him, peacefully awaiting whatever would come next. He thoughtfully but unhurriedly assigned to each a specific duty to be performed daily in connection with his own person. Some to dress him; some to work in the kitchen; some to do this and others to do that. The personal duties assigned, he turned to another select group and assigned to them specific duties in connection with the entire realm.

'I am the *centre* around which all revolve,' he thought aloud, 'and all will be well with my created world only when all is well with my own person and being. I am the *beginning* as well as the *end*. This is the *Dawn* and I am the first to witness it.' Then he gave an order that a mound of earth be erected in the court-yard of his dwelling. It was to be washed in white and there was to be no roof over it. No sooner was the order issued than it was executed. There were no questions asked because none needed to be asked. He watched the work being done and when it was completed, he examined it and signified his satisfaction. Then at a slow, deliberate pace, he approached the earth-mound reverentially, his attendants marching in slow motion behind him. He knelt beside the mound with all his attendants follow-ing his lead and ceremoniously planted the handle of his whip on the summit of the mound. At the base of the whip, he care-fully placed the empty snail shell, mouth down.

He rose, turned solemnly to the gathered crowd and announced, 'This is the shrine of *Osa*, the Almighty King in the Sky. With this whip, the Mighty *Òsánóbuá* ordered the world to be created. With it *Òsánóbuá* girds the created world into a single unit in which everyone and everything has a creative contribution to make for the general and overall good of all the inhabitants of this world. See to it,' he ordered, 'that no dirt and nothing black comes near this shrine. There shall be no blood sacrifice offered at this shrine.' Then, turning to an aged-looking man in the crowd, he beckoned him to step forward.

'I appoint you the keeper of this shrine,' said the creator-king, 'and henceforth you will be clad in pure white and you shall touch nothing that is black or dirty.'

The aged-looking man knelt at the foot of the creator-king and touched the earth with his forehead as a wordless sign of his acceptance of his charge. And to this day, no blood sacrifice is offered at the shrine of the Almighty who is recognised as too great to be appeased by the blood of what the Almighty has caused to be created. Any live sacrificial offering is presented whole at the shrine and then released to roam free. And the main gift offerings at the shrine are whitewashed unbroken coconuts and white kola-nuts, also unbroken. But occasionally, a live, white-feathered chicken is offered without being slaughtered. Such sacrificial offerings are meant to be taken away by any poor and hungry passers-by as Òsánóbuá's gift to them.

The glowing body up in the air, now named *Sun*, had slowly moved from its zenith towards its nadir, at the point where heaven and earth met and conjoined, when the creator-king returned with his attendants to his palace. He mounted his throne and decreed that the risen waters, now solidly hanging in the air within reach of everyone, were to be the single source of food.

'Just reach above your head,' the king ordered, 'and cut a slice from it to feed yourselves and your families. It is free,' said the king, 'but on no condition should it be wasted. Never cut more than you can eat.'

As the creator-king concluded his injunctions, the aged-looking priest of the new shrine inched his way towards the throne. He knelt before the king and touched the bare earth with his forehead in humble homage. Then, raising his eyes until they met those of the king, he said, 'Your Majesty, I humbly wish to make an annoucement.'

'Yes, God's priest,' replied the king. 'Speak freely.'

The priest slowly and purposefully turned round, careful not to turn his back to the king but to position himself so that the throne was on his right-hand side. Then, surveying the crowd from one corner to the other and back again, he raised his quavering voice and said, 'Hear me, all you inhabitants of this great realm. Our King-from-on-High, sitting before you in his mighty throne, is the earthly representative of our King-on-High, our Òsánóbuá whose mantle he bears and whose priest his majesty has made me. When you hear his majesty's voice, it is the voice of Òsánóbuá you hear. And when you appear before him, it is before Òsánóbuá you appear. His majesty has been divinely ordained to rule over us. All the respect, the honour, the reverence due to Òsánóbuá are due to him. And, henceforth, it must be said that when we see one another, we automatically see our king; and when we see our king, we automatically see Òsánóbuá. Forget what I have said at your own peril.'

There was a general sign of satisfaction with the priest's announcement.

After that, the sun rolled out of sight but not before first instructing his dutiful paramour, the *Moon*, to take charge of the universal supply of light without heat. To assist the moon in that task, it was granted the services of an unspecified number of *Stars*. So that, while the sun ruled by day, the night was to be ruled by the moon, assisted, especially when exhausted, as all the females of the created world must be at one time or another, by the brood of stars.

With all the *naming* completed and everyone duly assigned to their rightful places and duties, the creation of the world came to a fitting close.

2

Later Arrivals

*Before seeking Solutions, let us first know
that there are Problems.*

SINCE THE FIRST DAWN, when the world came into
being, till this day, there have been new arrivals. In Èdó they
are called Emọ, which, in a foreign tongue, means children.
Every birth is a re-enactment of that First Day and the birth of
every baby is a new Dawn. And each birth is a confirmation
that the King-on-High, known throughout the Èdó kingdom as
Òsánóbuá, has never abandoned the world below.

But, unlike the mass-creation of the First Day, every person is
now created individually by Òsánóbuá alone and sent down
into the world in total conformity with the greetings which the
child (Ọmọ) gave to the creator-king at the very beginning,
namely: 'I am Ọmọ, my friend, and as a child, I worship you
with my joyous innocence.'

To create a new human being, Òsánóbuá takes a piece of soft
clay and moulds it into the shape that has endured in his
own mind. The moulding is done with tender loving care and
nothing from the clay is ever wasted. No flaw ever exists in the
finished product: everything is perfect according to its eternal
design. It is only when the living creature arrives on earth that
human beings begin to imagine imperfections which they then
falsely ascribe to Òsánóbuá. The problem, of course, is that
human beings do not know what Òsánóbuá knows. They do
not know, for example, that in the realm where Òsánóbuá
dwells, nothing is good or bad but simply *is*, in accordance with
Òsánóbuá's conception of it. Only the King-*from*-on-High is

capable of knowing that, in addition to there being neither good nor evil in Òsánóbuá's dwelling-place-on-high, nothing there is beautiful or ugly, straight or crooked, tall or short, big or small. In short, where Òsánóbuá lives, whatever *is*, is right. But although the king is capable of knowing the truth, the king is, none the less, also burdened with the mantle of *Man* and is, therefore, unable to see as clearly or as deeply as Òsánóbuá.

During the process of creation, Òsánóbuá conceives a form, moulds that form in clay, its eventual function being allowed to precede its actual structure. Two identical forms are made. And when the moulding is completed, Òsánóbuá breathes into the nostrils of one of the two and it immediately comes to life. The duplicate, meanwhile, remains lifeless.

The form having come to life, Òsánóbuá speaks to it, saying, 'Now you are almost ready to descend into the world below. Whom would you choose for a father down there?'

The new life-form thinks carefully, makes a deliberate choice of an earthly father and announces the choice.

'So be it,' Òsánóbuá says, and then asks the same question about who the earthly mother is to be.

'So be it,' Òsánóbuá says again to the answer given.

Then Òsánóbuá asks what will be the circumstances of the actual birth on earth. More questions are then asked about how the new creature will live, what it will do, how it will die and return to its creator. Everything that is to happen when the creature arrives on earth is carefully chosen before hand. And to every choice named, Òsánóbuá says 'So be it'. Finally, the creator places into the head of the new life-form its twin, which then automatically comes to life. The two become one although only one of them, the first to receive life directly from the creator, will be visible on earth where the unseen companion acts solely as witness to its companion's destiny.

Carrying its companion in its head, the new life-form takes leave of its creator and descends into the world through the agencies of the parents it has chosen. Not a single one of the choices to which Òsánóbuá has said 'So be it' can ever be altered in the world, regardless of what attempts may later be made to change the course of its life. The silent partner ensures that the choices made before birth are kept; and, on the day of reckoning, when the man or woman or child dies on earth and returns to his or her creator to render account, it is the silent partner who bears witness. It is then – and never before – that the creator amends the creature. However, the amendment is never carried out on the returnee but on the former, silent partner who now prepares to return to the world in reincarnation. The birth and rebirth must be repeated fourteen times altogether, spanning an unspecifiable number of generations within the same family, the male always reincarnating as male, while the female always reincarnates as female. A man never reincarnates as a woman because his silent partner was a man. Nor can a woman reincarnate as a man since her silent partner was also a woman. For can a human being reincarnate as a plant or an animal since the silent partner of the human being is also a human being and neither a plant nor an animal?

The creator-king whose royal acquaintance we made in Chapter 1 had a favourite story which he enjoyed telling his audiences. He always said, 'If Òsánóbuá ever felt like laughing, the cause of the laughter would be that any man or woman, who had already told Òsánóbuá before birth what she/he would become on earth, should, on arrival in the world, be forced to be something different.' From that story, the audience always arrived at the same conclusion, namely: 'If Òsánóbuá has agreed that one should be king on earth, nothing and nobody can prevent it.' That suited and pleased the king enormously. It meant that his subjects understood the value and implications of divine kingship

No worse curse can afflict an Èdó woman than the curse of childlessness. Every woman desires to be a mother (regardless of the destiny she has chosen for herself before coming into the world to be born). But only those women who, at their creation, tell Òsánóbuá that they will be mothers on earth can be mothers.

In choosing a mother, therefore, the would-be child in the world carefully scans from on-high the state of affairs on earth to see who, among the women, deserves to be its mother. A child cannot be willed into the world by its parents. It is not the

11

parents who choose a child but the child who chooses its parents. And the child *owns* its parents, not the other way around. And parents are enjoined to be *thankful* to their children for having been chosen. The grateful parents are mere guardians who act out their parenthood strictly in accordance with their own chosen destinies.

Having been born as pre-ordained, children born to the same mother are closer to one another in affection than those only born to the same father. The reason for this, as the creator-king always explained to his subjects, is that children out of the same womb have all chosen the same mother while those born of the same father chose different mothers. The former, then, have more in common with one another than with the latter. A child without a same-mother sibling is one of the saddest and lone-liest creatures on earth. For, whereas a same-mother sibling will insist on following one and supporting one whatever one does and wherever one goes, a mere same-father sibling will say, 'Wait until I am ready'. Such waiting may make the difference between life and death. None the less, the child without a same-mother sibling receives great care and attention from its father and everyone else as sympathy for its lonely plight. Thus, even its life is not without compensation. After all, it is not for nothing that such a child has chosen at its creation not to have a same-mother sibling on earth. On the the other hand, the mother of an only child is the most insecure creature on earth and must thereby know the real meaning of filial love and the need for intense care of an only child.

The creator-king always told his followers that it is the human being alone who makes the choice of what becomes of him or her in the world. His Majesty always explained that human beings are responsible for what they do and for what-ever happens to them. Consequently, nothing should ever be considered by his subjects to have happened by chance. The king, then, spared no pain in establishing rules for the achieve-ment of successful parenthood; in enacting laws to govern children's duty to their parents; in specifying the duties of every adult towards the effective upbringing of children – even those children that were not theirs. Of all the laws enacted, perhaps the strictest was the one about the protection of pregnant women and nursing mothers throughout the kingdom. As the king always said, 'When I look at a child, I am looking at Òsánóbuá. To abuse or misuse a child is to abuse and a misuse Òsánóbuá, the creator-above. That, I will never condone in my kingdom.'

Under the laws, any man who knowing that a woman, other than his own wife or concubine, was pregnant yet forced her into sexual intercourse incurred the death penalty. And, confronted with famine and scarcity, after the disappearance of the sky out of human reach as a source of food, pregnant women and nursing mothers were given priority in the distribution of available resources. Women must never go to war; and, in time of war, women and children must be the first to be evacuated into safety. To this day it is still said, 'ai gbo'khuo gbọ'omọ'; any one who strikes a woman, seeing her to be pregnant or carrying a baby in her arms or on her lap or on her back, is guilty of a practice forbidden by the king. And women will say, 'Who, in her right mind, would wish to be a man when she is privileged to be born a woman?' Who indeed!

3

The Great Debate

*If we are all created equal, let some not be
more than equal than others.*

(*Èdó* saying)

T HE CREATOR-KING created a peaceful world. It was a
world whose centre was the city where the king perma-
nently resided. It teemed with life and activities. With the Sky
(*Iso*) always at hand to provide an abundance of food, and with
every man contentedly engaged in a craft and every woman
happily orbiting her husband in the gilded cage of her home
wherein the children orbited their mothers, the city was the
nucleus of a universe constructed on *Òsánóbuá*'s own blue-
print.

The husband-and-father was the sun in the family. The wives-
and-mothers were the satellites revolving around the sun, and
the children were the moons revolving around each satellite.
Father, mother and children held their respective orbits and, in
so doing, held one another firmly in place. The creator-king said
that such was the hierarchical ordering 'Above', where
Òsánóbuá, like the king on earth, rules over all. 'As Above,'
said the creator-king, 'so Below, and Below is an exact replica of
Above and nothing can change that order.' And nothing
changed it. At least not for a long while.

By divine right, the creator-king ruled wisely and fairly and
solely. His power was absolute and it was the power of life and
death. And, much like *Òsánóbuá* whom the creator-king per-
sonified on earth, the king alone had the power to take human
life, since the king alone had created that life on earth. If the

king ever told an offender, 'Take your feet off my land', the offender knew exactly what his majesty meant – he meant, 'go and commit suicide'. And the offender went and did as commanded.

The land on which the people stood and on which their dwellings rested and from which the inhabitants of the vegetable sphere drew their sustenance had everywhere been the king's sole property, and whoever stood on it did so at his majesty's pleasure. Beyond the sky was the king's ultimate home, to which he could return at will. He often warned – whenever he was somewhat vexed by events – that his abode on earth was only temporary.

'My real seat,' he would say, 'is up above. And,' he would add ominously, 'whenever I have had enough of you worthless mortals, I will simply pack up and return to my home above.' It was a constant source of joy to his subjects that his majesty never packed up and returned home. It meant that he had not had enough.

Although the royal judgment was unchallengeable, there were occasions when he realised that he might be wrong in his judgment and when being wrong would be offensive to the Almighty on high, who was known to be watching the events taking place on earth. On such occasions, when disputes became complex and the king felt insecure and inadequate, he had the privilege to call upon Òsánóbuá for direct intervention. If he did call, Òsánóbuá would be bound to descend and intervene. In principle at least, such was the understanding among the king's subjects But since the Great Dawn, the king had managed very well without having to use his reserved powers.

Then the need slowly arose.

The inhabitants of the earth had begun to squabble and disagree loudly among themselves over territorial rights. Those who inhabited the human sphere had begun to claim supremacy over the vegetable and animal spheres. Hitherto, the only unlimited powers over all three spheres had been the king's and that had never been disputed. It was not in dispute now. The Tiger, to whom the king had delegated the lordship over the animal sphere, had exercised his powers judiciously, strictly in

15

accord with the natural order. He killed only for food which was never wasted. His leftovers fed faithful scavengers and protected them from starvation. The *Uloko* tree, to whom had been delegated the lordship over the vegetable realm, had no opposition within that realm. *Uloko* set the example which all the inhabitants of that realm followed. When he began to shed his leaves it was the signal for all other trees to begin shedding theirs. His roots, on the other hand, went so deep that they loosened the earth, permitting the other trees to feed more easily. All was well in that realm. But the humans over whom the king himself held direct rule, had begun to interfere with the natural order and had thus set up a chain of confusion within creation. The confusion was mild at first, but later it developed into disagreement and even open hostility. Leopard had even begun to terrorise the humans in the city in daylight. And indeed, to everyone's horror, the cock whose duty, on pain of death, was to crow only at dawn, had begun to defy that order and was now known to crow at mid-day, an act which signified grave danger to one and all alike, including even the king.

The situation became so strained that when a man entered the jungle even for perfectly legitimate reasons, his presence met with hostility and he had quickly to beat a retreat just to save his life. A final showdown became inevitable and the king had to be told about it.

At first, his majesty took action to restore the divine order. But he failed. In desperation, he had to invoke his special powers by calling upon Òsánóbuá to come down and intervene. For there are conditions on earth which only the Almighty-on-High can handle successfully. The call on the Almighty is a legacy left behind by his majesty and it persisted until *Dusk*, when strange and foreign gods entered the realm and changed the natural relationship between Òsánóbuá and the created world. Even so, till this day, when situations threaten to get out of hand, the human inhabitants of what is left of the realm still call on Òsánóbuá to intervene. But Òsánóbuá no longer descends into the world. In fact, there is some doubt whether Òsánóbuá even hears the call these days. Yet it often helps just to call.

In response to the king's call for heavenly intervention, *Òsánóbuá* came down, accompanied by no retinue except for *Esu*.[1] *Òsánóbuá* went nowhere without *Esu*. In fact, *Òsánóbuá* could not travel without *Esu*. That was because *Esu*'s divinely ordained duty was to pull the chain which held and directed *Òsánóbuá*'s throne. For the Almighty to descend into the world below, *Esu* had to pull that chain (which the *Ẹdó* refer to as *Ogioro*) and for him to return beyond the sky, *Esu* must pull that chain again. In performing that duty, *Esu* had become very close to *Òsánóbuá*. Indeed, *Esu* had become *Òsánóbuá*'s closest, if not his only, real companion and confidant, although a passive and silent one.

Wherever *Òsánóbuá* was, there *Esu* must also be. And one important difference between *Òsánóbuá* and the king lay in the fact that the king was not granted the services of the likes of *Esu*. Therefore, although the king was mobile without the equivalent of *Esu*, his majesty could not travel to *Òsánóbuá*'s realm above the sky.

On this the first and only occasion that *Òsánóbuá* descended into the world, all the inhabitants of the three spheres of earthly influence – the vegetable, the animal and the human – gathered together to receive the Almighty. It must be noted here, to avoid any possible misunderstanding, that at this stage all the inhabitants of the three spheres still spoke a single language.

Òsánóbuá duly arrived, sitting on the eternal throne, unblinking, pensive, grand and mighty in every sense of the word. For the first time since the Great Dawn, the sun stood at

---

[1] *Esu* bears some vague resemblance to what the *Ẹdó* have now been taught to call the 'Devil' or 'Satan' or 'Lucifer', except that, for a start, *Esu* wears no horns on his divine head. His complexion, no doubt, is midnight-dark and he wears black. But that is as far as the analogy goes and no further. *Esu* is to *Òsánóbuá* what Caliban is to Prospero in Shakespeare's *The Tempest*. *Esu*'s shrine is placed just outside the front door of every respectable household in Benin City. And his duty is to guard the household and 'push' evil away from it. *Esu* does not *attract* human beings to himself. The relationship of the *Ẹdó* to *Esu* is not one of '*do ut des*' ('I give that you may give') but one of '*do ut abeas*' ('I give that you may go, and keep away'); and to him is ascribed the cause of any occurrence which results from human irrational thought or behaviour. *Esu*'s most cherished sacrificial offerings are the Tortoise and raw palm-oil. He is not worshipped as other gods are worshipped, having no priest or priestess. Close to *Òsánóbuá*, he is, however, not in any way godlike.

one corner of the sky, shedding light and heat while the moon stood on the opposite corner of the sky, reflecting the sun's light but not the heat. Never before had the two appeared together in that manner. And they were never to appear together again in that manner until long after the *Dusk*. Since this was the first and only time that *Òsánóbuá* was to descend, special dispensation was granted to the sun and the moon to appear together to witness the proceedings. For they themselves were part and parcel of the created world.

Seated at *Òsánóbuá's* right hand on a throne that was only a fraction lower than that of the Almighty, the king opened the debate, starting with the most obvious point.

'The Almighty has made this momentous journey,' his majesty began, 'because this is a very special occasion.' He paused and allowed his royal gaze to flow in a measured manner over creation. He felt a deep-seated pleasure at so impressive a sight spread before him. Not since the Dawn had a king seen the whole of creation gathered together in a single assembly such as the one that was spread before him. From the smallest to the biggest, they were all there, waiting calmly and peacefully. It was said later that the mere presence of the Almighty imposed peace.

'Who will present the issues?' challenged the king.

No one stepped forward. Neither man nor woman nor child nor tree nor plant nor beast nor bird. They all quietly held their peace and the silence was as immense and as mighty as *Òsánóbuá* would probably have wished. Even before anyone could have begun to speak, *Òsánóbuá* would already have known what was going to be said. Yet *Òsánóbuá* sat impassively on the eternal throne, ready to listen. As far as *Òsánóbuá* was concerned, it was not so much *who* spoke but *what* was spoken that would matter to the silent but secretly anxious audience.

Then the silence was broken.

Crawling out from beneath *Uloko's* discarded leaves, *Egui*, the Tortoise, approached the two thrones. His crafty eyes surveyed the great assembly from beneath a steel-like hood which served him both as protection and as shelter. Unafraid, the Tortoise inched his way slowly forward as if every step hurt, and then stopped at what he considered a respectable distance from the thrones. He cleared his throat and again looked around. *Ovbivbie*, the puff-adder, his head resting upon the folds of his coiled body, eyed the Tortoise with ravenous attention and was doing his best not to stretch out and strike. *Ovbivbie* had never before seen the Tortoise so scandalously and tantalisingly exposed at such close range.

'I do not have to kneel before your Mighty Majesties,' the Tortoise began humbly. 'I am already flat on my belly.'

The king nodded, shifted his royal weight slightly on his throne and looked on attentively.

'Whether we speak or remain silent,' continued the Tortoise, 'Òsánóbuá already knows what we all think.' He shot out his slender tongue and licked his thin lips. They said that he talked so well only because his lips were ever so thin! His eyelids flickered rapidly.

'The present situation,' he said, 'is unjust and unfair on all sides. It is unjust and unfair to the humans to be denied their supremacy in creation. In all of creation, the humans resemble our king – I mean, our creator-king – more than anyone and anything else, physically, at least. But for his majesty's undoubted divinity, the king could be any human being. That is how close the resemblance is . . . and that's where it must stop.' He cleared his throat coyly. A murmur of approbation rumbled through the human sphere. The Tortoise, they must have thought, was on the side of the humans even though he was himself a member of the animal sphere, strictly speaking. All eyes and ears were focused on the thrones. The king leaned back against his seat while the royal fingers quietly tapped the armrest. He nodded at the Tortoise who was thus encouraged to proceed.

'But it is equally unfair and unjust,' the Tortoise went on, 'that the humans, the *last* of all to be created, and the *youngest* and most *inexperienced* member in the whole of creation, should claim top position in the entire hierarchy.' He had made sure that emphases were placed where they should belong in his remarks: on *last, youngest* and *inexperienced*. Such emphases were not wasted on his audience. The humans, though,

19

murmured again, but this time in frustration and unspoken disapproval. They began to wonder what the Tortoise was up to. But the Tortoise was not, upon pain of death, to be interrupted.

'The oldest members of created beings,' the Tortoise continued, 'are the trees and plants – even to the smallest and weakest in that sphere. Without them, the rest of creation might never have come into existence.' He paused, as if exhausted with the simple task of speaking his mind. Then he looked furtively in the direction where *Uloko*'s[2] ponderous form stood, rooted firmly to the earth. *Uloko*, as if to acknowledge the Tortoise's wisdom, swayed lightly, his gigantic branches waving. The smaller members of the vegetable sphere followed *Uloko*'s example and began to wave their branches and leaves, too. But from the animal sphere emerged gentle hisses, paw-shuffling and sniffing. The king silently hoped that there would be no unrest.

'But,' said the Tortoise, undaunted, 'how far can the trees and plants go if all they can do is remain fixed to the same spot at all seasons? Their sustenance is buried deep underneath the earth where they dig deep to find it, while the rest of us roam above the earth in search of ours. They are immobile and can't even chase any prey as the lion or the tiger can. If any of us is pursued by our natural predators,' added the Tortoise, plaintively, 'not even the *Uloko* can offer any protection, certainly not unless you clamber up his enormous trunk, climb into and hide among his highness's leafy branches.' The Tortoise smiled mischievously and, in self-deprecation, continued, 'Can anyone here truly expect *me* to clamber up the trunk of *Uloko* to seek protection?' There were murmurs of amusement in the crowd. The Tortoise turned full circle to face *Uloko* who had stopped swaying and waving his branches and appeared to be brooding. '*Uloko*,' said the Tortoise somewhat rashly, 'you are the monarch of the jungle. But if you were to call me and I were to refuse to come to you, what could you do about it? You could not walk over to me and drag me by the neck, could you? And, however slowly I might crawl, I could still outrun

[2] The *Uloko* is known to western scientists as '*Iroko*' and is named as *Clorophora Excelsa* or *Clorophora Regia*: it 'reigns' in the jungle.

20

you any day or night.' A quiet voice chuckled among the humans and whispered to a neighbour in the crowd, 'Uloko can stop shedding his leaves. Then where would the Tortoise hide himself?' Òsánóbuá noted the whispered remark but said nothing.

But still directly addressing himself to the silent *Uloko*, the Tortoise went on, 'You never move at all from the same spot. You can only sway and let your branches wave. Yet, it is you who must shed the leaves that protect me and I do not have to lift a finger to pluck them down over my head. I am grateful to you, of course, but I cannot see you as my master. After all . . .' The Tortoise paused again. There was a ripple of amusement among the human group. From the animal group, not a sound was heard while the vegetable group seemed to react by swaying and waving their branches and leaves. But the Tortoise still commanded the full attention of the multitudes. The only impassive visage was that of Òsánóbuá. Even the king managed a barely concealed smile. No one in the huge assembly was sure anymore of the correctness and legitimacy of any claim in the Great Debate. Everyone was convinced, however, that only Òsánóbuá could sort out the situation. That conviction justified the king's invitation which had brought the Almighty down from the clouds. Baffled, the crowd waited. The Tortoise obviously had not done yet. Otherwise, he would take his leave and crawl into some cover. He turned again to the thrones.

'Your majesties,' he said, 'we in the animal sphere were created *after* the immobile trees and plants but *before* the contentious humans.' He had carefully emphasised the *before* and *after* in his statement to ensure that no one missed the next point. 'We move about,' he said somewhat accusingly, 'and we gather whatever we can find. And much of the time, we ourselves get eaten by our animal-kind – the weaker among us is prey to the stronger. But speaking for myself,' he said plaintively, 'I am alive at the moment because of this adamantine cover which I carry on my back and into which I can easily withdraw at the slightest sign of danger. Even so, my attacker, if sufficiently hungry, will defy all my protective armour and suck me out.' He moved his outstretched head up and down in

21

undignified self-deprecation. But at the sound of 'suck me out', the puff-adder, who had pretended to be asleep throughout the proceedings, blinked his eyes beneath the folds of his muscular body as a ripple of excitement ran down his spine. Sucking out the fleshy part of the Tortoise was the puff-adder's method of feeding on the speaker whenever the huge snake had the chance.

'But the humans,' said the Tortoise, now at the end of his long advocacy, 'are in sole possession of and have the exclusive right to the sky (*Iso*), which none of us in the animal sphere, let alone those in the vegetable sphere, can ever hope to reach. So, both the animal and vegetable spheres, unlike the humans, are denied the blessings of getting our sustenance from the sky without risking our lives in our search for food. Since we can never reach down into the earth to find food as the trees and plants can do, it is we alone who must toil for our food and get eaten in the process. Yet . . . er . . .' The Tortoise daringly looking straight into the king's eyes, and his majesty's eyes meeting those of the Tortoise turned away as if feeling guilty about some aspect of the Tortoise's predicament. The king threw a rapid sidelong glance in *Òsánóbuá*'s direction. If his majesty had not been *Òsánóbuá*'s human equivalent on earth, he would have been suspected of feeling somewhat ashamed of some error of omission.

The Tortoise fell silent at last and slowly crawled back under cover. Then, like everyone else in the assembly, he waited.

No one else spoke after the Tortoise. It seemed that there was nothing else to be said. The king had thought about it all before and his royal confusion had not been eased by the Tortoise's thorough and detailed analysis of the situation. But he, too, had to wait for *Òsánóbuá*'s final arbitration. He did not have to wait too long.

Òsánóbuá, speaking in a sombre voice, said, 'Your problems are well known. They existed even before you were created by your creator-king, my personal embodiment in your midst, although they could never have surfaced until you were ready to have revealed to you the innermost workings of my Laws, which can manifest themselves only as you mature in your abode here on earth. Now, hear my judgment by which you are bound to abide forever.'

'Have we any choice?' sniggered the Tortoise under his breath from the safety of his hiding-place. None but *Òsánóbuá* could have heard the Tortoise's cynical remarks.

'Henceforth,' continued the Almighty, 'the three spheres of influence shall exist side by side autonomously, living in mutual respect and admiration.' Except for *Òsánóbuá*'s voice which could only be felt rather than heard, there was no sound anywhere. Kindly but firmly, the Almighty laid down some new rules, not otherwise in existence in the world, saying, 'There shall be boundaries between one sphere of influence and another. Within those boundaries, the assigned ruler shall hold sway. And I say to you, whosoever shall cross a boundary shall be guilty of trespass and shall pay the price demanded by the injured party.'

Òsánóbuá spoke slowly and calmly and there was no doubt about the authority behind the words. The king's gaze was fixed on his royal feet while the Almighty spoke.

'And henceforth,' *Òsánóbuá* continued, 'the three spheres shall each speak in its own tongue; and even within each sphere, there shall be variations in the language. There shall be no usurpation. Each species in all of creation shall be free to invent and perfect its own language which shall constitute nothing more or less than its own peculiar sound that serves as a code for some meaning.'

The Almighty paused. The creator-king lifted his royal gaze from his feet and transferred it to the assembly, as if saying to the respectful audience, 'I didn't quite expect that.' From that moment on, every sound in the animal and human spheres, in particular, became a code by which every species in those spheres could communicate with each other to the exclusion of all others. Thus, when a lion roared or an elephant trumpeted, only another lion or another elephant could decipher the true meaning of the roar or the trumpeting. And, so, among the humans, even the grunting of the foreigner would never convey the same meaning as that of the *Èdó*. Had the creator-king been anyone but his divine self, he would have been somewhat uneasy about this edict. For it meant that, even within the palace itself, language would now contain hidden meanings from its connotations in the city. Òsánóbuá is great, he thought, and held his peace.

'That peculiar code,' continued the Almighty, 'each species shall pass on to the sub-species immediately below it so that the mystery of its transmitted structure shall become the acceptable language understood within the sub-group but meaningless outside that group.' If the tiger could no longer decipher the meaning of the antelope's cries when pursued as a prey, then the antelope's plea for mercy would never again be understood by the tiger. That might make hunting easier for the tiger; but it would hardly make escape easier for the antelope, since the latter could no longer hope to appeal to the former's conscience. The antelope in the assembly immediately projected a silent appeal to the Almighty for additional protection against his predators. The Almighty felt the projection and immediately granted the antelope the ability for increased fleet-footedness. Meanwhile, among humans, language would diversify so far that, soon afterwards, mankind would divide and sub-divide to form a multitude of clans and tribes, speaking dialects and sub-dialects.

Having spoken, Òsánóbuá waited for Esu to pull the chain that would lift the heavenly throne back beyond the sky. And, as silently and majestically as it had arrived on earth, Òsánóbuá's throne rose and slowly disappeared behind the clouds. The assembly dispersed in various directions, leaving only the trees and plants and the rest of the vegetable sphere where they had stood rooted throughout the Great Debate.

Followed by his adoring retinue, the creator-king returned to his palace, somewhat bewildered. I have suffered no loss, he reassured himself. Although his overall control of all the spheres seemed to have been somewhat curtailed, he reflected, he had not been dethroned. Interrupting his thoughts, a gentle voice spoke out, saying almost in a whisper, 'Your majesty is no less king of all creation than hitherto.' The voice was that of the recently named Ohen-Osa (priest of the Almighty). The king silently admired the priest for his words. He nodded his royal head several times. The priest continued in his soft, gentle voice: 'Only your majesty can order the felling of *Uloko*, ruler of the vegetable sphere though he undoubtedly is.' He cleared his throat and continued rather sycophantically, enjoying what he considered unassailed intimacy, 'And only your majesty can still order the tiger, ruler of the animal sphere, to be brought alive before you and to be sacrificed at the shrine of your head.' He cleared his throat again. But before he could add another word, the Tortoise cut in. No one had noticed his presence among the king's retinue as it processed under the blazing sun towards the palace. He said, 'Come to think of it', he said, 'only his majesty can still order a human being to be brought before him and sacrificed at the shrine of his head.' The Tortoise's addition to the list of what or whom the king alone could still order to be slaughtered in sacrifice startled the priest and set everyone else in the entourage reflecting on their vulnerability. A numbing silence descended on them as the king himself nodded his royal agreement with the inimitable Tortoise. Then the great palace doors, fashioned out of the body of an old *Uloko*, rolled back and the king disappeared into his royal abode.

4

On Their Own

Born out of necessity, mankind can thrive
only through necessity.

WHILE IN THE BEGINNING all people, animals and trees spoke in the same tongue, different languages sprang up after the Great Debate. And with different tongues wagging, different manners of being arose. The changes were much more profound in the human sphere than elsewhere in creation. In the jungle, much as of old, there existed well-kept order, smooth-running governance and uncomplicated peace and co-operation. Knowing exactly who they were within the natural order of the jungle and knowing, too, what they had been ordained to perform by day or by night, the animals lived beside each other without any conflict, rivalry, jealousy or envy. If for example, one was privileged to be born into the jungle as an antelope, one had no reason to wish to be a leopard. And, just as the shrub on whose succulent leaves the antelope fed never complained, so the antelope never complained when chased, captured and fed upon by the leopard. The antelope's only natural defences against his hungry predators were speed and lightness of foot. In the same way, the shrub's natural defence against the antelope and his like was to shed its leaves and pretend to be dying or dead. In the jungle, wherever there was anything to be eaten, there was always someone or something to eat it. To be able to escape with their lives in the jungle, animals had been endowed by the creator either with deceitful skin colour or good hearing, or a keen sense of smell or agility. But if, in spite of their natural defences, they strayed into the path of a hungry predator and were captured for food, they did not live to regret anything. The main point was that in the jungle, particularly after the Great Debate, no one was permitted to waste any food. Kill, if you must, but waste no part of what you have killed: that was the law. In this way, the jungle remained relatively orderly and trouble-free for all the animal inhabitants.

When the sky fulfilled its ordained function of shedding those portions, those drops, which the humans did not need for food but merely for drinking, the wet earth found great pleasure in increasing its own productivity. The fallen leaves, discarded by trees and plants all over the jungle floor rotted more thoroughly and the crawlers and non-killers like worms and insects were grateful for the abundance of sustenance. But when the shedded drops had dried up and the earth itself had caked, the vegetable inhabitants of the jungle soon began to shed their leaves in order to eat less, so as to avoid committing suicide through starvation. The scarcity of leaves and fruit sent forth the likes of the deer and monkey in a more frantic search for food. And that was when the flesh-eaters increased their own vigilance in their search for prey. The search everywhere, all the time, was for food alone. Plucking, tearing, killing – none of that was for fun. The compulsion to find food had been pre-ordained only as a means of maintaining and prolonging the pre-ordained existence of the various species that populated the created world. The creator-king had repeatedly made that point clear to the elders who later passed on the message to later generations of humans. From the Dawn, through its numerous generations and maturing stages, life in the created world was orderly, each being acting according to type, obeying only the dictates of his or her or its own peculiar character within overall Nature.

Humans, too, at the beginning, were no different from the inhabitants of the other two spheres. They hungered and thirsted and searched endlessly for food and drink. But theirs was a privileged existence, since the creator-king had honoured them by providing them with sky as the source of food. All they had to do was reach over their heads, cut a slice of sky and prepare it for their table. According to Tortoise, the humans were so privileged only because they were the last to be created and because, more importantly, they looked far more like the king himself than anyone else from the other spheres.

Sky was food for humans alone from the beginning of time. Not even birds who flew high up needed sky for food. Birds merely hovered beneath sky and then alighted on earth to find food. As the bounteous gift to humans, sky had to be protected by a strict law, which was that under no circumstances whatsoever should the food sky provided be thrown away as waste. Thus, by Divine Decree, all greed was to be eschewed lest it led to the temptation to waste the food provided by sky. The law was strictly obeyed. Stomachs were filled, and, without any worry about where the next meal would come from, the humans were saved the difficult and risky job of looking for food all over the place. But, more than that, it meant that the humans were free to devote their time to art and craft and thinking and, above all, the worship of the numerous deities that surrounded them and guided everything they did. There were deities representing the head, hand, foot and every part and little portion of the human body. They were all highly venerated. In addition to the deities of the body parts, which were personal deities, there were also more venerable ones, such as dead parents and relations and other remote ancestors who were never far away from the home from which they had long departed. These were family deities. Above them were the mountains, hills, rivers, streams – all of which were collective deities venerated and worshipped by everyone. The greatest deity of all was *Òsánóbuá N'Oghodua*, whose mantle the king wore on earth. Thus the king himself was a living deity. And humans were fully engaged in their daily lives and could never be idle.

Then came the shock.

Sun had climbed towards its zenith and every creature had sought the mid-day shelter. A child began to scream at the top of its voice. 'Food', the child yelled, 'food now. Mother, food.' Husband-and-father could hear where he lay sprawled on his back in the shade of the silk-cotton tree. The young mother, fresh from her father's protection and determined to make a good mother-and-wife in her new home, and thereby earn her own industrious and dutiful mother the high praise of her neighbours, rushed out to the back of her dwelling and cut a bowlful of sky. In the rush to feed the yelling child, the inexperienced mother-and-wife was unmindful of the care it required to take the exact amount – just enough for her child and herself. The careless woman shredded sky into a pot, broiled and seasoned it and waited. As the pot boiled, so did the restless child simmer. But soon the food was ready. She sat her child on her lap and fed it. She, too, ate till her stomach was full. But to her horror there was much of the food left. She panicked and rushed out in search of any other child she might feed but found none. Distraught beyond words, she didn't know what to do. There was nowhere to hide wasted sky.

She would take the bowl of sky to her mother, she thought, and hoped her mother had not yet eaten. But, she reasoned, to do that would be to call attention to her crime. She had never had any reason before to take food to her mother from her husband's house. How, then, would she justify the sudden urge to do so now, she wondered?

She called her father's name but it did not help. Nor did her mother's or her husband's. Nothing helped her in her distress. She faced death if anyone else knew what she had done. She must conceal everything, she thought, and pretend that nothing had happened.

But pretence was certainly not going to work, especially not with a husband around who could never be deceived. Suddenly, she thought she would run over to her mother for help. She dashed out of the house and ran. Halfway there, she remembered that she had left her little child alone in the house. Hurrying back to fetch her child, she stumbled into Tortoise who was crawling up the path.

'Look where you're going, woman,' cried Tortoise. 'You nearly stepped on me. You are running as if pursued by who knows what. Have you done something you don't want the world to know about?'

'Me?' she replied, out of breath. 'Me, done anything I don't want the world to know? Never! Not me.'

'Well,' said Tortoise, 'if you run too fast, you may run past the thing you're pursuing.'

'If the pursuer does not relax,' she answered as Tortoise crawled slowly away, 'how can the pursued stop? Òsánóbuá, please help me. Oh, my father, help me. Mother, what shall I do?' She beat her head with both fists, slapped her cheeks with open hands and tore at her buttocks with her nails in the frantic but futile search for an answer to her problem. She was completely beside herself with grief, driven almost to distraction for guilt and fear of reprisal.

But at last she calmed down sufficiently to think of a practical solution to her problem. She scraped the surplus food from the wooden bowl, wrapped it in plantain leaves and took the bundle far into the bush and left it where, she thought, no one would find it. No human eyes saw what happened that day in the home of an unfortunate mother who found herself under pressure which she could not control. Her husband was not around to notice anything. Without realising the full implications of her situation, she slowly drifted into a false sense of security and breathed a heavy sigh of relief. Inwardly thanking the household deities for their supposed help and assistance in concealing her crime. She returned to her dwelling and sat down to play with her child.

Unknown to her, however, sky had seen what had happened. It was never possible to hide anything, any deed, from sky. What he did not see, he heard; and what he did not hear, he felt. For as long as the sun was on parade in the day and the moon on the prowl at night, nothing could escape sky's notice.

Vexed by what happened, sky appealed directly to Òsánóbuá.

'Look what has happened,' sky complained. He was in a towering rage.

'That's me, cooked, uneaten and thrown away! At this rate, how can I ever guarantee to keep humans alive?'

Òsánóbuá, of course, already knew what had happened and sympathised with both sides. Òsánóbuá never condemns. Òsánóbuá is never taken by surprise. 'I saw what happened,' Òsánóbuá told sky undramatically. 'It was meant to be.'

Sky waited as patiently as he could, heaving in fury and trying very hard to restrain his urge to condemn the criminal.

'The humans,' Òsánóbuá said, 'have just arrived at the next stage in their pre-ordained maturity. They now must take on the added task of creating their own source of food. Their days of easy-to-reach food from above are over.'

Sky neither spoke nor moved, but remained patient and reverential before the Almighty.

'From henceforth,' said Òsánóbuá, 'you are released from your divine duty of supplying food to the humans. Move as far away as you may desire out of their reach. Continue to provide necessary protection from the heat of the sun on his daily journeys and see to it that he, too, is not abused. Continue,' added Òsánóbuá, 'to provide only water to the whole of creation.'

Sky wasted no time but rose steadily higher and higher, until nothing on earth could touch him. The highest-soaring bird fell far short of sky in his new position and so did the highest of mountains.

The first of the humans to notice the disappearance of sky were the members of the king's household. They were utterly dumbfounded. Someone, they thought, ought to inform his majesty immediately that sky had moved out of human reach, although not out of sight, and that there was no food anywhere for anyone. But who would take his life in his own hands and approach the king with such news of total disaster?

Then, amidst the consternatioon and despair, an idea struck the Umoẹmwaẹn[1] who happened to be absent from the king's company at that particular moment. Umoẹmwaẹn said, as calmly as his high status dictated, 'I know who should bear this terrible news to the king.'

'Who?' chorused the servants in unison.

'Tortoise, of course,' he replied, 'Who else? Only Tortoise can break such news to the king and still live to tell the story.'

Tortoise was hurriedly sent for.

Let it be noted that since the Great Debate the king had

---

[1] Umoẹmwaẹn was the king's personal adviser and consultant in all matters. The king was not bound to accept his advice, although he always did so.

secretly admired Tortoise's wisdom and had later openly culti-
vated Tortoise's friendship. The friendship rapidly reached the
point where Tortoise became for the king almost what *Esu* was
to Òsánóbuá. Almost, but not quite. For, unlike *Esu*, Tortoise
had no power to transport the king anywhere, let alone Above.
The king's secret hope was, in fact, that through his deviousness
and ingenuity, Tortoise might indeed one day devise a means to
perform for him what *Esu* performed for Òsánóbuá. Tortoise's
reputation, meanwhile, had spread far and wide as the standard
against which all humans were assessed for wisdom, cunning,
roguery, impudence, lying, cheating and plain tomfoolery.
Tortoise would openly challenge and even defy the king and get
away with it. He was too clever ever to lose an argument. Yet he
was practically incapable of any sustained physical activity. For
him even walking was an ordeal.

To Tortoise, therefore, was the word about the sky disaster
urgently sent. Sensing an opportunity for some personal gain
from the situation, Tortoise immediately crawled to the palace.
Quickly briefed in whispers by the king's distressed household,
Tortoise sought urgent audience with the king.

Employing all his tricks, Tortoise slowly broke the terrible
news to the king. His majesty was struck dumb for a long while.
Then, in a most unsure tone, almost groping for words and
desperate to appear calm, he asked, 'But Tortoise, how could
that have happened? Who committed the crime? What is to be
done? How are my subjects to find food?' The king was so
agitated that questions tumbled out of his month in cascades,
waiting for no answers. And more questions might have poured
forth had Tortoise allowed them to do so.

'Well,' Tortoise said thoughtfully, 'Your Majesty should
set up a Council of Elders to work out this matter. Make me
the head of the Council and give strict orders that mine will
always be the final word in the Council's deliberations. Do that
and I will bring you the solution to the problem in no time
at all.' If the king thought he had a choice in the matter, he
showed no sign of it. A Council of Elders was immediately
set up with Tortoise at its head and his word was to be final in
all deliberations.

Tortoise, meanwhile, saw that the humans soon knew about the disaster, because of the hunger which rapidly hit them. There was panic and chaos, so much so that it did not occur to anyone to even ask who had been responsible for sky's sudden defection. Thus the offender remained concealed. All roads led to Tortoise's door where everyone went to seek advice and, possibly, assistance. Tortoise made everyone pay in one way or another for whatever he told or gave them. In no time at all, Tortoise could count wealth greater than the king commanded in the royal treasury. Or almost. For if it came to counting wealth, the king would count Tortoise and his newly acquired opulence as all belonging to the king's treasury.

When Tortoise next returned to the palace, he reported that the Council of Elders had reached unanimous agreement that henceforth all male humans must grow the food they needed.

'Grow?' queried the king in unconcealed perplexity. 'What do you mean by grow? How is that to be achieved?' Food had never been grown before by humans. Nor had they ever known how to kill for food. Sky had been all they had for food and sky had been quite sufficient.

The assembled populace gasped, looking from one to the other with open but wordless mouths, and then turned their gaze on Tortoise, speechlessly demanding more enlightenment. Tortoise alone, they all thought, knew the answer and they waited for it.

Unknown to anyone, since the Great Debate, Tortoise had secretly learnt how to cultivate the little patch of jungle which had become his second home. Known only to Òsánóbuá, Tortoise had, in fact, perfected the art of cultivating the soil and producing his own food. He had had all the time necessary to do so, when he'd had no other engagement to occupy his time. He never hunted for food in the jungle but simply crawled around and scavenged what the flesh-eaters and the non-flesh-eaters left behind. Thus Tortoise had long become omnivorous, while the taste of flesh still remained a secret to the humans.

It was *Uloko* who taught Tortoise how to farm. *Uloko* knew what it meant for the soil to be loosened up and he revealed to Tortoise the advantages of such loosening up of the soil.

'Tortoise,' said *Uloko* late one evening, just as Tortoise was preparing to go to sleep under *Uloko*'s shedded leaves.

'Yes, what can I do for you?' asked Tortoise cheekily.

'It is not what you can do for me that I am about,' replied *Uloko* good-humouredly, 'but what I can do for you.'

'In addition to shedding the leaves under which I sleep? How generous of you, *Uloko*!' replied Tortoise, tongue in cheek.

'Do you know what it means for the soil to be loosened?' teased *Uloko*.

'No,' replied Tortoise truthfully. 'But I'm sure you're about to tell me.'

'Well,' said *Uloko*, 'when the soil is loosened, it makes it easy for all vegetables to feed well and grow strong.'

'So?' queried Tortoise, sceptically.

'So,' replied *Uloko*, 'it means that some of them will be able to produce what you can eat. You can make them produce food for you.'

'How?' queried Tortoise.

'You dig up the soil to loosen it. Then you put in some of the vegetable plants and let them grow and they will yield you your food.'

Tortoise said nothing more. But he kept in mind what *Uloko* had told him and later tried it out. It happened exactly as *Uloko* had predicted.

Tortoise was able to capitalise on his secret knowledge about cultivation after sky's disappearance. He carefully explained to the bewildered populace how to grow food. He undertook, for a price to be paid by the king, to teach the humans how to cultivate the earth and how to hunt for animal flesh, which they at first were reluctant to learn to eat. It took them some time to overcome their consanguineous feelings towards the inhabitants of the animal sphere, feelings which made them averse to what initially seemed a form of cannibalism.

The price which Tortoise demanded from the king was the hand of the king's eldest daughter. He received what he asked for.

The humans were, at first utterly shattered. But, as *Òsánóbuá* had revealed to sky, the time had come for them to fend for themselves. They were on their own and *necessity* forced them to find the answers to their problems of hunger. For the first time since creation, humans knew what it meant to compete for scarce resources, especially food. They had to learn the rules of the jungle and to live by those rules. Sanctions existed for the violation of the territorial boundaries set up by the Almighty at the Great Debate. But as Tortoise had suspected, those boundaries could still be crossed, with impunity, by those who knew how. The know-how rested on mutual agreement and the give-and-take co-operation necessary for peaceful co-existence. First, as Tortoise painfully, if spitefully, explained, those whose boundaries were to be crossed had to be placated and reassured that no excesses would be perpetrated within their territory. Second, those crossing any boundary must study the nature of the owners of the territory they were invading. To do that, the would-be invader must know and respect the deities that controlled and guarded that territory. Those deities and they alone could grant permission for the invasion.

The crisis had led to a new area of learning for which the humans were ill-equipped. But they had to shoulder the new responsibility because sky never returned as the source of human food. And what became obvious was that, cultivation or no cultivation, humans would have to compete among themselves. For that they were also ill-equipped. Later, competition was to lead to the protection of vested interest. That was strange at first, and in turn it spread into the formation of interest-groups. The birth of language-within-language was at hand. And soon it was to become necessary for individual groups and sub-groups to apply to the king for permission to migrate to new and previously uninhabited regions. If the king refused them permission, he risked plunging them into greater difficulties than they already faced.

Thus it came about that humans began to disperse, carrying with them their new-found languages as shapers of their future.

5

Leopard and Its Spots

*He who seeks to kill his enemy in haste
may die before the adversary.*

(Èdó proverb)

P ROBABLY THE MOST remarkable physical feature of
Leopard is his skin which is spotted. There is, of course, also
the fact that his eyes are usually red, or pinkish at the best of
times, and that he always looks shame-faced and shy, if not
morose. But Leopard was not created that way. His skin was
once all white in colour, marvellously smooth; and his look was
once arrogant and haughty in the extreme. Something forced
him to change.

Long before the Great Debate, no one in the animal sphere
trifled with Leopard. No one, that is, except Tortoise who was
his friend and close confidant. At that time, all the inhabitants
of the animal sphere, from the highest to the lowliest, from the
largest to the smallest, from the strongest to the weakest, from
the most ferocious to the mildest, had a single mother in
common. She was called Mother by all of them and she was
highly respected and cherished. She lived alone in a hut in the
middle of the jungle and all her children visited her in her hut
twice daily. Oh, and one more fact: they all practised the art of
pottery. Perhaps it was a family hobby. They all made clay pots
of different shapes and sizes, the size being dictated by the size
of the potter. After a whole day's search for food through the
jungle, they spent most of the night making their pots from wet
clay. In the morning, they carried their still wet and soft pots to
their mother's hut to be baked in the heat of the day's sun. Their

mother's sole responsibility was to keep an eye on the baking pots. Then, at sundown, as they returned from their search for food, her children stopped at the hut to collect their baked pots and to give their mother some food.

The separation resulting from the Great Debate led to the closer unity among members of each sphere in which separate languages later prevailed. Within each sphere there was mutual respect, with every individual knowing his place and staying within it. Their shared belief was that if one knew one's place within a group and stayed within that place, one succeeded better in fulfilling one's personal destiny. Thus, for example, if one was a flesh-eater and had fed oneself on a jungle rabbit and remained healthy and alive as a result, in turn, one would in due course be eaten by, say, the lion who would, as a consequence, stay healthy and alive. In that way, the belief went, the eaters, like the eaten, fulfilled their personal destinies without any waste of resources. Obviously, the creator who devised that rule abhorred waste. And in the animal sphere, perhaps more than in the other spheres, only four activities constituted living: searching for food, procreation, making pottery and sleeping. The most regular and persistent of those four activities was searching for food. But one noticeable aspect of the arrangement was that however hungry and voracious the flesh-eater might be, he never killed any member of his own immediate family for food. The lion, for example, would never kill another lion for food, nor would the tiger kill another tiger for food. That sort of cannibalism was strictly forbidden by Òsánóbuá's orders which the creator-king enforced on earth.

The arrangement worked quite well until one day disaster struck when one of the clay pots fell from the mother's old hand and broke into pieces.

What actually happened was that after her children had all gone in search for food, leaving her to keep an eye on their pots as they baked in the sun's heat, the sky slowly darkened. Following Òsánóbuá's strict injunction, sky had protected the sun by hiding him behind a thick layer of water which was to be shed later, also according to Òsánóbuá's orders. Mother knew from long-standing experience that when sky let down a deluge over the baking pots, they would dissolve back into the original soggy clay from which they had been formed. She never wanted that to happen to her children's pots. Therefore, she set about carrying the pots into her hut, storing them out of reach of the approaching storm until their respective owners returned to retrieve them. Knowing the nature of each of her children, mother exercised great care in handling each of the pots. None must be broken through her own carelessness; but some of the pots must be more carefully handled than others.

As she carried the pots one after another into the hut, there was a mishap and one of the pots, a rather big and heavy one, fell from her hand and shattered into pieces.

Perhaps there would not have been much trouble over the broken pot had it belonged to, say, the gentle Elephant or the humble Jungle Mouse, both of whom were extremely understanding although for different reasons. Elephant was gentle because, being large and strong and powerful, he disdained to use his strength to bully others. He preferred to maintain the dignity of one who would receive insult but scorned to return it, since he knew he could never be defeated in any show of strength. As for the Jungle Mouse, he was humble because he was so small and weak that he dared not risk any confrontation with any of his brethren. His policy was that of using one's own strength as a defence against attack. However, the broken pot on that fateful day belonged to Leopard and that put a totally different complexion on the whole affair.

Mother's solution to her grave problem was to go into hiding. She locked herself in her hut and bolted the door as tightly as she could. She barely allowed herself to breathe for fear that she would be detected. Even so, she was sure that, as far as arrogant and haughty Leopard was concerned, there was no hiding-place for her. He was perfectly capable of smashing down the door, searching her out and ripping her to pieces as small as those of his broken pot. Leopard was that unreasonable and irrational when roused to anger.

The first of her children to return to pick up his pot was the humble Jungle Mouse. Small, harmless and fragile, Jungle Mouse was delicate and sensitive and totally inoffensive. He knocked gently on his mother's door and in an effeminate voice and manner to match he said, 'Mother, please let me in.'

'No, my son, never,' replied his mother in a tremulous voice.

'Mother,' pleaded Jungle Mouse, 'it's me, Jungle Mouse.'

'I know who you are,' replied his mother. 'Just go away for your own good.'

'Mother, why?'

'Because,' replied mother from behind the door, 'while taking in the pots one of them dropped and broke into pieces.'

'Mother, whose pot was it?'

'It belonged to your fearsome brother, Leopard,' replied his mother, a fresh shudder shooting through her spine as she mentioned the name. Her throat was so tight that her words could hardly squeeze through it. 'You know what your brother is like,' she continued, 'ferocious, unkind and deadly in anger. On his approach, both the ground on which he treads and the sky above quake in fear.'

'Mother,' shuddered Jungle Mouse, 'do hide yourself well. I won't hang around here longer than is good for me.' He disappeared into the forest, leaving his pot behind and in his hurry forgetting to leave any food remnants for his mother.

One after another, the animals returned, asked the same question, got the same answer and disappeared into the jungle as Jungle Mouse had done much earlier. Last but one to return was Ram.

He knocked and his mother gave him the now familiar reply. But instead of beating a hasty retreat he insisted on the door being opened. 'Open this door,' he bleated loud and clear, 'or I'll break it down.'

Unsure whether it would be worse for her to face Leopard's fury or to let Ram break down the door, thereby exposing them both to the grave danger that threatened them, the mother pleaded, 'I'll not expose you, my child, to this danger. If Leopard . . .'

Ram interrupted his mother angrily. 'I say open this door or . . .'

His mother reluctantly opened the door and Ram pushed his way past her into the hut. 'Now, mother,' said Ram in as quiet and reassuring a voice as he could muster, 'you go and hide yourself as best you can. Leave me alone to deal with Leopard.'

'You, my son?' mother gasped, shaking with amazement.

Ordinarily, Ram was mild-mannered, somewhat sheepish but quite accommodating, even friendly in his own quiet way. He was a loner who never picked a fight nor displayed any temper. Always tender-hearted and co-operative, no one in the animal sphere had ever heard Ram raise his voice. None even gave Ram any chance, let alone encouragement, to show what a blessing he could be to have around. There were some who thought Ram was nothing but a spineless coward, deserving of no attention. His most ludicrous feature was the sack that housed his huge testicles and dangled hideously between his thighs, giving him the ungainly walk for which he was treated with contempt. In fact, Ram's single claim to the attention of his fellow-animals was his insatiable sexual appetite.

'Go,' Ram said, 'go now'. His mother slipped away into a far corner of the hut and hid herself. Ram dragged out the grinding-stone and, one after the other, removed his horns, sharpened them to a needle-point and replaced them. He pressed each horn firmly back into place to ensure that it was secure and ready to do business. Then he dragged the grinding-stone back into its usual corner and let himself out of the front door, carefully shutting it behind him, and began to plan a strategy for tackling Leopard.

'If only I could protect my testicles,' he said aloud with a heavy sigh, 'things might not look too grim.' He looked around as if searching for an ally. There seemed to be nothing and nobody within sight or earshot. There was no doubt in his mind that he was facing a grave and life-threatening situation. 'Leopard,' he soliloquised, 'is so mean that he will go straight for my testicles. And if he grabs them . . .' A shudder shot down his spine as the thought flashed across his mind. But although there was still time to abandon his mother to her fate, Ram remained where he was, determined to defend his mother to the death.

As he pondered his own fate, Ram did not hear Tortoise creep up behind him.

'Mother is in trouble,' said Tortoise with a show of indifference. The sound of Tortoise's voice startled Ram who spun round aggresively to face him.

'Oh, it's you!' sighed Ram, obviously relieved. 'What do you want?'

'And you are going to defend her?' continued Tortoise, disregarding Ram's question.

'Yes,' replied Ram defiantly, almost with a show of bravado, belied, however, by the rapid intake of breath through his flared nostrils. 'Only . . .'

'You're handicapped,' interrupted Tortoise, sniggering. 'Your large . . . er . . . He let it be known that he was steadily, almost rudely, gazing at Ram's huge sack dangling between his thighs.

'I know,' snapped Ram, panting heavily while his eyes restlessly scanned the horizon.

'That makes you vulnerable,' continued Tortoise mischievously. 'What are you going to do about it?'

'I don't know,' replied Ram, showing signs of irritation. 'I was just pondering the matter when . . . when . . .'

'When I interrupted your thoughts,' Tortoise added, completing Ram's unfinished sentence.

'Why don't you sit on it?' suggested Tortoise.

'Sit on it? What do you mean?' asked Ram.

'Let me see,' said Tortoise, his head tilted to one side and a glint of amusement in his eyes. He projected his wrinkled neck another inch out of its shell and looked around. Then in a conspiratorial tone, he said, 'Dig a hole in the ground, bury your testicles in it and sit on top.' Tortoise, noting the cloud of uncertainty that swept across Ram's face, continued, 'Have you a better idea?'

Ram shook his head in a negative answer.

'No,' Ram said. 'At a time of crisis anything is better than nothing, I suppose.'

'Very wise,' returned Tortoise, encouragingly. Ram dug a hole, inserted his testicles into it and Tortoise helped him to close up the hole with loose earth. Ram sat on top of the mound, adjusted himself into a more comfortable position and waited. Tortoise withdrew his head into his shell, turned round

41

and crawled away under a nearby bush. There he waited quietly.

Leopard soon burst out of the jungle into the clearing where his mother's hut stood. He was arrogant, boisterous and as self-assured as ever. Ram made no attempt to acknowledge Leopard's presence.

'Are you deputising for Mother?' sneered Leopard with a sarcastic grin. 'Where is she?'

'She's hiding,' replied Ram, sternly watching Leopard. 'She broke your pot accidentally and she is scared.'

'She broke my pot? Mine? I'm going to kill her.' Leopard dropped his bag of food remnants and made for the door. Ram barred his way.

'No,' he said, 'you're not going to kill her. You're going to fight me.'

Leopard could not conceal his shock. He could hardly believe his ears. Ram's suicidal challenge was most unexpected. And even Ram himself knew that Leopard did not take him seriously.

'I am going to fight you?' Leopard asked. It sounded neither like a serious question nor a statement, but just a stupefied repetition of Ram's words.

'Yes,' replied Ram, half boldly and half uncertainly. Whatever fear assailed him was overcome by a feeling of inevitability. It was too late to withdraw from the situation.

Infuriated beyond words, Leopard roared, 'Then let's fight.' He hauled himself at Ram. With only a slight flick of his head, Ram caught his wild assailant with his razor-sharp horn. Leopard felt the sharpness of the horn tearing a gash beneath his raised left paw. It was not so much the sight of his own blood or the pain that accompanied it that drove Leopard into a wild, uncontrollable fury, but the fact that the wound had been inflicted by Ram.

'I!' Leopard thought in a flash of anger. 'I, the monarch of all the animal sphere! I, the feared but fearless!' The humiliation was unbearable. He lurched forward again, this time with renewed determination and ferocity. Ram remained rooted to the same spot, determined and unshaken.

The fight went on and on and on until it began to grow dark.

Leopard attempted to seize Ram from all possible angles but to no avail. Meanwhile, he bled in frustration and despair. Having gained enormously in self-confidence and self-esteem, Ram noticed that Leopard's fury was beginning to wane. The blood had begun to clot in Leopard's eyes which were slowly but surely getting dimmer with pain and exhaustion. It was time, Ram judged, to pull his celebrated testicles out of the hole and stand erect for the final assault on his adversary. He pulled himself up and, from a crouching position, launched himself forward at Leopard, blood-stained horns poised murderously. But Ram's attack, successfully repulsed, galvanised Leopard to mount a counter-attack. He leapt forward only to impale himself fully on Ram's horns. Straining all the muscles of his neck, Ram rose with the burden. He lifted Leopard as high in the air as he could and, with one mighty heave, tossed him into the spiky branches of a nearby young palm tree.

'Leave him there,' said a voice from the undergrowth, 'and let him wriggle out of the thorns.' The voice was Tortoise's. He had watched the fight from the safety of his hiding-place and just as Ram's memorable victory seemed assured, Tortoise emerged from hiding to applaud the victor. 'Well done, my brave Ram,' Tortoise enthused. 'I have always known you've got it in you. Let him wriggle.'

Ram was panting heavily. He could not believe what he was seeing. His eyes blurred with fatigue, incredulity and pride.

'You may come out of hiding, mother,' shouted Tortoise. 'We've done it, You're safe now.'

Ram ignored Tortoise's 'we' but managed to say through a grimace, 'I thought Leopard was your best friend, Tortoise.'

'Not any more,' replied Tortoise. 'He's too much of a bully for me.'

Their mother emerged timidly from her hiding-place, convinced that her son, Ram, was dead. But, as she looked around, she saw Ram standing beside Tortoise, grinning. She blinked, shook her head in disbelief, and stepped forward an inch or two. Then the shaking and rattling of the fronds of the young palm tree caught her eyes. She looked again more closely and saw, to her utter amazement and grief, her proud son, Leopard, wriggling among the thorns. He was completely perforated and bleeding from every part of his body. His mother rushed forward, intending to help free her son from the thorns. Tortoise barred her way.

'Let him wriggle out by himself,' he told his mother. 'After all, but for the brave young Ram, you would be dead by now.' His mother withdrew tearfully into her hut and shut her door.

Leopard was left to wriggle out of his trap as best he could. It took him a long night of pain and struggle to free himself. And, when he did, it took even longer for the thorns to be picked out of his body.

The scars remain to this day as the spots which now characterise Leopard. And, to this day, Leopard fears two implacable foes. They are the Ram and the palm tree. He will go nowhere near them, whatever the circumstance. After the fight, the inhabitants of the animal sphere, like those of the human one, split into separate groups, each with its own beliefs about Ram. But although Ram had earned the respect of most of the animals, he still continued to tread warily, giving the other inhabitants of the sphere the clear message that the strong man who does not show off his strength possesses the same virtue as the beautiful woman who remains chaste. That was the message Tortoise later spread all over the Èdó kingdom.

6

✕⁓⁓✕

Never Too Weak to Help

There is no limit to what one being may do
for another in time of need.

(Èdó proverb)

THE FIGHT BETWEEN Leopard and Ram took place shortly after the encounter between Spider and Deer. At the time of that encounter, all the inhabitants of the animal sphere were still speaking the same language and had not yet split into subgroups with specialised languages of their own. Spider, then, was still able to communicate directly with Deer in a common tongue, allowing for no misunderstanding.

Also, when Spider and Deer met, humans had only just begun to accustom themselves to growing their own food, since sky had moved out of their reach. Humans had actually become very like the inhabitants of the animal sphere in their lifestyle: all they did, and needed to do, was search for food, to procreate, to play and to sleep. There was nothing else to living but these four pursuits. As Tortoise kept saying, 'The history of humans is but the story of a hungry beast in search of food.'

Social status and position, of course, were important among humans, as indeed was the case among the animals; but status also involved great responsibilities. For the higher the status of the human within the human sphere, the greater the amount of food to be grown, because of the increased number of mouths to be fed.

In their endless search for food, the inhabitants of the human sphere could gather what those of the vegetable sphere produced but could not devour themselves. There was always an abundance of fruits in the jungle, since each sub-group of plants produced its own special brand of fruit, which weighed down the branches in the appropriate season, ripened and then dropped to the jungle floor where the inhabitants of the animal and human spheres gladly gathered them for food. A plant was forbidden to eat its own fruit, just as humans and animals were forbidden to eat their own offspring. Cannibalism was rigidly controlled by a taboo which decreed that no one in any of the spheres should feed upon his or her own brood or kind. The message was loud and clear: no matter how hungry one was, one did not eat one's own children or any member of one's own family. The *Divine Duty* was said to be to hunt for food for self and family and to protect family from harm. The inhabitants of one sphere could feed on those of any of the others, always provided that nothing was wasted. For, however bad suffering might be in life, if hunger was removed from it there was but little or nothing in it to hurt the individual. A widely accepted truism was that one gets used to everything except hunger.

Nevertheless, there was now a special law which everyone, regardless of sphere, had to obey. It was the *Law of Caution*, which decreed that, regardless of who an individual was either within the animal or human sphere, he must be careful never to pick from the vegetable sphere any fruit which was unripe, since it might contain some dangerous but invisible substance that might not only ruin future appetite but could, in fact, cause Ọfọe[1] to pay a visit to the individual who ate such a substance.

To ensure that the precocious humans and the often thoughtless animals recognised their natural limitations in their dealings with the vegetable sphere, Ogi'uwu[2] had consulted with Òsánóbuá, quite some time previously, and sought permission to provide members of the otherwise relatively unprotected vegetable sphere with some special hidden power which was often concealed in their unripe offspring. If ever any human or

---

[1] Ọfọe is known among the Ẹ̀dó as the 'messenger of death'. No one dies unless Ọfọe has visited him and invited him away to meet Ogi'uwu.

[2] Ogi'uwu is known to the Ẹ̀dó as the 'god of death'. It is he who authorises the death of anyone. Having authorised it, he sends Ọfọe to visit the victim and to invite him over.

any animal was careless or stupid enough to eat such fruits, they would automatically invite Ọfọe's visit. Ọfọe, of course, was Ogi'uwu's own personal and faithful messenger who never returned empty-handed from a visit.

Òsánóbuá gave the required permission and in addition loaned Esu to Ogi'uwu as the agent by whom to convey the special hidden power to the vegetable sphere, provided there was a witness at the hand-over. Esu chose Tortoise as the witness, having first sworn him to secrecy.

As time progressed, the inhabitants of the human and animal spheres learned exactly which vegetable food to eat. It had to be ripe; it had to drop to the jungle floor by the force of its own weight; and it had to agree with the physical and spiritual character of the individual who ate it. Otherwise, that individual could be in mortal danger. To assume, therefore, that, since the plants were standing still and rooted to the same spot throughout the seasons, they could never harm anyone, would be foolish. At least, that was what Tortoise went about telling everyone without actually revealing any secrets.

In addition to being able to pick up plant food from the jungle floor and hunt for food in the animal sphere, the humans had also learned, thanks to Tortoise, to grow their own food just where and when they liked. In effect, what Tortoise had done was to bring the human and animal spheres into closer co-operation and mutual help in their struggle for survival.

The arrangement was meant to be flawless. Hunger might not have been fully banished from any of the spheres but it had become a motivation towards creative activity and against idleness. And that was the situation when Spider encountered Deer.

Spider was hanging on to the underside of a dried-up leaf, with all 16 spindles which he called legs, on the bank of a slow-moving stream, and hoping that he would not drop off as a result of a sudden gust of forest wind which always seemed to blow upwards from the jungle floor, scattering the dry leaves into the air as if trying to put the fallen leaves back in their original places on the branches. If he did drop off by accident, Spider could easily get trampled underfoot by any of the animals and humans who were marauding in search of food all over the jungle.

The water in the stream sparkled and beneath it Spider saw a number of carefree movements in all directions. Fish, too, Spider reflected, were probably not exempt from the endless search for food. But Spider was slightly baffled. He wondered what food there could be in the water for fish to rush madly after. But his main concern interrupted his curiosity and brought him back to the problem of his own position, which was how to cross the stream to the opposite bank. Spider was not a swimmer and, in fact, he was terrified of water and would never go anywhere near it. He had concluded that if one has 16 spindles for legs and a rotund under-belly full of slimy spittle and could only spin sticky webs for flies, one should be terrified of water which seemed to have no limbs at all but yet was able to move its whole body endlessly forward in a single direction and in a single, smooth and silent elasticity regardless of obstacles.

Spider, like Deer, was out searching for food; and, like Deer, Spider felt certain that across the stream lay some fresh source of food. As Spider wavered between confusion and despair, Deer, somewhat hurriedly, appeared on the scene. Deer was always nervous. His sharp eyes dashed in all directions as if he expected to be attacked by some concealed enemy.

'In the jungle,' Spider often said, 'you can never tell who is watching you whether friend or foe. There are more foes than friends.' Deer's hearing was excellent. His long ears twitched ceaselessly, collecting both near and distant sounds. Deer's proverbial insecurity was such that he was always on the look out for danger. Ram once made the joke that among all the inhabitants of the animal sphere, Deer was the only individual who might be able to hear a sound that had not yet been made. What he did not actually hear, he imagined. Only a few of those present laughed at Ram's joke about Deer. But Deer himself always boasted, whenever he gave himself enough time to talk to anyone, that he possessed the natural ability to expect the unexpected. Perhaps only Deer himself could clearly understand what he meant by his claim.

'I can always hear something approaching,' he claimed, 'and I prepare myself for flight.'

As Deer stood quivering on the bank of the stream, looking restlessly this way and that, it flashed across Spider's mind that if only Deer's earlobes could stop flapping quite so continually, he could crawl silently behind them without even being noticed. In that case, he could be carried across the stream without having to beg for a lift and facing the chance of being turned down.

Deer stopped only briefly on the bank of the stream before putting his right paw into the water as if testing it for something. Spider shut his eyes. Just to think of anyone putting a paw in water, Spider thought, was too much of an experience. Deer then drank cautiously, his earlobes bobbing in the air, collecting sounds. Having satiated his thirst, Deer lifted his muzzle from the stream, shook his head sharply and looked around.

'Hello, Deer, my good friend,' said a clear but ingratiating voice. Deer jumped involuntarily and nervously edged away from the apparent source of the voice, for the sudden sound startled him almost out of his wits.

'Don't be alarmed,' said the voice. 'It's only me, Spider.'

'You!' gasped Deer, practically out of breath with fright, 'Where are you hiding?'

'Right here behind a brown, withered leaf.'

'What do you want? Why do you have to startle me so? Eh?'

'Well,' replied Spider, frantically searching through his head for something soothing to say that might placate Deer. 'I am not stupid,' he said. 'With your likes around, I would not stand on the bare surface of a green leaf and take the risk of being eaten alive. You, surely, won't chew a brown and withered leaf, will you?'

'I! Chew a brown, withered leaf!! Of course not. What do you take me for?' Deer looked around apprehensively. 'You are wise, though, to be cautious,' he said.

'Thanks to Tortoise,' returned Spider, ignoring Deer's rather condescending compliment. 'He has taught me some worldly wisdom, if you know what I mean.'

49

'I know what you mean. Tortoise is the wisest of us all. That's the truth.'

'Well,' said Spider, anxious to hold Deer's attention long enough to make known his need to cross the stream. 'If you know Tortoise and I know him too, then you and I have something in common.'

'I doubt it,' replied Deer without the slightest hesitation. His earlobes twitched relentlessly. 'What on earth can I and Spider ever have in common?'

'Good question,' teased Spider. 'But who knows!'

'I know,' replied Deer. 'What do you want anyway?'

'Since you've been so kind as to ask,' replied Spider. 'I wonder whether you would be good enough to carry me across the stream to the other side. That is if you are crossing over.'

'I am crossing over,' said Deer truthfully. 'But carry you across? Carry Spider? Ho? Why would I want to do that?'

'Slow down, brother,' coaxed Spider in his most conciliatory tone, realising that the beggar's arm is always longer than the benefactor's. 'You are asking too many questions all at once. You are agitated. Give me a chance to answer your questions one at a time.' Fearing that Deer was almost at the point of hopping off into the water, Spider was anxious to delay him.

'Be quick, then,' Deer retorted brusquely, earlobes pricked up and waving vigorously. 'Everyone knows that I am always agitated. It is my nature and I can't help my nature. Even the stupid Ram knows that.'

'I know,' replied Spider apologetically. 'You want to cross the stream and so do I. So, it is you who must help me by carrying me across, since I cannot cross over by myself.'

'Must? Who said I must?'

'Excuse the must. Forget it. It was the wrong word to use when asking a favour. But, you see, there is no telling where and when I, too, might be in a position to help you in life.'

Deer's immediate impulse was to jump into the water and swim across without another word. He felt insulted. But he waited long enough to reply to Spider's ludicrous suggestion.

'You! A Spider to help me, Deer! You must be joking or you are out of your mind.'

'Neither,' said Spider. 'I am in deadly earnest. You may not think it possible now; but you can never tell what . . .'

Deer interrupted impatiently. 'I can tell,' he said. 'There is no time in my life when I shall need the likes of you to help me. You can't even walk properly in spite of your 16 wiry legs. What . . .'

It was Spider's turn to interrupt although softly and solicitously. 'I know all about my wiry legs, as you call them. I didn't make them. The creator who made you who you are also made me who I am. Everything and everyone in creation has a reason and a purpose.'

'Maybe,' Deer grudgingly conceded, his nerves growing increasingly taut with impatience.

'All you need to do is allow me to perch on your back while you're crossing the stream. And as long as my wiry legs do not touch the water, I'll be fine.'

'You on my back! Whatever next? All those legs and your slimy underbelly to stick to my glossy hair?' Deer shuddered with revulsion just talking about it. 'Why would I want to permit such horror?'

'Because, helping me now in my moment of greatest need will open the way for me to help you in the time of your greatest need, too.'

Deer could not believe his ears. 'I wish you wouldn't keep saying that,' he complained. 'Look, if I carry you across the stream, it will only be because I am kind and generous, not because . . .'

'Fine. Forget that I said I might one day help you. Just carry me across on account of your kindness and generosity. Listen,' Spider continued pleadingly, 'Tortoise has said . . .'

'Never mind what Tortoise has said. Tortoise is Tortoise, not Deer; and Deer is Deer, not Tortoise. Tortoise is only one of us, despite his so called wisdom by which he lies and cheats. Tortoise is not God Almighty. Understand?'

'Yes, I understand. I meant no offence. Please forgive me,' Spider replied meekly, almost in despair. The thought that crossed his mind, however, urged him on to further attempt to win over Deer. Spider thought, 'One must play the fool in order to outwit the wise.' All was quiet for a brief while. Then Spider said, 'Help me across the stream anyway. Forget that I said anything about Tortoise.'

'I think I am wasting my precious time here listening to your drivel. If I carry you across this stream, it will be because . . .'

'I agree,' interrupted Spider, 'because you are kind and generous,' he added, preventing Deer from completing the sentence.

'If I carry you on my back,' warned Deer, 'make absolutely certain that you leave none of your sticky, webby mess on my glossy hair. Do you hear me?'

The hope that leapt into Spider's throat nearly choked him. He could not reply for a while. Then, recovering quickly, he said, 'I hear you. And I promise, I shall leave nothing on your glossy hair. Trust me.'

'Your web is found only in cold, deserted, decrepit, abandoned places,' jeered Deer, 'but my back, as you will find, is fresh, smooth and alive due to my careful feeding.'

'Yes, I know,' returned Spider, not daring to say anything that might anger Deer and make him jump into the water without him. 'I know and I am grateful for your help. May I climb onto your back now?'

'Climb on if you can. Can you manage or do I also have to . . .'

'I can manage, thank you. But. please move a bit closer.' Only someone who has known the depth of abject despair and been rescued from life-threatening hopelessness may be able to comprehend Spider's relief. Hope has the habit of enveloping its unhappy victim in the blackest shroud and then suddenly ripping itself apart to display the brightly lit path to the fulfilment of what it has threatened to deny.

Deer grudgingly edged to towards the leaf under which Spider had been sheltering until the left side of his haunch touched the edge of the fragile leaf and Spider quickly clambered onto his side. From the slight touch of Deer's body, the leaf shook and fell off the branch, with just enough time to allow Spider to climb on Deer's back. Spider inched his way until he was resting on the middle of Deer's back.

'Are you up yet?'

Spider was so light that Deer could not even feel his movement on his back.

'Yes, thank you, well and truly. I couldn't be happier.'

'Don't you weigh anything at all? I can't feel any of your legs on my back, in spite of their number.'

'I didn't think you could feel my weight. Your hide is thick and you are a great deal heavier than I am. Can Elephant feel the weight of a tsetse fly on his back?'

Without any answer to Spider's banter, Deer stepped into the water and swam across the ever-moving, gently rustling stream. Deer emerged on the opposite bank, shook his head sharply and waited just long enough for Spider to disembark. Deer did not wait to be thanked. He went off at a hop and disappeared into the undergrowth.

Perhaps it was a mere coincidence that Spider and Deer found themselves at the same new source of food in the jungle clearing. It was a site which the human food-growers had recently sown with crops which had germinated and given rise to a fresh gathering of flies for Spider to trap in his webs and a huge supply of fresh and succulent leaves and shoots for Deer to devour. Both found an enormous store of food on the site which the food-grower and his family were sure would shortly yield an excellent harvest. Thus, on that single site, the food grower's, Deer's and Spider's hopes of abundant food coalesced.

Deer went to work frenetically, jaws grinding zealously. Spider, on the other hand, began to lay traps for his prey. Both Deer and Spider fed sumptuously throughout the night until next morning when dew-drops began to sparkle in the unused parts of Spider's webs and Deer's ears began to detect distant human voices approaching. Although Deer had virtually forgotten Spider's existence, Spider kept his benefactor constantly in mind.

At the first sign of human presence in the clearing, Deer disappeared into the jungle, leaving fresh paw-prints on the dew-drenched earth. Spider, meanwhile, settled on the underside of a dried-up leaf on the edge of the clearing, quite out of sight or reach of anyone.

The farmer's senior wife was the first to offer joyful compliments to her husband on the successful growth of the crops. 'Oh, my husband and master,' she enthused, 'look how well my okra is doing! Look at the Spider's web spreading over the sprouting shoots. It is only a matter of days before I begin to take the pods off the trees. Òsánóbuá be praised.' She seemed very pleased with herself and the entire world.

'Your okra patch,' said her husband, 'will always be untouched by any blight or flies if the Spider's web spreads over it every night. It prevents flies from chewing up the sprouting shoots.' He, too, sounded pleased with himself and the world.

Husband and senior wife smiled contentedly at each other, each recalling the fruitfulness that might be reproduced on the farm by events of the previous night on the mud-bed which they shared at home. I have always felt, the woman reflected with a coy smile, that going to bed early at night stimulates productive energy. If only I could make my husband and master agree with me more, she ruminated. Her husband's thoughts were, in fact, not that far from hers. He was wondering how to reduce the amount of time he spent at the Council of Elders meetings in the evenings and was slowly discovering that it might be an excellent excuse to say he had to rise early to head for the clearing. None but the lazy and irresponsible, he concluded, would dispute that.

The intimate thoughts of the farmer and his wife were short-lived. For, from some distant corner of the clearing, the raised voice of the youngest son assailed his parents' ears.

'Father, look!' the young man called, 'some animal has cropped the young yam shoots which I saw sprouting only yesterday. Look!' he moaned, 'there's nothing left of them. All eaten overnight.'

His parents rushed to his side to take a closer look.

'It is Deer,' said the father. The mother nodded vigorously in agreement. She was speechless.

'It must be Deer,' said the man. 'I was afraid all along that this would happen. Deer has invaded my territory without permission. That's against the law. Deer must pay the price. He must be stopped before further harm comes to the crops.'

Before returning home that evening, the farmer and his family held a conference beneath a nearby tree which provided much needed shade from the midday sun. They sat not far from Spider's hide-out.

'Deer must die,' vowed the eldest son.

'Yes, son,' affirmed the father, 'that must be seen to at once.'

'If you speak to the Elders at the Council meeting tonight,' suggested the wife, 'they can arrange for help. Two or three additional hands, well-armed, should be enough.'

'True,' said the father, disappointed at the thought of having to stay late at the Council meeting that night.

'Well,' thought the wife, with a shrug of resignation. 'Damn that Deer,' she swore beneath her breath. 'I hope they kill him soon.'

'Early tomorrow morning,' said the father, 'we will all come back, surround the clearing and wait for Deer and hunt him down. He can't escape.'

'Not if we're early,' declared the eldest son.

'But,' ventured the younger son, 'why not find Deer's path into the clearing and set a trap for him? Deer is senseless and will soon step into a trap.'

'That, too, is a good idea,' replied the elder brother, condescendingly, 'but father wants Deer dead quickly and I agree with him.'

It was agreed that Deer should die the next morning. It seemed a well-laid plan for which there would be ready support at the meeting of the Council of Elders, since other farmers would benefit from its results.

Unknown to the farmer and his family, Spider heard all that was said. Later that night, Deer galloped mindlessly into the clearing and thoughtlessly began to eat yam shoots. Deer had totally ignored the part of the clearing which had been covered by Spider's webs. That side, Deer thought, was old and contained nothing fresh or succulent.

'Oi,' called a voice, 'it's me, your friend, Spider. I'm over here.'

'You again? I'm not going back to the stream, just in case you want another piggy-back across it. There is enough fresh food here to last me quite some time yet.'

'If you live to eat it.'

'What do you mean if I live to eat it? Of course, I'll live to eat it.'

'They've planned to capture you.'

'Who's planned to capture me?'

'The farmer and his family. I heard it all.'

Deer, in shock, hopped over close to Spider who then revealed the farmer's plot. Deer was struck dumb with fright. He breathed in gasps as the hammer of fear battered the anvil of his heart. 'What am I to do?' he gasped, half pleadingly. The lure of the fresh field of yam shoots was too strong to be lightly abandoned by him. Yet the fear of imminent death was overwhelming.

'I will help you out,' said Spider.

'You? How?' Deer could not disguise his scepticism. 'How can you help me?'

'Calm down,' said Spider and he carefully outlined a counter-plan, little of which could Deer fully comprehend.

'You may eat as many of the yam shoots as you wish,' said Spider, 'but just before dawn, even if I am fast asleep, you must wake me.'

'Then what?'

'Never mind what. If you want to remain alive, then wake me. Here is where I will be.'

'Of course. Except . . .'

'Except nothing,' Spider interrupted, 'eat your bellyful of the crops while you can. The hunting party won't be here until first light.'

Having no option, Deer went about eating up as much of the crops as he could, leaving paw-prints everywhere. Even the okra plot was not spared. At first light, Deer surprised himself by actually remembering to wake Spider before disappearing into the jungle. No sooner had Deer vacated the clearing than Spider went to work, weaving thick, impenetrable webs over every fresh paw-print left behind by Deer. Even the stunted yam twigs that had lost their leaves to Deer's busy jaws were carefully covered with Spider's webs. And the smooth path which the careless Deer had made from the jungle into the clearing was meticulously covered so that it looked as if nothing had passed through it for many years. Everything and everywhere that Deer had touched the previous night was thoroughly obliterated with ancient-looking webs. Then, just as the jungle cockerel began to announce loudly that the sun was on his way up, Spider withdrew to the underside of a withered leaf and waited.

Faithful to their plans, the farmer and his team arrived; they were armed and took their positions around the clearing, but Deer was nowhere near the farm. Then, wondering what might have happened, the members of the hunting team began to inspect the clearing for clues. All they could see were what looked like ancient paw-prints covered over by Spider's web.

'But there's no fresh paw-prints around,' said one member of the team.

'I know,' said another. 'Where are the fresh paw-prints you said you saw?'

'The only path through which Deer might have entered this clearing,' said a third, 'is so old that it doesn't seem to have been used even by the Jungle Mouse in recent times.'

There was some confused talking over the whole futile affair. The farmer and his sons, thought their companions, must have been imagining things. Spider watched and listened as the confused discussion proceeded.

'We must return to our own farms,' said one of the disappointed companions. 'Enough of my time has been wasted here already.'

The others agreed and they left the clearing. The farmer, dispirited, asked his sons to put away their hunting weapons and to do some weeding.

The working day drew to a close and the farmer and his sons left for home, their hopes vanished and their pride beneath their feet. Later that evening, Deer bounced nervously into the clearing.

'Hey,' Deer shouted, 'where are you, Spider, my good friend?'

'Over here,' replied Spider with a giggle. 'You are safe. They've all gone home with their cudgels and disappointment.'

'What did you do?'

'Nothing much,' replied Spider somewhat nonchalantly. He ran over the events of the day and told Deer how the farmer and his hunting team had been successfully fooled.

'I don't know what to say,' admitted Deer without guilt or shame. 'You seem to have saved my life.'

'Seem, it is!' sneered Spider. 'Just as you seemed to have carried me across the stream?'

There was an uncomfortable silence. Then Spider said, 'If there wasn't a law against saying "I told you so", I would readily say to you "I told you so".'

Deer stared foolishly at Spider as if attempting to come to terms with the fact that Spider had, in fact, helped him in his time of need.

'I told you that you can never tell where help will come from,' added Spider for additional effect. 'Remember? There's no limit to what one being may do for another in moments of need.'

Silence descended on the jungle clearing.

7

Tortoise and the King

*Things are elaborately connected, and it is
impossible ever to be totally objective.*

(*Ẹ̀dó* proverb)

AFTER THE GREAT DEBATE, humans had a good many
lessons to learn. As the last to see the Dawn, they were
backward and slow to understand what life is about. It was this
hard road to understanding that led to the birth of social norms,
ethical values and moral imperatives among the *Ẹ̀dó*; and all
those later became encapsulated in parables and proverbs.

The fight between Ram and Leopard and the encounter
between Spider and Deer taught humans two important lessons
about life. The first was the lesson of humility and the dangers
of arrogance. The second was the lesson of respect for others,
regardless of their outward appearance. Indeed, the narrative
about 'Later Arrivals' teaches many valuable lessons, notable
among which are that things are never the same *here* as they are
in the *hereafter*; children choose their parents, not the other way
around; caring for children is an act of gratitude and demands
a great sense of duty; and, since humans choose their own
destinies, they alone are responsible for their lives.

The lessons taught by the Great Debate are, of course, quite
obvious in that narrative. But in the story of what happened
between Tortoise and the king, there is yet another lesson
of great importance. Who better to teach this lesson than the
inimitable Tortoise and who better to learn it the hard way but
the king himself, the fountain of human wisdom!

Shortly after the humans had recovered from their initial

shock of having to produce their own food, when Tortoise taught them the art of cultivation, the king himself decided to become a farmer. That way, his majesty must have thought, his subjects would have no qualms about farming, since they would have the king's divine example to follow. For, among the Èdó, as their saying goes, when the king laughs, all his chiefs and subjects knock their heads against pillars in hilarity. So, the king must have concluded, if there was a royal farm, no one else throughout the kingdom would find any reason for not farming. Sky's sudden departure would rapidly be forgotten if everyone had full stomachs.

The king's decision to farm was taken privately, in consultation with Esagho, the king's senior wife.

'Your food-growing plot, my lord,' she enthused, 'will be so large that no one on earth could traverse it.' She was well known for enthusing at the wrong time and over the wrong issues. She was, in fact, the personification of evil in the harem and an endless thorn in the royal side. Half the personal and national disasters that had so far befallen the king and the kingdom could be laid at her door. Yet the king could not get rid of her. As the Èdó would say, she was something that could neither be kept nor thrown away.

However, having decided that the king was to become a farmer, it was arranged that his subjects should be mustered to work on his plot. A huge multitude of able-bodied men got ready to begin work a few days later.

Tortoise waited until all the arrangements had been agreed upon. Then he hailed his king. 'Your Majesty,' said Tortoise, eyeing Esagho furtively and edging away from the reach of anyone who might wish to elbow him in the neck. 'This whole arrangement sounds excellent in many ways,' said Tortoise, 'in almost every way, I should say. But . . .'

The king looked somewhat displeased.

'But what, Tortoise?' cut in Esagho with her usual vehemence. She and Tortoise were avowed enemies and would give everything they owned to thwart each other whenever possible, although Tortoise had to use clandestine means because of Esagho's position as the king's senior wife.

'Your Majesty,' continued Tortoise unabashed, 'there is only one thing missing.'

'And what might that be, Tortoise?' queried one of the chiefs who was standing away from the throne and slowly fanning himself with his elaborately embroidered fan. He was one of those who secretly admired Tortoise and who successfuly concealed his detestation of Esagho.

'When the king made these arrangements,' replied Tortoise, 'his majesty should have added a proviso, saying "barring any obstacle".'

Esagho was seized by a paroxysm of hate and was almost overcome by the desire to take Tortoise by his wrinkled neck and wring it. The chiefs in attendance looked anxiously from one to the other and desperately at the king. His majesty managed to contain any royal expletives which Tortoise might have deserved.

'When arrangements are made for a future event,' said Tortoise, turning on the charm which he used when engaged in delicate negotiations, 'especially an event as important as the king's food-growing enterprise, it is wise to say "barring any obstacle". That way . . .'

Tortoise was not allowed to complete his sentence. The king interrupted. 'What obstacle,' asked the king, 'can ever stand between a king and his arrangements, Tortoise? Can you name one?'

'The king of heaven and earth, the lord of life and death', elaborated an exasperated chief, dressed in the ceremonial scarlet that defined his high status beside the king. 'What obstacle can ever prevent his royal will from taking effect?'

Tortoise eyed the chief disdainfully from under the hood of his eyebrows, silently dismissing him as a sycophant. Everyone in the audience began to talk at once, expressing their hostility to Tortoise and trying, in the process, to be seen to identify themselves with the king's will. That way, they all thought, they stood to gain the king's favour.

In the din that followed, no one noticed Tortoise slipping away out of reach and out of sight. The arrangements for work on the king's farm remained unaltered.

61

Over a period of time, Tortoise's frugality had yielded him a secret hoard of maize and groundnuts which he stored carefully away, out of reach of anyone. Tortoise's own private food production had been successful, but what he did not harvest from his own farm he obtained by deception from other food-growers. Back in his lair, Tortoise opened his store of dried maize and groundnuts and began the long and arduous task of roasting and salting them. He carefully packed the finished product in bags and hid them safely out of harm's way. On the day that work was to begin on the king's farm, Tortoise had ready a large store of roasted and salted maize and groundnuts, well mixed. Before first cock-crow, Tortoise began transporting his bags of roasted maize and groundnuts to the top of a tree on the path to the king's farm-plot. By sunrise, when the workers took to the path, Tortoise had installed himself firmly among the branches of the tree, surrounded by his bags of roasted maize and groundnuts.

As the first of the workers approached the foot of the tree, Tortoise released a downpour of salted nuts which rained down on the workers' heads and strewed the path. The leading members of the team stopped and picked up some of the nuts for inspection. Then, the more adventurous among them put the nuts in their mouths and began to chew. They tasted like nothing they had ever known.

'Try these,' said one of them.

'What are they?' asked another.

'We don't know. But they seem to be falling from sky.'

'From sky?' asked another.

'But sky has gone. Gone far away,' cried yet another, with regret easy to discern in his voice.

Soon, the entire body of king's workers put down their tools and began to collect Tortoise's tasty nuts. They ate as much as their stomachs could hold and began to store the remainder in every container they could lay their hands on. The more they collected, the more Tortoise let drop. All day long they were trapped halfway between the projected plot and their homes. And, to their surprise, the sun had shifted his position far down to where he usually met with the earth and darkness was falling fast. They had not reached the king's farm and not a single blade of grass had been cut there that day. The workers returned to the city and, in trepidation, had to report to the king that they had not done any work on his farm.

No sooner had the last of the workers left the foot of the tree than Tortoise climbed down and headed for the city. He found his way to the palace before any of the others and waited under cover.

The king was waiting for news. It arrived. But it was not what he had expected. The first to arrive hailed the king, knelt before his majesty and touched the earth with his forehead.

'Well?' asked his majesty, a touch of anticipation in his voice. 'How did the work go?'

'Your Majesty,' replied the worker, remaining on his knees and not daring to look up at the king's face, 'we didn't actually reach the farm.'

'You didn't actually reach the farm?' cut in a chief, shocked rather than surprised.

'And why not?' said the king, astounded.

'Your Majesty,' continued the petrified worker, 'a miracle prevented us from reaching the farm.'

'What miracle?' asked another chief, more out of curiosity than anger.

'We think sky has changed his way of providing food. The food now rains from above, Your Majesty, and it is not like anything we have ever tasted on earth. We brought some of it back to show Your Majesty.' He pulled out a parcel of roasted and salted nuts, poured some out on his palm and held his hand out.

A chief stepped forward, took some of the nuts and began to chew them. The slow movement of his jaws and the way he slightly inclined his head to one side indicated that the chief relished what he was chewing. 'Your Majesty,' said the chief after swallowing. 'I think they're right. This new sky food is better than anything we have ever known.'

There was a stampede to taste the new sky. Even the king was curious and could not resist the temptation to taste the new find.

When all the excitement had died down, Tortoise inched his way out of hiding and placed himself in the direct path of the king's gaze. 'Your Majesty,' Tortoise began with a solemn look on his wrinkled face, 'do you remember my advice when the arrangements were made for the work on the royal farm? I said then that . . .'

A chief interrupted. 'Yes, Tortoise, we were all present and we remember what you said.'

Ignoring the interruption, but withdrawing his head slightly into his shell, Tortoise continued, speaking slowly as if trying to make his words clear. 'I said that when you make any arrangement for a future event, you should never forget to say "barring any obstacles".'

'Yes, Tortoise,' said the king. 'Where is the obstacle in what happened today?'

Tortoise cleared his throat. 'What your workers brought back from the path to your farm,' Tortoise announced with a show of indifference, 'was nothing but my roasted maize and salted groundnuts.'

'Not new food from sky?' asked an astonished chief. 'Is that what you are telling us, Tortoise?'

'Yes,' replied Tortoise, 'that's exactly what I'm telling you. I roasted them myself,' he said, 'and I sat on top of the tree to throw the nuts down on the heads of your workers as they passed by.' He withdrew his head almost totally out of sight and waited for reactions.

The general reaction was one of dismay mixed with admiration. From the edge of his shell, Tortoise gave his final verdict. 'Òsánóbuá alone,' he said, 'needs fear no obstacle. Òsánóbuá does not gamble. Òsánóbuá alone knows both the past and the future.' Then Tortoise withdrew totally into his shell and listened to the noise of crowd as they slowly passed out of the palace.

8

⁓ᴄᴀᴏ⁓

The Undaunted Destiny

*They who have seen only a little vociferate about how
much they have experienced while they who have seen a
great deal cannot even find the words to express what they
have gone through.*

(Ẹwuare *Ogidigan*, an Ẹ̀dó King)

O GUN, THE SON OF OHEN, had a natural predilection for
the supernatural and in that sense alone he could be said to
have been a 'born magician'. Otherwise, his great knowledge of
herbs and medicines was taught him by the animals and trees in
the jungle where he spent the seven years immediately preceding
his accession to the Ẹ̀dó throne. And it was because of his supernatural powers and the wonders which he performed with them
that his loving subjects nicknamed him *Ogidigan* – 'The
Awesome'. To describe Ẹwuare *Ogidigan*, as Ogun later came
to be known, as 'The Great' is to insult his memory. He was
more than just great. He saw the *before* and the *after* of every
event and foretold Benin's dusk some 400 years before it closed
in. He saw the monarch of death face to face. He knew the king
of life, too, for he was that king.

Next to Ẹwuare in Ẹ̀dó history is Ehẹngbuda the magician
(the Ẹ̀dó refer to him simply as '*Ehẹngbuda N'Ọbo*') who, in
defying death, cut off a finger on one hand. Later, followed by
his faithful and adoring subjects, he marched into the sea rather
than submit to the indignities of a mortuary. One of the songs
sung about Ehẹngbuda as he challenged and defied death may
still be heard today in some circles in Benin. It runs as follows:

Ehẹngbuda n'ọbo – o,
ee – tayo, tayo'wa

They were words of subtle advice to the king by his wise men
and translate as

Ehẹngbuda, the magician,
All must return home

'Home' is the hereafter or, as it is commonly called these days,
'heaven'.

It is well known among the *Ẹdó* that the king comes to earth
straight from above and that his real 'home' is above. And what
the wisemen were reminding the king in that song was that
immortality is not a viable proposition among human beings,
even if they are divine kings. This advice was necessary because,
as the *Ẹdó* elders say of Ehẹngbuda, he spent 200 years (*ikpu'ri*)
as a prince, 200 years as *Edaikẹn* ('crown prince') and 200
years as a reigning monarch. Yet, when a message came to him
from above, recalling him back 'home', he refused to return.

Ẹwuare *Ogidigan* was greater even than Ehẹngbuda. Early in
his life, he was other-worldly and heavily involved in the practice of magic, witchcraft and the supernatural. Affairs of his
father's court had no attraction for him. His principal interest
lay in the medicinal properties of animals, trees, herbs, birds,
insects and reptiles. Anything at all that existed – even a dead
leaf – interested Ẹwuare. Everything had something to teach the
young prince. They did not only teach him their own languages
but also initiated him into the various mysteries of their own
natures. One of his earliest revelations was about his own
destiny, which he later fulfilled in its entirety.

Prince Ogun's father, king (*Ọba*) Ọhẹn, was born crippled in
both legs but the fact was successfully concealed for many years.
Only the king's closest personal attendants knew the secret. It
was they who carried him into the audience chamber long
before the arrival of his courtiers. And it was they who carried
him out of the audience chamber long after his courtiers had
departed from the palace.

In due course, the senior chiefs, overcome by curiosity, persuaded their leader to spy on the king. He hid behind a door and discovered the secret. But he, too, was discovered and, of course, he paid the price. He was killed on the spot where he was found hiding and his body was secretly disposed of. But the chiefs later organised an insurrection and murdered the king themselves.

While all the court intrigues were in progress, Prince Ogun was roaming the forests of the kingdom, collecting herbs and increasing his supernatural powers. The chiefs feared him even more than they feared the gods of the kingdom, and to protect themselves they made up their minds that Ogun would not succeed his father to the throne. They banished him from the city and installed his younger brother, Uwaifiokun, in his place.

Banished from the city and deprived of his divine birthright, Prince Ogun remained in the jungle with his bag, called *Agbavboko*, at his side. The bag had been given to him by a jungle spirit in payment for a favour done at a great moment of crisis and at grave risk to the prince's life. The main property of *Agbavboko* was that the more he put into it, the more room there was in it. And whatever was put into it remained safe. Finally, whenever the prince dipped his hand into it, he brought out whatever on earth he desired, even if it had not been previously stored away in the bag.

For a long time, the prince moved about the jungle. He did not build himself any shelter but slept anywhere he fancied. He spoke freely with the various inhabitants of the jungle. He learnt, among other things, that to master anything, whether alive or dead, animate or inanimate, all he needed to know was its true name. With that knowledge he could control everything around him.

Prince Ogun was wandering through a thicket one morning when his eyes caught sight of a hawk (*Ahua*) who was shooting through the thin air like an arrow. The prince's eyes followed the bird in flight until it perched on the topmost branch of the tallest tree some distance away. From that vantage point, Prince Ogun imagined, the world below was at the command of the hawk's dreadful talons; and from that height, it could swoop down at will and pick up whatever it wanted.

'One day,' Prince Ogun said to himself, 'I may be able to rise to such a height in the Èdó kingdom.'

Led only by his instincts, the prince followed a straight path that took him to the foot of the tree on top of which the hawk was perching. It took him three jungle daybreaks to reach it. And what he found on arrival did not surprise him. The tree was an *Uloko*, monarch of all the trees in the jungle, most ancient, tall, majestic, strong and powerful. Beneath the towering branches, nothing could grow. Around it were dwarfed trees struggling to catch momentary glimpses of the sun.

In Benin, nobody – and nothing – except the king could touch *Uloko*. There were three reasons for the tree's exalted position. First, it was the only tree that was sacred and strong enough to supply the lintels that held up the walls of the king's palace, as well as the carved doors that guarded the outer palace gates, and the ornate and ornamental doors of each of the 201 secret chambers into which the palace was divided. Thus, *Uloko*, the monarch of the jungle, belongs to the king alone. But the second reason for its exalted position was that it was the principal host, superior even to the silk-cotton tree, to the witches and warlocks who held their nightly meetings among its branches. At midnight, they flew from great distances to the top of the *Uloko*, carrying with them the life-forces which they had ripped out of men, women and children to be shared among themselves at their banquets.

A person is a witch, not because he or she is evil by nature but because he or she has decided to live by doing evil deeds. Such a person turns into a witch usually by being given some magical potion along with food or drink by an already established witch. A witch never does anything good. Witches are haters of their fellow human beings, especially those human beings whom the witches perceive to be more prosperous than themselves. Witches possess the evil-eye and one is wise to steer clear of them, if they are known.

Prince Ogun knew witches by sight; but he was neither scared of them nor hated them. He preferred to press them to work on behalf of himself and the kingdom. The witch would approach Prince Ogun and volunteer knowledge of whatever might be in the offing. So that the prince knew before anyone else what to expect and was able to plan for it in advance. Nothing ever took the prince by surprise.

The third reason for *Uloko*'s superiority over all other trees in the jungle was through association with the magical powers imparted to it by the witches who used its branches during their feasts. No magician in the Ẹ̀dó kingdom, who aimed at producing effective magical potions, could do without some part of the bark or the leaves, of *Uloko*. Whatever part of *Uloko* is taken however, must be paid for with some libation. Thus, at the foot of *Uloko*, there is always found huge quantities of sacrificial matter which has been deposited there by various supplicants. The foot of *Uloko* is, itself, a shrine.

Thus, after three jungle daybreaks of walking through the jungle, Prince Ogun arrived at the foot of *Uloko*. There his instincts told him to stop and wait. He did not know exactly what he was waiting for. But he waited all the same because, as he was later to learn and to tell his people in Benin City, '*ozine'gbe orhi'uwa*' (it is only the patient person who succeeds).

Several jungle nights rolled by, each night announced by the jungle cockerel, *erhumohi*. The prince sat and waited patiently at the foot of *Uloko*. When hunger struck, he simply dipped into *agbavboko* and took out whatever he wished to satiate his hunger. When thirsty, he followed the same procedure. Every night, while sitting at the foot of *Uloko*, Prince Ogun overheard the chattering of witches who were holding their feasts among the branches of the tree. From what he overheard, he learnt a great deal that was to be of use to him later as king.

On the seventh night, just before dawn and while the witches were leaving for their respective homes in the ordinary world of humans, *Uloko* spoke. 'Ogun, the son of Ohẹn,' said *Uloko*, 'your life in the jungle has been as hard as it has been rewarding. For seven years you have lived in the jungle. Now you will soon have to leave and return to your city. What you have learnt here will make you the greatest and most powerful king in the world.'

Prince Ogun had never even thought of being king. Since his

banishment from the city, he had simply wandered through the jungle, talking to plants and animals, doing the best he could for them, collecting herbs and learning new magical tricks. Surprised or not by what *Uloko* told him, he accepted the prophesy with complete equanimity. If it was his destiny to be king, he thought, then nothing would prevent it. '*Ai s'agbọn rhi'ọba,*' he said aloud to *Uloko,* '*ẹrinmwin ake rhiọrhe*' (kings are made in heaven, not on earth).

While dwelling on that thought, he heard *Uloko*'s voice again, saying, 'Go deeper into the jungle and meet your other friends and take your leave of them.'

'And then what?' Prince Ogun asked.

'Then,' replied *Uloko,* 'you can go forth into the city of your birth and claim your throne.'

Uloko's 'go deeper into the jungle …', reminded Prince Ogun of the lyrics to a song which he had once heard from an old slave who had been his personal servant in his father's palace. The old slave's name was *Ẹ̀dó.* The song contained the lines,

> *Ovbiogue n'agbọn*
> *Sikẹ odaro kherbe,*
> *Uwa rhivb'odaro*

> (You who are stricken by
> suffering and pain, take one
> more step forward, there's relief ahead).

As the jungle dawn broke, Prince Ogun went deeper into the jungle. And as he roamed, he received friendly acknowledgements from all sides. He knew he had nothing to fear since he was among faithful and devoted friends and trustworthy allies. The jungle animals and trees, he reminded himself, were much more friendly than the human beings in Benin City. Both the city and the kingdom were so remote from his thoughts that he would not even have been able to guess which direction led to either of them.

Then he arrived at a clearing. The elephants, he imagined, had frolicked there recently. But as his eyes roamed over the clearing, he caught sight of a lion lying with one front paw stretched out limply along the ground, the other tucked away beneath a painfully heaving chest, his eyes half closed.

Prince Ogun inched his way cautiously towards the lion until he was well within reach of the half-closed eyes which had opened a fraction wider and had tears slowly rolling down their reddish corners. 'Did I wake you?' asked the prince, apologetically, managing a thoughtful smile.

The lion's head rolled mournfully from side to side.

'There's something wrong, then,' suggested the prince. 'Let me help you.' The lion made no attempt to lift his damaged paw. But the prince soon found out what the matter was. He found that the outstretched paw had a huge jungle thorn buried deep in the paw. Blood had caked around the entrance of the thorn into the lion's flesh. The paw was swollen.

'You stepped on the thorn of life,' the prince whispered into the lion's ear, 'and you have bled.'

'I stepped on a giant thorn,' moaned the lion, 'and now I can't walk.'

'That will soon be put right,' said the prince. With gentle tenderness, he lifted the lion's damaged paw and examined it with meticulous care. Then he dived into *agbavboko*. Out came in his hand a steel needle and a phial of herbal concoction. He slowly and carefully extracted the thorn from the lion's paw, cleaned out the wound, applied the medicinal balm and bound it up. The lion breathed a deep sigh of relief and stood up. He could walk again without pain.

'I can't say how grateful I am to you,' said the lion to the prince. 'Ogun the son of Ọhẹn,' said the lion, 'I have nothing of great value with which to pay you. Only this tiny token.' The lion then opened his mouth, his chest heaving, and a shining talisman fell out. 'Take this,' said the lion humbly. 'It's yours for life. And wherever you may encounter any opposition, you will overcome it by touching your tongue with the talisman and speaking your wish. That wish will immediately turn into reality.'

'So, if I touch my tongue with this talisman and curse,' asked the prince, 'it will be done as I say?'

'Yes,' replied the lion. 'And if you touch your tongue with it and bless, it will come to pass, too.' With that, the lion walked away into the jungle.

Prince Ogun dropped the talisman into his *agbavboko* and wandered off. Shortly afterwards he came face to face with an antelope who had been caught by her hind limb in a trap set by a human hunter. She had been desperate to free herself from the trap and had only succeeded in getting her limb almost severed from the rest of her body. Only a main tendon held the lower part of the limb to the rest of the antelope's hindquarters. She was at the point of complete surrender when the prince made his appearance on this scene of terrible pain and sorrow. Deeply touched by the antelope's plight, the prince took her tenderly by the neck and cut the rope that had held her prisoner and had damaged her beautiful limb. He applied a balm and bound up the wound and carried her in his *agbavboko* until she was well enough to walk free again.

On being released from *agbavboko*, she said to the prince: 'Ogun, the son of Ọhẹn, I have nothing of value to give you in payment for saving my life. But from this day onwards, whenever I may be overcome by any human or animal predator, the whole of my left hindquarter, from the waist to the smallest toe, shall be earmarked for you as a tribute.' Her promise has been kept ever since among hunters throughout Benin kingdom.

That same night, sitting with his back against a tree, the prince heard a sad and mournful voice complaining. The cry was like a dagger piercing through the still, cold night air and tearing through his own heart. It kept him awake almost all night. Who on this earth, he wondered, could be suffering such pain? He resolved to find out at dawn. Meanwhile, to mark the location of the cry, he held out the index finger of his right hand in the voice's direction.

'Another sleepless night,' wailed the voice, 'and more pain. When will I ever be rid of this merciless worm that eats through my heart? Who will rid me of it?'

'I will,' said the prince to himself in the jungle darkness. 'Come dawn', he solemnly promised himself, 'and I will rid you of that worm. Just hold on until dawn.'

At the crack of dawn, as the jungle cockerel proclaimed the

arrival of the new day, the prince rose and followed the direction indicated by his index finger. As he searched through the jungle, his eyes soon caught sight of a young, healthy-looking tree. He let his jungle-trained eyes travel up and down the trunk of the young tree. Then, with a sharp intake of air, he stopped searching. For he had found, he hoped, what he was looking for. At the point where one of the main branches grew out of the main trunk of the young tree, the prince saw some fresh white sap oozing out and flowing down the tree trunk earthwards. Here it is, he concluded and dived into his *agbavboko*. Out came a short dagger with which he went to work. He dug out the worm that was eating into the tree, applied some balm and bound up the wound with the soft, watery leaves of a nearby plantain plant. He found his way back to the tree at whose foot he had slept the night before. There he sat and waited.

Later that night, Prince Ogun heard the voice for which he had been waiting. 'Blessings on the one that has rid me of my pain,' breathed the voice. 'I can now spend a night free of pain. I wish I could see this great magician. I could at least give him my thanks.'

Prince Ogun heard all that the tree had said and was convinced that he had helped the right sufferer.

'However,' added the joyful voice, 'if it was Ogun, the son of Ọhẹn, who has saved my life, all he has to do is sacrifice a tiger to his head and he can safely return to his father's throne.'

Prince Ogun knew at once that such a sacrifice would be impossible, since he would never, under any circumstance, capture and slaughter any animal, let alone tiger.

'That,' Prince Ogun said aloud, 'is out of the question. I will kill no animal in this jungle deliberately for my own benefit. If I can't sit on my father's throne without sacrificing tiger to my head, then so much the worse for my father's throne. I am contented where I am,' he affirmed, 'and I will remain in this jungle where I have no enemies.'

With that resolution firmly lodged in his mind, the prince leaned back against the tree and prepared himself for sleep. But, unknown to him, that was to be his penultimate night in the jungle. Only one more night was to pass before he went out of

the jungle in accordance with the dictates of his destiny. For the
next night, his last and final night in the jungle, the sacrifice of a
tiger to his head was, in fact, made.

It happened in the following way.

Having roamed the jungle all day, Prince Ogun settled down
as usual for the night at the foot of a tall, leafy tree. He was
almost dropping off to sleep when he felt some liquid dropping
on to his forehead. He wondered what it might be, but he was
confident that it would result in no harm to himself. Perhaps, he
thought, it was a raindrop which had lingered among the leaves
of the tree after the downpour of the evening before. But before
finally drifting off to sleep, he touched the liquid with his finger
and, rubbing the finger against his thumb, he surmised, accu-
rately, that the liquid was sticky. With that knowledge in his
mind, he fell asleep.

The sticky liquid dropped steadily onto his forehead all night
long. And at dawn he raised his eyes to the branches of the trees,
only to meet the steady gaze of a tiger who had been lying up
there throughout the night. With his face turned downwards,
tiger had bled from his nose and it was the blood from that
source that had dropped on the prince's head.

'Fine,' he said aloud. 'My sacrifice of a tiger to my head has
been achieved and I didn't have to slaughter tiger, after all:' He
then rose and headed in an unpremeditated direction which
took him to the very outskirts of Benin City.

He emerged from the jungle at a point called Ọkhọrhọ, which
to the Èdó meant *peace* or simply *peaceful*. He hid behind an
old lady's hut. The city was seething with celebrations. His
younger brother, Uwaifiokun, was celebrating customary ceremonies in connection with his coronation. It was a sort of
thanksgiving and the city was alive with singing and dancing.
The words of one of the songs hit him and made him laugh. The
words went,

> *Uloko, nọzọ vbe ẹrhi'ogie,*
> *Ughu w'ọmọ do,*
> *Ẹguae ghi rhọ . . .*

(The singers appealed to '*Uloko*, that had grown in the king's harem' to give their 'greetings to the king' and to wish that 'his palace may never be deserted'.)

Ogun, the son of Ọhẹn, wondered silently what his people knew about *Uloko*. The singing and the dancing went on. Sweat bathed the faces of the people. Their shuffling feet raised dust which muffled the air and rendered breathing well-nigh impossible. They coughed and wheezed and sneezed but carried on dancing and singing while the sun blazed down on them. Witnessing the proceedings in the relentless heat, Prince Ogun wondered how human beings could be feeling such joy when everything about them signalled a great deal of pain and suffering. As he was to tell his followers later, after he had become king,

> Rather than grow tall as a result of illness, it would be better to remain short. And why eat hot food with mouth open and head rolling from side to side with the pain of burning, when one can patiently wait for the food to cool!

From his hiding-place behind the old lady's hut, he reached into *agbavboko* and out came in his hand the talisman which the lion had given him in the jungle. As if deliberately testing out the efficacy of its magical powers, he touched his tongue with it.

'Let the city burn.'

Instantly, the city burst into uncontrollable conflagration. The great fire which seemed to begin spontaneously from nowhere, raged fiercely all around the city, burning from the outskirts towards the centre. Most of the dancing and singing crowd scattered in a great panic in all directions. Unable to run out of the city, they began to congregate towards its centre. Prince Ogun watched what was happening attentively filled with secret approval. He would let them gather together at the middle of the city, he thought, where he could corner them and tell them who he was.

Meanwhile, the crowd of dancers and singers surrounding his younger brother, Uwaifiokun, the usurping king, continued with their celebrations regardless of the fire that was consuming the city. And when he had become king, Ewuare, Ogun, the son of Ohen, prophesied a repeat of the conflagration which, 500 years later, was to consume Benin City, this time caused by foreign hands.

The old lady behind whose hut Prince Ogun was hiding, went forward, waving her withered hands in the air and shouting, 'Ogun, the son of Ohen, has returned. Get him and give him back his rightful inheritance. Otherwise, he will destroy us all.' Then she burst into a song of her own,

> Ogun n'ovbiohen
> darigho, dasue,
> Ogun n'ovbiohen
> darigho, dasue

No one in Benin City, then or now, has been able to explain the full meaning of the old lady's song. 'Ogun n'ovbiohen', of course, was 'Ogun, the son of Ohen'. No one could be mistaken about that. But 'darigho, dasue' could not be explained. The ancients of the city claimed that the old lady's 'darigho, dasue' was a witch's special language which contained a hidden meaning.

Uwaifiokun's procession proceeded through the confused city streets until it passed through Okhorho. Prince Ogun spied his brother from the safety of the bush. He dived into *agbavboko* and out came a magical bow, accompanied by a poisoned arrow. He pulled the bow and let fly the arrow. It hit the new king's forehead and he sagged at the knees. In vain, his faithful and devoted attendants supported the king under his arms and attempted to keep him upright. The sight of the usurper being held under his arms by attendants reminded Prince Ogun of his father being held upright and carried by his dutiful attendants before being assassinated by treacherous chiefs. This sight re-awakened his inner anger.

The young king died on the spot. His supporters fled in all directions. Something awesome had arrived, they feared, and they were struck with a feeling of dismay beyond description.

The old lady returned to her hut to find Prince Ogun waiting. She fell on her knees and paid him homage. But since she could not accommodate him safely in her hut, she took him next door to the abode of a man called Ẹ̀dó. This was the man who had been the slave of Prince Ogun while he still lived in his father's palace. Ẹ̀dó was overjoyed to see his old master again. For Ogun's safety, Ẹ̀dó took him out of doors and hid him in a dry well which he covered over with dry grass. Soon the prince's opponents arrived at Ẹ̀dó's dwelling which they turned inside out. They grabbed Ẹ̀dó from his humble abode and killed him.

When Prince Ogun ascended the ancient throne, he took the name, Ẹwuare to which the kingmakers and other senior chiefs immediately appended the nick-name Ogidigan ('The Awesome'). His first act as king was to immortalise the city and the kingdom by renaming it Ẹ̀dó in memory of his devoted servant who was murdered.

Then, employing all his magical powers to the utmost, he set to work to protect and fortify the rebuilt city. Nothing evil was to be allowed to enter the city. To ensure this, he placed at each of the seven city gates a potent and invincible charm so that, when any dangerous influence approached the city, the harm it bore died at the gate.

It was Ọba (king) Ẹwuare who established the legendary Ẹ̀dó hospitality which friendly foreign visitors to the city found profoundly welcoming. 'Never make a stranger suffer,' Ẹwuare ordered, 'and whatever else you may do to a foreigner, you must not kill him. Forgive his transgressions because he doesn't know the laws by which you live. Give him time and teach him the laws of your land.'

Other profound laws and decrees were to follow through his long reign. And a great number of the proverbs, of which the Ẹ̀dó are justly proud, came into existence during his reign. The kingdom prospered beyond everyone's wildest dreams during his reign; and long after Ẹwuare's reign there lingered the legacy of orderly and good governance which he had established.

The newly crowned Ẹwuare understood his subjects as no one else before or after him could understand them, and realised to the fullest extent that those among them who cried 'praise and glorify him' in one breath, would, in the very next breath, also cry 'curse and vilify him'.

9

All or Nothing

If death is beyond words, so is life.

(*Ẹ̀dó* proverb)

THE Ẹ̀DÓ ELDERS say that trouble does not come singly but always in legions; one problem, they believe, always produces another in an endless succession. Therefore, they counsel, to avoid trouble (*ukpokpo*, as they call it) one must steer clear of any avoidable difficulty. But, paradoxically, they also say that out of tears always comes laughter and that there can be no gain without pain.

When they remember Ẹwuare *Ogidigan*[1] and Ẹsigie[2] and Ehẹngbuda N'Ọbo,[3] not to mention the numerous lesser mortals who have risen to great heights of human endurance and achievement in their history, they cannot help but accept the apparently contradictory claim made by their own elders. Thus one is forced to agree that, in order to succeed in life, one must first face failure. For out of the grip of despair will hope always rescue one and out of the jaws of death will life always snatch one.

Such was the case among the *Ẹ̀dó* throughout their long history. And no one among them, therefore, was ever seriously afraid of pain, knowing that in the end there would be compen-

[1] Ẹwuare the Awesome, an early king of Benin. See Chapter 8 above for his full story.

[2] Ẹsigie, a later king of Benin. He established diplomatic relations with Portugal early in the 13th century, and sent his own son to Portugal for education.

[3] Ehẹngbuda N'Ọbo, another early king of Benin, mentioned in Chapter 8 above. It was he who, according to legend, refused to die when he might have done so naturally and, later, defiantly marched into the sea, accompanied by his attendants.

satory relief. And, indeed, it was the intensity of their pain that
made their pleasure more cherishable. It was death, they always
said, that gave meaning to life; and it was life that gave meaning
to death. Ẹwuare, for one, taught them that '*ama rukhọ, ai wu
khọ*' (if one does not live an evil life, one will not die an evil
death).

However, experience showed them that early success and a
trouble-free life must be handled with extreme caution and even
circumspection. For the child that is strapped to its mother's
back can never know how long is the distance to be covered by
a journey.

Such was the case of Idẹn. The highly favoured wife of a
much-loved and venerated king, Idẹn had not the slightest
personal experience of human suffering, although she had constantly shared the pains and suffering of those around her.

Anyone among the Èdó, ancient as well as modern, who
knew nothing about Idẹn would be better dead. Young, beautiful and generous, Idẹn was the toast of every homestead in the
kingdom of Benin and basked in her royal husband's and his
court's adoration. The beauty of her soul made everything
around her seem ugly. Even her harem-mates, never short of
causes to grumble and complain about one another, found no
grounds on which to complain about Idẹn. No one, however
malevolent by nature and discontented by circumstance could
have considered plotting Idẹn's downfall. In the harem, Idẹn
was always the first at the scene of trouble or discord. And
her presence alone was an immediate balm to all hurts and
injuries. Idẹn's sole affliction in life was her barrenness. There is
no life without some blemish and the only blemish in Idẹn's life
was that she had no child of her own. And for an Èdó woman,
childlessness is the worst possible affliction that life can inflict.

On the city as a whole, Idẹn's influence was no less felt than it
was in the king's harem. She was the surest and safest gateway
into her royal husband's heart; and any chief or commoner was
soon restored to the king's favour if only he could reach Idẹn
with a plea for mercy. Thus it was impossible to count the
number of lives she saved by merely a word in her husband's ear.

The king could deny Idẹn nothing, not even the life of a con-

79

demned criminal. And her reputation so spread throughout the kingdom that she was deified in her lifetime in many remote areas of the land.

It was universally accepted that Idẹn's pre-birth choices in front of Òsánóbuá had been perfect, even the choice of barrenness. And in that respect, it was said that she chose to be barren in order to devote her time and care to all the needy children who would otherwise have been deprived of the true affection of a mother. And there was not a single woman in Benin who did not, in one way or another, aim to make Idẹn-like pre-birth choices in her next incarnation.

'If you choose as Idẹn has chosen,' every one believed, 'you will be bound to succeed in life as she has done.' So, in numerous cases older women began on their deathbeds to prepare for their next incarnation by praying to be like Idẹn. Such prayers, made during any lifetime, are believed to be stored up by Òsánóbuá to be added to an individual's choices before she/ he returns to the world again in the cycle of birth and rebirth.

That Idẹn's birth and origin lay buried in total obscurity had raised no eyebrows or comments. But, even had it done so, the only possible explanation would have been that the general lack of knowledge of her birth, parentage and early childhood was an inevitable part of her special pre-birth choices.

'That was the way she told Òsánóbuá she wanted things to be,' everyone would have said. And the matter would have been dropped.

Presently, 'Idẹn-Ọba' (the king's Idẹn) became the standard term used to describe one's dearest and most cherished child or wife or even friend. An Idẹn-Ọba was so dear and so highly cherished and so totally indispensable that she/he was untouchable. And everyone in the kingdom aspired to be or to have an Idẹn-Ọba in his or her own life.

Then, slowly, gradually and imperceptibly, the royal fortunes began to change for the worse.

'Whatever is good for the Èdó,' so the saying has developed over the years, 'never lasts long.' So it was with Idẹn and her loving husband.

It all began as a harmless joke, but in the end, it gave birth to the belief that it is in harmless jokes that one encounters the most deadly seriousness in human life. The gentle voice of Èdó wisdom warns, therefore, that jokes must be treated with extreme caution. This is not to suggest that the Èdó are kill-joys. Far from it. In fact, they are extremely humorous and can tease the hair off anyone's head.

The joke concerning Idẹn originated from Esọn, the king's first wife and head of the harem. It was during an evening audience when the wives and daughters gathered in the inner sanctum Ovb'ikun, of the king's palace, an outer chamber next door to the royal bedchamber. There they told folk tales, sang and generally made merry. In the course of the general hilarity that evening, the king, addressing his senior wife, mother of three and mistress of thirty maids, teasingly said, 'There is no doubt about my senior wife's loyalty and devotion. I know she will not hesitate to die in my place if asked to do so.'

'Die in Your Majesty's place, my lord?' asked the senior wife. 'Yours is the power of life and death, my lord, and Your Majesty can order my death at any time it please Your Majesty. Long may you live and reign, my lord and royal husband,' she added coquettishly, 'but it won't fall to me to die in Your Majesty's place.'

'Oh, why not?' teased the king.

'Your Majesty,' she returned, 'because our Idẹn will do that before anyone else has the chance to even try.'

All eyes, including those of the king, turned in Idẹn's direction, some quizzical, others blank, while yet others were disinterested.

'Quite so,' Your Majesty, cut in Iden, coyly. The king looked from his radiant Idẹn to his senior wife and back again. It was as if he was trying to assess some weight of hidden evidence before making up his mind which of the two wives was speaking honestly.

'The head of our harem, Your Majesty,' cut in one of the other senior wives, 'did not mean it. I know she was only joking. You *were* joking, Esọn.' She spoke from a corner of the chamber where she sat with a sleeping daughter on her lap.

'I know,' said the king. 'I know.'

81

The rest of the evening passed peacefully and joyfully into night, when the palm-oil lamps were lit and carefully tended until they bathed the room with a yellowish light over the ensuing gloom. Then, one after the other, the wives took their leave of the king and returned to their respective houses in the harem.

Idẹn remained behind with the king.

The next day passed uneventfully as the king conducted his routine court business among his chiefs and his subjects. The palace was never quiet or dull. It was a hive of activities and endless rituals from dawn to dusk. And as dusk approached and the various activities drew to a close, the palace emptied into the city, leaving the king, his most senior chiefs and his usual personal attendants to enjoy the private jokes and gossip that would eventually usher in the end of sunlight.

This particular day was no different from any other normal day. Relaxed among his trusted city leaders, his majesty fell into a jocular mood. In the presence of the king, though, none but the court jester, who was called *Aka-ẹrọnmwọn*, was permitted to make jokes unceremoniously. The court jester was usually a decrepit-looking elderly man and somewhat disabled. He owed his privileged position to the fact that he was not only the court jester but also the 'bell', as he was referred to, who rang in the opening of the king's day and tolled its closing. His functions were, therefore, highly respected, being vital to the maintenance of the king's health and well-being and that of the kingdom as a whole.

As the king sat with his chiefs and numerous other functionaries around him late that afternoon, the court jester, the tiny brass bell dangling from his neck and tinkling monotonously, fanned his twisted face with his ancient leather fan, and addressed his majesty.

'Long live Your Majesty,' he began.

'*Isẹ-ẹ!*' (Amen) chorused the assembled chiefs and attendants.

'What now, *Aka-ẹrọnmwọn*,' smiled the king benevolently, 'hungry again as usual?'

There was a hum of laughter round the audience chamber. As it died down, the court jester replied,

82

'Hungry, Your Majesty? Who can be hungry in Your Majesty's service?'

'No one,' cut in a chief, sycophantically.

'Who indeed!' smiled the king.

'What I was about to say, my lord and master,' continued the court jester, 'was that I desire that Your Majesty should ask your loyal chiefs one question. Best to start with their leader.' The leader in question was called Esǫn (his counterpart in the king's harem was also called Esǫn, the king's senior wife).

'And what may that question be?' asked Esǫn, somewhat uneasily. He was secretly embarrassed and a little apprehensive, knowing as he did, from long experience of courtly life, that the court jester's jokes could sometimes be quite dangerous. Such jokes had been known to lead to revelations of the most dangerous and treasonable intrigues among the city leaders. Whoever was the butt of the court jester's joke in the presence of the king had good reason to be apprehensive.

'The question, Your Majesty,' replied the court jester, turning to face the king. 'The question is who, among these great chiefs will be prepared to die in Your Majesty's place if asked to do so?'

The king smiled broadly and the chiefs went into hysterical laughter. When it died down Esǫn cleared his throat, adjusted the chain of beads that hung round his neck, and rose to the court jester's challenge. He said, '*Aka-ęrǫnmwǫn*, that is a foolish question. The need will not arise.'

'Then,' said the court jester, 'answer the question, even as a joke.'

With that, it became a life-or-death duty for Esǫn to give an answer. 'Your Majesty,' said Esǫn, passing a wet tongue over quickly drying lips, 'long may you live to reign over us. Yours is the power of life and death and you may order my death at any time it pleases you to do so. But I will never be asked to do what the court jester is suggesting. Your wife, Idęn would give me no chance to do so.'

The silence which followed Esǫn's answer was only short-lived. Another senior chief by the name of Ezǫmǫ cleared his voice and said, 'Well said, Esǫn. I would have said exactly the

83

same thing had I been asked that pointless question.' It was Ezọmọ's diplomatic way of preventing himself from being asked the same question. The rest of the chiefs looked from one to the other as they anxiously awaited the king's next comments. But since no comments came, the evening came to a close early and the chiefs took their leave of the king and returned to their respective homes scattered all over the city.

Having set the disquiet in motion, the court jester slipped out of the audience chamber to carry out his other, more important, palace function, that of bringing the king's public appearance to a close. Presently, his voice rang out loudly and sonorously from the palace courtyard,

> *Wa dia ghalọmwan*
> *Wa dia ghalọmwan*
> *O- Ogbe – e*
> *O- Ogbe – e*
> *O – egbe naigbe – o*
> *Kpa owẹ!*

('Listen,' the words went, 'there's curfew afoot; There's curfew afoot; all clear; all clear; all that must not be man-handled, move away.')

That cry cleared the palace of all those who did not normally live in it. The ritual horn sounded within the palace after the *Aka-ẹrọnmwọn*'s cry, summoning the king to the next ritual ceremony before finally retiring to his private chambers.

Not long afterwards, the joke's wishful thinking began to crystallise into concrete, albeit undesirable, reality. The unwished-for, untoward, transformation first began when Esọn began to send excuses to the palace for his 'unavoidable absence' from palace duties. Then followed one after another the other powerful chiefs. Then the lesser ones. And then came what could only be described as a general boycott of the palace, which rapidly degenerated into a city-wide abandonment of the king. It soon spread throughout the kingdom. All tributes from near and far trickled to a complete halt. No one, least of all the king, knew what was happening or why, until it was too late. The palace guards, other servants and retainers disappeared as if by magic. Those in the city and in the outlying areas of the kingdom who had sent their sons and daughters to the palace as men servants and maids withdrew their children from the king's service. Even the women in the harem left until it was the king and Idẹn alone who remained.

Idẹn remained close by her husband's side night and day. When he moaned, she tried to comfort him.

'So, it has come to this!' his majesty groaned, 'deserted, friendless, destitute. Yet I am king.'

'Yes, Your Majesty,' replied Idẹn in a soft voice, meant to console. 'You are the king in every way. Your kingship was bought and paid for in Heaven with the full approval of Òsánóbuá N'Oghodua.' (This was how the Èdó referred to the father of all their gods and goddesses.)

'I don't believe that anymore, my Idẹn,' groaned his majesty. 'The days of my majesty are well and truly over. Mark my word.'

'May the gods forbid that to be the case,' prayed Idẹn, earnestly. 'Your days are far from over, my lord. They will never be over. One can't be born a king and yet wish one were born a commoner. That saying is as old as time itself. You told us so yourself.'

'I thought I was right when I said that,' said the king. 'When I said all that, I was just following the tradition of this kingdom. I know now that I was wrong.'

'The gods will . . .'

'The gods!' sighed the king hopelessly. 'Where were they when my downfall came?'

'My lord,' pleaded the faithful Idẹn, 'Òsánóbuá forbid I should argue or dispute with you. But I can't ignore the fact that whoever curses the gods perishes.'

Her words struck a cord of dread at the centre of the king's being. He cleared his throat nervously.

'I do not curse the gods, Idẹn.'

'I know, Your Majesty. Òsánóbuá be praised for that.'

Day after day and night after night, the king's moaning and

85

groaning continued without abating. Idẹn could rouse no hope in his heart. If only she could make his majesty do something – anything – she thought, that might ease his royal mind a little through diversion. But what could she, a mere wife, make a king do? A king who never lifted a single finger to flick a grain of dust from his royal regalia! What could he do for himself? No, she concluded, sadly, that would not do any good. She could entertain him with songs and dance, she reflected; and, whatever else she might have lost in the world, she recalled, she still had her sexual dexterity which, even in the recent past, had never failed to keep his mind from depressing thoughts. She resolved to try everything in her power to help lift her husband's spirit out of the depths.

She made little headway. Kings' sorrows, she discovered, were as monumental as their joys were overwhelming, she realised. Kings would not be kings if that were not the case, she conceded.

'I climbed a mere hill,' sighed the king, as Idẹn entered the second refrain of a long-loved harem song of royal praise. 'I have rolled off the side of a rugged mountain.'

Idẹn realised that his majesty had not been listening to her song at all. She withdrew silently into a far corner and wept quietly. But soon she wiped her face with the back of her hand and returned to her husband's side.

Little by little, they sold off what was left of their worldly possessions and were left with a single loin-cloth which, at his majesty's insistence, they shared between them. Idẹn wanted him to wear it while she remained naked.

'What need have I of a loin-cloth in Your Majesty's presence?' she reasoned with him. 'It is not as though I have ever had any child, which might have made a difference.'

To go to the king's market to beg for scraps of food, Idẹn tied the loin-cloth round her waist, leaving her husband naked in the bed chamber. At night, when they went to bed, they spread it over their nakedness to protect them from the cold.

For several years, the king and his Idẹn lived in crushing poverty. While he lived, the king could not be dethroned. Therefore, the Èdó elders and senior chiefs never thought of crowning another king in his place. They were simply waiting until his death before they did anything about a new king.

Meanwhile, morning, afternoon and evening, the king would sit himself on the edge of the famished palace and sing. The words of his song were invariably the same and they went as follows,

> Esǫn, ri'ugi'gho gun mwẹn momo
> Iyasẹ, ri'ugi'gho gun mwẹn momo
> niya de atẹtẹ, niya dẹ'bo
> ni miẹn yagha wa ẹki'ǫba n'agbado,
> ri'ugi'gho gun mwẹn momo.

(The song was an appeal to Esǫn, his former senior chief, and Iyasẹ, the prime minister of Benin, requesting them to lend him a little money in order to buy the trays and the baskets which he needed to begin to hawk his wares at the Agbado Market.)

Needless to say his pleas fell on deaf ears.

One night, just before retiring, the king said, 'What on earth am I doing here? Why don't I just end it all once and for all?'

Idẹn slapped her hand over her mouth, horrified by what she had just heard. 'My Lord,' she pleaded tearfully through her fingers, 'please, never say that. Don't even think it. I will die in your place, if that is what you desire. Kill me first, my lord, before you do anything that will harm your divine person.'

'Kill you?' the king said in horror, 'kill my Idẹn? Òsánóbuá forbid.'

As the king sat, watching the last flickering of the palm-oil lamp, Idẹn knelt at her husband's feet and held her hands together in front of her. 'Your Majesty,' she said, 'my beloved husband, I pray permission to go out later to night.'

'Go out? Go out where?'

'May it please Your Majesty,' she answered tremulously, 'there is an important mission I must accomplish.'

'Mission? What mission? Where?'

Idẹn refused to be awed. She would stand her ground, she

thought. The worst that could happen was that he strangled her with his bare hands. But that, she reassured herself, he would not do.

'I have to see someone, my lord. And it is urgent and extremely important.'

'Someone? Whom do you know to go to see at midnight? Who knows you today?' Idẹn held her breath. She hoped he was not thinking what she feared he might be thinking.

'It is someone I haven't even ever met, my lord,' she said, panting. 'I'm going to meet him for the first time, my lord. Trust me. You've always trusted me.'

'At long last,' said the king in a whisper, as if absent-mindedly talking to himself. 'I always wondered when you would have enough of this suffering and, like everyone else, leave and save yourself. You are free to go.'

'My lord,' said Idẹn frantically. 'You've done me an injustice. I will never desert you, my lord. Only death and death alone will separate me from your side. The oaths of loyalty I took will always remain in my heart.' She wiped the tears from her eyes with the back of her hand. 'I will explain when I return. I shall be back here before second cock-crow.'

'If you must go out at dead of night,' his majesty said after an uneasy pause, 'I will go with you.'

'May it please Your Majesty, my lord and master,' she replied, 'what I have to do must be done alone, by myself.' She waited with baited breath for his reaction which was miserably slow in coming. And she added, hesitatingly, 'We can't go out together, anyhow, my lord. There's only one loin-cloth between us.'

He relapsed deeper into morose silence. He was crying quietly. Idẹn could not bear the sight. She put her hands over her eyes. He lay on the bed, naked, rolled over and faced the blank wall.

Idẹn plunged into midnight darkness, not really sure where she was heading. She tore an unsteady path through the thick, deaf, dumb and sightless darkness of a sleeping city that bore all the appearance of peace on a full stomach after an honest day's toil. She tripped over unknown obstacles, fell flat on her face, picked herself up and pressed on. All the witches in the land, she imagined, must be settled on some *Uloko*, sharing their feast. And the old lady of the legend must be seated on her favourite branch of the silk-cotton tree, twirling her silk thread slowly through her slender fingers. But none of that, she thought, was her concern. There was nothing on earth or in heaven, she reminded herself, to stand between her and her destination, unknown though it so far was.

'I must hurry,' she said to herself aloud. 'I can't bear to leave my husband alone by himself for too long.' Her pace quickened, breaking through the solid night, a human vessel bearing an unknown fate. A quiet voice in her womb whispered an oath. She would find out what she was seeking that night, she swore silently, even if she died in the search. Determination can sometimes be preternatural in its depth and ability to motivate a mere mortal in desperation. And Idẹn's motivation to find Ọbi'ro⁴ that night was preternatural. The night, creeping towards daybreak, was cold and freezingly indifferent. Idẹn broke into a sweat in spite of the cold. She felt gripped on all sides by unkown and unseen walls, like the upright walls of a grave. Her

---

⁴ Ọbi'ro was the great invisible Oracle. Everyone in the ancient kingdom of Benin knew about Ọbi'ro by name only but none had ever seen the Oracle. No one, therefore, could describe what Ọbi'ro looked like. It could not be said whether Ọbi'ro was male or female or half-male and half-female. No one knew where Ọbi'ro resided. But everyone knew that the Oracle could be sought and found at times of the greatest human need. Ọbi'ro, it was said, always knew when any mortal was seeking to make contact, and then the Oracle disappeared into the spirit world to find the answers to the questions the seeker would pose. Ọbi'ro manifested an awesome presence in various disguises – sometimes as an ant-hill, sometimes as a lion, sometimes as a whirlwind or a cyclone, sometimes as a pool of water. When Ọbi'ro spoke, the hearer was enveloped by the sound alone without any vision of the source of the sound. How Ọbi'ro received callers depended upon who the caller was. But precisely where Ọbi'ro was to be encountered, was an impenetrable mystery. Ọbi'ro, as the Ẹ̀dó elders said, possessed the power to burn spontaneously and to rise again out of the ashes and speak to a seeker of truth. For anyone in desperate straits in life, Ọbi'ro was the last resort. Ọbi'ro never failed those who were granted audience. To those who were not granted audience, Ọbi'ro paid no attention at all. It was said that the only mortal who ever set eyes on Ọbi'ro was Ewuare the Awesome. It was Ọbi'ro, according to popular belief, who gave Ewuare the power to dematerialise at will and to appear at more than one spot at once. So that, while holding court in the palace in Benin City, he was simultaneously sorting out problems in other parts of his beloved kingdom.

feet felt as if they were moving of their own volition, pointing in a direction that they had chosen entirely for themselves without Idẹn's conscious connivance. The name Ọbi'ro clung to her mind with the same tenacity as the old loin-cloth which clung to her torso. What must be done, she thought, in a haze of uncertainty, must be done, come what may.

As she pierced through the cold night, a solemn voice suddenly wrapped itself around Idẹn from head to foot like a wet shroud.

'Idẹn, my daughter,' the voice called out of the night all around her. It penetrated her entire being and held it tightly together. 'The king's Idẹn, I got back as soon as I could, my child, from the land of the dead. The answer to your question was not easy to find.'

The sound stopped her in her tracks. Before her quivered a yellowish body of light. It was soft and woolly to the eye. She broke out in a cold sweat again, passed the back of her hand rapidly over her eyes, and sniffed. The tips of her fingers curled into the palms of her hands and her feet remained rooted to the earth as if frozen.

'Ọbi'ro, my father,' began Idẹn in an unsteady voice, 'I don't know how far is the land of the dead. But I haven't much time. I must be back at my husband's side before second cock-crow. Please, Ọbi'ro, what answer have you for me?'

'My child,' replied the Ancient of days, 'they say you and the king, your husband, the husband of all the Èdó kingdom, must make one human sacrifice to the deity of fortune.'

'Is that all, my father?'

'Yes, my child, but not quite.'

Then Ọbi'ro proceeded to give Idẹn the whole message. The yellowish light extinguished itself as suddenly as it had lit itself, leaving Idẹn once more in the belly of total darkness. She turned and headed back for the palace through the slowly fading blackness of approaching dawn. As she knelt at her sleeping husband's bedside, she heard the distant sound of the first cock-crow. 'I've made it,' she sighed to herself and, climbing beside his limp, cold and naked body, she lay behind him and threw the loin-cloth over them both.

Dawn broke speechlessly and, as always, morosely for the king. But for Idẹn it was as if there was spring in the air.

'*Lamogun*,[5] my dearest husband,' she chirped sonorously. The king eyed her suspiciously. What she was so cheerful about he could not tell.

'So you came back!' He sighed heavily. 'Why?'

'My place, my lord,' she answered unwaveringly, 'my destined place, alive or dead, is by your side. Where else on earth or in heaven can hold your Idẹn?'

He did not answer immediately. He had first to beat back the tears of appreciation mixed with despair that were rapidly rising within his soul. When next he spoke, in a low tone that Idẹn had to strain her ears to hear, he said, 'You still haven't told me where you were last night. Don't you think I have a right to know?'

'Your Majesty,' replied Idẹn, dropping on to her knees at his feet and clapping her hands together in front of her face. 'You have every right to know where I was last night. I went to consult Ọbi'ro.'

'Ọbi'ro!' he repeated with undisguised astonishment. 'You?'

'Yes, Your Majesty. I had to.'

'And you saw Ọbi'ro, I suppose?'

'Yes, Your Majesty, sort of. I spoke to Ọbi'ro anyway, Your Divine Majesty, and Ọbi'ro gave me the message from the land of the spirits.'

'And what was the message?'

She didn't think it would be fair to keep him in suspense. He had been patient enough, she thought, and to keep him guessing any further would be a crime. She relayed to him, carefully and truthfully, the entire story. They sat, looking in different directions, each lost in secret thoughts.

'So, we are to sacrifice a human being to the deity of fortune,' he said, after a long pause.

---

[5] *Lamogun* is the Family Salutation especially used by members of the Royal Family in Benin. Among the Ẹ̀dó, particularly the 85 leading and original families that make up the kingdom, every family has its own special Family Salutation. It marks the natural boundary between one family and another and its use identifies each of its users – rather like an emblem or coat-of-arms granted to the patrilineal head by Òsánóbuá from time immemorial.

'Yes, my lord, just one,' she replied. She secretly wished he would reach out his arms, as he frequently had done many years before, and fold her in his royal embrace and even . . . She quickly banished the thought. The memory was hurtful in the extreme.

'That, my Idẹn,' the king said in a soft voice which he meant to sound kind, 'is one human being too many. Where does Ọbi'ro say we would find this one sacrificial victim? Doesn't Ọbi'ro realise that we no longer have any access to anyone or, for that matter, anything anymore? Is Ọbi'ro . . .' He stopped himself before he said anything he might later regret.

'We will find one, my lord,' Idẹn reassured him, gently stroking his exposed, thin arm. He was so emaciated that the skin all over his body had become crinkled into folds, while his bones stuck out at every joint. He was not the man he used to be, Idẹn moaned inwardly.

'We will find one,' she repeated. 'Òsánóbuá will provide.'

He said nothing.

To let him brood too long on the issue, Idẹn feared, might jeopardise any chance of securing his co-operation in the task that lay ahead. 'Your Majesty,' she said, 'you keep forgetting that I am still a woman and your devoted wife. How have I . . .' She turned away her face to hide the tears that had welled up in her eyes.

'How have you what?' asked his majesty.

'I . . . er . . .' Idẹn began shakily. 'I can't remember the last time you did to me what caring husbands do to their devoted wives. Yet I keep wondering whether the gods will not punish me for neglecting my wifely duties.'

The king, feeling accused, remained silent.

'My lord,' resumed Idẹn, 'may the gods forbid that I should blame you. But this Uhe[6] which I tend with meticulous care is still yours and yours alone. I don't exactly know why you have totally neglected it.'

'There's been too much on my mind, my Idẹn,' the king con-

[6] Uhe is the Ẹ́dó word for the female genitals. The word is rarely openly used in polite conversation. But Idẹn employs it here to shock her husband; it was effective, if shocking.

fessed bitterly. 'I have not deliberately neglected that aspect of our lives, my dearest Idẹn, believe me.

'It is never too late, my royal husband and master,' she replied. 'I'm here beside you and Your Majesty can take me whenever you like. There can be no resistance whatsoever.' That said, Idẹn lay on the bed, threw her frail arms around his middle and pulled him down on herself.

A mixture of excruciating pain and profound joy rolled over them. It was as if they had both been virgins all their lives. As if they were discovering for the first time ever what it meant for a man wholeheartedly to enter a wholeheartedly submissive woman, penetrating her to her very core. They fused and merged into each other and once more became a complete whole, not separate individuals thinking their own thoughts about the same subject.

Neither of them knew exactly how long they were held together in each other's arms. Time had stood still while they lay together; when they came to, the king looked far more radiant and alive than he had done for a very long time. Idẹn, too, looked quite alive. She shook her hair, looked sideways at her husband, and smiled broadly.

'You see,' she teased, 'you haven't lost the knack, my lord.'

'Neither have you, my Idẹn,' he smiled as he had not remembered to do for many years.

'Tomorrow, my lord,' she began . . .

He had long forgotten the use of the word 'tomorrow'. He had ruled that word completely out of his vocabulary. 'Tomorrow', he had come to believe belonged to those who *hoped*. For him, hope had died and must be forgotten.

'Tomorrow, my sweet lord,' Idẹn continued, 'we must repeat this reunion. It will brighten our existence somewhat. The Èdó may take from us all that we once had, although it does not belong to them. But they haven't taken, nor ever can take from us what the gods and, especially, Òsánóbuá, has freely guaranteed us since life began.'

'And what is that, my Idẹn?'

'We still have each other,' she smiled, 'and we shall continue to have each other until the end of time.'

'You're right,' he said without hesitation.

'But why tomorrow? Why not today? Why not now, this very moment?'

'Why not, my lord? I just didn't want to wear you out too quickly. There are still many days and many more nights ahead of us.'

'True,' said the king. 'But . . .' He rolled onto her and drowned himself and whatever was left of his sorrow in her.

She began to feel that there was some hope, however slight, of securing his full co-operation in the task ahead.

The rest of that day passed with much less tension and fewer moans and groans. Iḍẹn's spirit was buoyant as it had not been for many years. She even managed to make the king watch her perform a ritual dance and listen to one of her improvised odes. Sad memories of the distant past flooded both their hearts; but it caused no bitterness. For, as Iḍẹn believed, if it was done in the past, it could be done in the future. And that mattered a great deal to her.

Two days went by quite quickly. The king had begun to mention 'tomorrow' in his talks with Iḍẹn, just to please her, he thought, and to take her mind off her crazy idea about human sacrifice. The sun was setting and the room they shared was getting dark. Iḍẹn lit a fire which supplied the only flicker of light in the darkened room.

'My lord,' she said, placing her hand on his thin arm. 'I think we should start tomorrow to collect the sacrificial items as ordered by Ọbi'rọ.'

'You still wish to carry out that task?' he asked.

'Surely, my lord,' she affirmed. 'Don't you?'

'I'll go with you, if that will help you forget your misery.'

'I thank Your Majesty from the bottom of my heart,' she said, falling on her knees at his feet and clapping her hands in front of her face. He was slightly apprehensive that a refusal might lead her to turn away from the sexual fulfilment which had only recently begun to lighten their burdens of sorrow. Having eaten for long the bread of sorrow, the king no longer felt he had anything to lose except his wife, Iḍẹn, a prospect he dared not even contemplate. Without her, he told himself, there would be no life. Indeed, he recalled silently, it was her presence around him that had prevented him from applying the final solution to his condition. It would have been over long ago, he thought. For, if you have nothing to fear from living, he reasoned, what could there ever be to fear from dying?

Led by Idẹn, the king allowed himself to step into the arena of new hope. He postponed sulking until the task in hand was completed. Idẹn knew, as every Èdó woman knew, that in speaking to her husband, she must not only pick the right words but must also select thoughtfully the appropriate moment to speak. This suited the king perfectly and encouraged him to listen attentively to whatever his wife had to tell him.

As Ọbi'ro had ordered, they had to collect for their impending sacrifice 201 torches made out of dried palm-tree fronds, 201 head-pads (which Èdó women placed on their heads before placing any load on them), and 201 fragments of calabashes which had been used previously to carry palm oil to the markets. Having collected all of this, they had to be disposed of in a special manner which Idẹn was later to reveal to her husband. It took a long time to assemble the items. But in the end the task was completed to Idẹn's satisfaction.

When all was ready, a night was arranged for the ritual to take place. The night before the event, the king virtually went wild with sexual excitement. He simply could not take his hands off Idẹn. She, of course, rose to the occasion, never complaining, but urging him on to higher levels of performance. Tomorrow, she thought, is the night to end all nights. Tonight, she felt deeply, it was time to dance the dance of a lifetime before going home.

It was close to first cock-crow when his majesty finally fell asleep in Idẹn's arms. He dreamt. He had not dreamt for a long time, he later recalled. In the dream, he was walking beside Idẹn in the open air, touching green, succulent leaves on the roadside, plucking twigs and showing them to Idẹn who was paying very close attention to everything. He saw a bright light rising over the harem wall. Idẹn seemed to have seen the light too and was calling his attention to it with excitement. He turned and, to his astonishment, all the weeds and saplings around the deserted harem metamorphosed into servants and maids, all rushing around, bowing down low as Idẹn passed by them. Then, the ground in front of them opened up and Idẹn walked straight into it. He rushed foward to prevent her from falling into the hole in the ground, but he was too late and could not stop her. He began frantically to call for help. He was shouting and his arms were flailing everywhere. Idẹn woke him.

'You've had a nightmare, my gracious lord,' she said, wiping the sweat off his soaked forehead with one corner of the shared loin-cloth.

'Yes,' he confessed, 'it was horrible.'

Idẹn held him close to her chest and rocked him as any Èdó woman would rock her whimpering baby. He climbed on top of her, visualising himself in the process as mounting a flat-top table-mountain from which he looked down at a busy world below. Idẹn threw apart her thighs and carefully, dutifully coaxed his manhood into her being. Then the cock crowed for the first time. By daybreak, he had almost completely forgotten about his dream.

The sacrifical ritual began at midnight at *Urhokpọta*, which is the name the Èdó gave to the main gate into the Benin palace. It was said that, standing at that gate, one could not hear the noise raised by the busy voices in the king's market just across the street. The reason, it was believed, was that the gate represented the intersection of the *here* and the *hereafter*. The significance of *Urhokpọta* was that it demonstrated the well-known belief that the cry in the *hereafter* is never audible to the *here*.

The ritual seemed simple enough in practical terms. Each of them carried a quantity of the sacrificial items. When Idẹn lit a torch, her husband lit one from her own. Then they threw the half-burnt torch away and with it went a fragment of the calabash along with one of the head-pads. They did this throughout the sleeping city. At the gate to the palace of every senior chief and king-maker, they threw a burnt-out torch, a fragment of calabash and a head-pad. They travelled from one end of the city to the other until all the items were used up. Then they started homewards towards the long-deserted palace.

At Agbado Market, Idẹn stopped her husband. She placed her hand lightly on his bare arm. 'Stop here, my lord,' she said casually. 'This spot will do quite well.'

'Do for what?' asked the slightly bemused husband.

'For the final stage of the sacrifice,' she answered wistfully, not daring to look into his face.

'Now what?'

'Now we dig the hole, my lord,' she answered.

'The hole? Which hole?'

'The hole for the human sacrifice, my lord,' she answered. 'You haven't forgotten!'

He swallowed. 'But where is the victim?' he asked.

'Let's dig first, my lord,' she cajoled. 'We must not let the first cock-crow catch us here.'

She handed him the blunt machete which she had carried with her all night long. Reluctantly, he began to dig. As he dug deeper, Idẹn handed him the loin-cloth which he had taken off. 'You can use it, my lord,' she said, 'to carry the loose earth from the bottom. I will take it from you and empty it out here.'

He dug until the hole was deep enough to cover all of him so that his fingers could just touch the outer edge. Then Idẹn leaned foward, took him by the wrist and helped him out to the surface. And, as he regained firm ground and began to shake the loose earth from the loin-cloth, Idẹn slipped into the hole.

'Fill up the hole, my lord,' she said urgently.

'No,' he cried, 'never! You're all I've got,' he pleaded. 'I won't do this. I can't,' he wailed.

'Do this for me, my lord,' Idẹn pleaded from the hole. 'And when I'm gone, please see to it that no man or woman or child steps on this grave. You will recover your kingdom. Ọbi'rọ told me so.'

He was in tears and in great turmoil. But with a heavy heart and heavier hand he filled up the grave and made a mound of earth on top of it. Then he turned his weary steps towards the empty palace where, he thought, he would quietly end his own life. Now that Idẹn was gone, the king thought, there would be nothing to stop him from carrying out the suicide he had once contemplated.

As the light of dawn crept over the palace walls, the servants of Esǫn came out of doors. They were shocked to find, scattered at the gate, the burnt-out torch, the fragment of calabash and the head-pad left there the night before. In a panic, the excited servants rushed indoors.

'Wake up, Esǫn, or you're undone, the head servant shouted at the door of Esǫn's bedchamber. Hurry, you've been betrayed.'

'Betrayed?' cried Esǫn from inside his bedchamber.

'Yes,' the servant brayed, 'betrayed by your fellow-chiefs and the Ȩdó elders. Overnight. Hurry or you will pay with your life.'

Esǫn emerged, confused, from his bedchamber and followed his agitated servant to the gate of his palace. There he saw what the servants had seen.

'See?' they shouted. 'While you slept, your fellow conspirators were making their secret peace with the king. They crept in during the night, carrying their tributes to the king's palace.'

In feverish haste. Esǫn ordered his retinue to collect whatever tribute was ready to hand. He dressed hurriedly in his ceremonial regalia, ordered his drummers and pipers to strike the familiar chanting and headed for the king's palace.

The servants of another high chief, hearing Esǫn's drumming heading for the king's palace, hurriedly gathered together whatever tributes they could lay their hands on and beat their way to the king's palace. One after the other, all the senior chiefs and the leading city elders rushed to the king's palace with their tributes. Each of them, as they arrived, threw himself at the king's mercy, begged for forgiveness and took his place in the normal queue and waited for the king's orders. And the commoners all around the city, witnessing what was happening, picked up whatever they could afford and headed for the king's palace.

In no time at all, the rampant weeds that had taken over the palace and its surroundings fell to the machete. The able-bodied men and artisans began work on the broken walls of the palace and by sundown the walls were upright and loaded with decorations. And soon the palace was teeming with life and court activities. Every city chief, as he arrived, brought with him his sons and daughters to serve as the king's servants and as maids in the newly refurbished harem. Adult women were offered as wives.

The king's forgiveness was freely and generously given to his repentant subjects. And, in no time at all, the rest of the kingdom caught up with the city and everything returned to normal.

Meanwhile, the king, moved to tears by all the changes that were taking place around him, led his chiefs and the city elders to Agbado Market. He showed them Idẹn's grave.

'Here, Ẹ̀dó,' he announced joylessly, 'on this spot lies my Idẹn. She who gave her life in her prime to save mine and to return this kingdom to its rightful owner.' His majesty paused to let his sorrowful words take effect on his audience. 'From this day forward, anyone, man or woman or even child, who sets a foot on this grave shall die on the spot. There is no exception to this decree.'

'So be it, Your Majesty,' the audience responded with a great shout.

10

More Powerful than Death

The knot of Death comes undone as we try to pull it tight.

(*Èdó* proverb)

WHEN UGI'OMO DIED, the entire neighbourhood was
stunned into fearful silence.

The *Èdó* elders say that the screaming in the land of the dead
('Heaven') is never audible on earth. And they also say that, on
the contrary, the screaming on earth is as clearly audible in the
land of the dead as the tears are visible. They claim, too, that
although to the earth-dweller the land of the dead is infinitely
far away and inaccessible, to the dweller in the land of the dead,
the earth is just around the corner, shielded by a thin veil of
unknowing. But, as they repeatedly say, only those who once
dwelt on earth but later took up permanent abode in the land of
the dead can understand and correctly interpret the earth-bound
screaming and tears that keep the earth on its toes.

Babies, until they are named seven days after their birth, still
belong to the realm of the spirits who inhabit the land of the
dead and can still see and hear what goes on over there. And
when still in their infancy, they can freely communicate with the
inhabitants of the land of the dead. Which is why nursing
mothers must be extremely careful how they handle their babies
and little infants and what they say to them.

In spite of all his efforts to reconcile the world of mortals with
the world of the immortals, even Ewuare the Awesome, like
Ehengbuda N'Obo. failed to establish the same value system on
earth as the one that operates in the hereafter. How much the
gap between the two can widen, none can tell. But to this day, it

is the value system that operates in the hereafter that the earth-dwellers aspire to emulate. And among the Èdó, the elders are less concerned with living long than with dying well.

'Enọtọe ẹse, mahe wu ẹse' (he who has lived long has not necessarily died happily), as the Èdó proverb warns. In other words, in order to be judged to have died well (happily), a man must be survived by all of his children; and they must play their full roles in his funeral rites, and all those who know him, must hold him in loving reverence.

The only natural death known among the Èdó is death from old age. Every other death is caused by a witch and the evil-eye. But the route by which one returns to the creator is chosen by oneself even before birth into the world. So, even though it is reprehensible for a witch to cause a person's death, it is still held that such a death was chosen by that person and sanctioned by Òsánóbuá even before their birth.

'Èhì mamie'gho, ẹi gi'ọbo gbe' (if one's destiny does not permit it, no witch can effect one's death), as the Èdó believe. Such, then, was the case of Ugi'ọmọ, the third wife of Ogieva.

As a wife, Ugi'ọmọ lived only because she was a mother. And, according to her pre-birth choice, she had been chosen for a mother by two children, a boy and a girl. She could never have desired any further blessedness as an Èdó woman. Ugi'ọmọ was strong, healthy and happily devoted to her husband and her children. Faithful to her destiny in the presence of Òsánóbuá, she performed to perfection all her duties as a wife, an Èdó woman and a mother, and she was admired both at home and outside of it. She was the pride of her mother for as long as her mother lived. Her husband, Ogieva, treated her with the respect due to the mother of two of his children, but although he was foolish enough to let that show, his great affection and adoration were for his second wife, Imade.

Imade had the physical beauty and the graces of a princess and her manners were so impeccable that she was used as a standard by which to judge other young wives all over the neighbourhood and even beyond. When Ogieva compared Imade's smile to the early morning rising-sun, he knew that he was only understating the reality. Whenever he had any cause to be depressed, it was Imade's presence alone that restored him to his usual joyful nature. That Imade was barren did not detract in any way from her husband's adoration. Indeed, that fact, sad though it was to the household, tended to make Ugi'ọmọ seem less valuable as a mother because Ogieva never lost any opportunity to demonstrate that, had he his way, Imade would be the natural mother of Ugi'ọmọ's children. The situation did not please Ogieva's mother at all, but there was little she could do about it. As for Adesuwa, Ogieva's senior of the three wives, she was past everything. Elderly and lugubrious in appearance, her own two daughters had grown up and were living away from her with their own husbands. That freed Adesuwa to carry on as if the rest of the world did not exist, let alone matter. She remained faithful to her husband and kept all the oaths of allegiance and loyalty to which she had freely and willingly subscribed when she first entered Ogieva's home as a wife. Although she was no longer invited to Ogieva's bed, there was nothing to fear from her. She was the *Iy'owa*,[1] fully trusted and highly dependable.

Unknown to anyone, however, the gorgeous Imade, pride of her husband, was an arch-witch. It is the disarming irony of the work of the gods that anyone who compared so favourably to a goddess in appearance, as Imade did, should also be so foul in her soul as to be an arch-witch; she would fly out through her vagina at midnight, night after night, to a feast on top of an *Uloko* tree – a feast concocted from the life-forces of other people or their innocent children.

The only fear that might have touched Imade's vile soul was on account of the household gods and spirits who might call her to account for her evil practices. And they might have done so had Imade attempted to harm any of Ogieva's children by his other wives. For the main responsibility of each of those gods was to protect the children and their father from any harm that might come from a household witch. In any case, as an arch-witch, Imade's supernatural powers were of such potency that,

[1] *Iy'owa* is the term used by the *Èdó* to describe the senior wife in her husband's house. In the *Èdó* tongue, '*Iye*' means 'mother' while '*Owa*' refers to house or home. In combination, *Iy'owa* connotes 'mother of the home or house'.

with the greatest of ease, she could neutralise the powers and influences of such gods and household spirits, thus keeping herself alive and flourishing. The trick in this matter was ingenious.

The devious Imade could easily hurt Ugi'ọmọ's children via another witch who would actually deliver the blow, leaving the household gods in Ogieva's home unable to trace the real source of the trouble.

As a further sign of his admiration, Ogieva appointed Imade the surrogate mother of Osagie, Ugi'ọmọ's son and it was Imade whom the little boy was consciously encouraged to refer to as 'Mother'. The two were inseparable; and, from all appearances, it looked as if Imade truly adored the child and sincerely treated him as her own son. Ugi'ọmọ was duty-bound to be satisfied with the arrangement, since it was the wish of her husband. Had Imade's darker side been known, Ogieva's domestic arrangement would have been hailed as evidence of first-rate in-family diplomacy because, by giving Imade sole motherly charge of Osagie, he would automatically have prevented the arch-witch from ever harming the child. For, as the Èdó elders would say, 'Oyi -i- rhi'emwin na rhienẹ dayi' (the thief does not steal what is kept in his charge).

The only soul Imade could steal was that of her fellow-wife, Ugi'ọmọ, whom she envied. The soul of Ugi'ọmọ's younger child, the baby Imasuen, was to some extent protected by the household gods and spirits, but mainly as a consequence of the child's own *destiny*.

Imasuen was not even a year old when her mother became ill. Ogieva reacted to his wife's illness with words of disdain and a show of indifference. He even declared that, but for Imasuen, he would have sent Ugi'ọmọ packing because he was fed up with her frequent illnesses. Ugi'ọmọ was deeply hurt by her husband's remarks and his show of indifference to her health and well-being, since she was well known for her good health and happy disposition. But she had to swallow her resentment for fear of reprisals from the household gods and spirits.

As her health progressively deteriorated night after night, serious efforts were made by Ogieva's aged mother, ably assisted by Adesuwa, to call in various witch doctors and diviners. And while one witch doctor attempted to contact various spirits in order to discover the real cause of the woman's illness, another supplied various medicines that might help alleviate her nightly pains and suffering. Nothing was to any avail. Ugi'ọmọ's health went from bad to worse.

Then the spirit-oriented witch doctor, in the course of a prolonged divination, declared what the spirits had revealed to him.

'The cause of this illness,' he said, 'lies in this household.'

'What can it be?' anxiously inquired Ogieva's mother.

'They do not say,' admitted the diviner, 'but they warn that unless something is done quickly, this woman will die.'

'But,' interjected the old lady, 'what do they say we should do?'

The witch doctor consulted again.

'They say that she is still alive only because the spirit of her father-in-law is protecting her.'

'My dear, dear husband,' the old lady exclaimed jubilantly, 'he's as protective now as he ever was while alive. I knew he would not sleep wherever he may be.'

'I think,' said the witch doctor, 'you had better sacrifice a he-goat to his spirit as soon as you can. Any delay will be dangerous.'

'We will,' said the old lady. 'As soon as my son comes home I shall inform him and whatever has to be done will be done urgently.' She then thanked the witch doctor profusely and he departed with his bag of tricks and gifts.

When Ogieva returned, his mother gave him the witch doctor's message and stressed urgency in the matter. Ogieva screwed up his face, his lips curled. It was his boyhood habit of showing resentment.

'In that case,' he said in a rumbling voice, 'Ugi'ọmọ has committed some secret abomination. Otherwise,' he added, 'the spirits of the household would not be after her.'

'How on earth can you accuse Ugi'ọmọ of doing wrong?' asked the old lady in a flash of anger.

'How can I know?' argued Ogieva, his temper rising. 'How can you know what Ugi'ọmọ is up to when we are not looking?

Women these days; who knows what they are up to when one is not looking?'

'Never,' cried his mother, 'I will never stand by while you falsely accuse that poor, innocent woman. Ugi'ọmọ never steps out of this house alone. When she goes to the market, she goes with me or with Adesuwa. She is never out of sight night or day. And she devotes all her spare time to Imasuen. What time would she have to commit any abomination?'

Ogieva relented but remained obdurate, trying to conceal his reluctance to provide the sacrificial he-goat. His mother pursued her son with vigour.

'If my Ugi'ọmọ dies through your negligence,' she screamed tearfully, 'Ọsánóbuá will never forgive you. The spirit of your father will pursue you to the end. You know as well as I do that Ugi'ọmọ was his favourite while he was alive.'

Ogieva felt overwhelmed with guilt. He relapsed into sullen silence.

'If it had been Imade . . .'

'Keep Imade out of this,' Ogieva panted, 'don't tarnish her name with it.' He felt as if he was about to choke with rage. His eyes bulged with fury and he was gasping for breath.

The old lady, sensing victory, pushed on. 'You would have done anything in or out of your power to save Imade,' she moaned. She knew she was speaking a painful truth but it was too late to stop herself.

Ogieva turned in fury and disgust and walked out of Ugi'ọmọ's sick-room. But the next time he appeared before his mother, it was silently to hand her a he-goat on a leash. Reluctantly, he supervised the sacrifice and his mood was soon improved when he retired into his bedroom, accompanied solicitously by Imade. Soon they were heared giggling behind the closed door.

While this melodrama was in progress, Imasuen was showing increasing signs of inseparable attachment to her mother. She screamed, which was out of character, when anyone even as much as took her away from her mother. Her previous fond ways seemed to have deserted her. The fear was growing that she, too, might be feeling unwell.

105

During the day, Ugi'ọmọ seemed to recover slightly although she remained weak and bed-ridden. She could not recover her otherwise rich and healthy appetite. Imasuen was an additional source of worry both to her sick mother and her grandmother as well as the matronly Adesuwa.

However, Ugi'ọmọ's condition worsened every night. Had anyone suspected Imade's influence, Ugi'ọmọ's nightly conditions might have been easy to explain. For, it was only between midnight and the first cock-crow that Imade made free with Ugi'ọmọ's life-force among her fellow-witches on the *Uloko* tree. When she climbed into bed with her husband, as she did every night now that Adesuwa was no longer invited there and Ugi'ọmọ was busy nursing her baby, they raced through their sexual performance and Ogieva soon fell asleep. He slept all night without stirring because Imade employed her magical powers over him and put him to sleep at will. Then she lay down, threw her legs apart and drifted off into deep sleep. At midnight, the bird (the witch) living within her flew out through her unguarded vagina and headed for the top of the *Uloko*. She would not be back until second cock-crow. But on her way to the *Uloko* she would take with her the life-force in Ugi'ọmọ. Thus every night the sick woman got worse and worse.

A dull day opened upon the world. Ugi'ọmọ had had a particularly bad night in which all hope of her seeing the dawn had been all but abandoned by those who tended her. Imasuen was particularly uncooperative. She clung to her mother like a leech and hardly stopped whimpering. She rejected her feed and even when her mother strained nerves and sinews to suckle her, she turned away from the breast and continued to cry. There were moments when she screamed and everyone was frightened.

'My main worry,' said her grandmother to Adesuwa, showing clear signs of anxiety, 'is that the baby sees what the rest of us cannot see and knows what the rest of us do not know. You understand me, my child?'

'Yes, mother,' replied Adesuwa, thoughtfully. 'You think the baby has been told about her mother.'

'That's it, my child,' replied the old lady dispiritedly. 'Babies talk to spirits and the spirits always show them what they do not show us. I fear that . . .' What she was thinking frightened her so much that she couldn't put it into words. 'Òsánóbuá! Please don't let this happen to Ugi'ọmọ,' she prayed.

'Isẹ – ẹ, Iye' (amen, mother), said Adesuwa, sharing the old lady's fears and apprehensions.

'Do you remember what happened to Ọmọrogbẹ?'

'Yes, mother,' returned Adesuwa, 'who can ever forget that?'

'Didn't they say that Ọmọrogbẹ screamed all night before his father died in that ghastly accident?'

'Mother,' pleaded Adesuwa, 'please don't remind me. It's too frightening.' The old lady took Imasuen from Adesuwa's arms and strapped the baby to her own back and danced around the floor of the sick-room. Imasuen would not stop whimpering.

Later that night the worst happened. Ugi'ọmọ died in her sleep with Adesuwa sitting at her bedside, dozing from sheer exhaustion. Adesuwa woke up suddenly, saw what had happened and raised the alarm. Ugi'ọmọ had died shortly before the first cock-crow.

Chaos broke loose in Ogieva's house. He was summoned from his room and he hurried to his third wife's sick-room. He confirmed that the woman was dead. He beat his head with both hands, struck his chest with his fists and stamped his foot on the floor in agitation.

'They will call me uhumwun dan [unlucky],' he moaned aloud, tears rushing down his face. 'They will say I'm a bad husband. That I killed her with neglect. No woman will look at me twice ever again after this. Why me?'

No one could console him.

The cock-crow rang out somewhere in the distance. Adesuwa was grieving openly for her dead friend. The old lady had her head against a wall, with Imasuen asleep on her back. She was weeping profusely. 'Ogieva, my son,' she was saying, 'where is your new god now? Where is your foreign miracle now? What will you tell the neighbours, eh? And what will you tell Ugi'ọmọ's mother? Poor woman! Ugi'ọmọ is her only child!'

As the sun rose sluggishly over the tops of the trees in the backyard, Ogieva dashed out of his house to set in motion Ugi'ọmọ's funeral arrangements. Her body would have to be taken to her mother, of course, carefully wrapped in white linen. He wished her father were still alive. That, he believed, would have made some difference because the old father-in-law would certainly have understood and conceded that his daughter's premature death was not his fault.

In the confusion which ensued, no one remembered Imade. All thoughts were centred on the dead woman and her children. Imasuen woke up on her grandmother's back and immediately resumed screaming. This time a good deal louder than before.

But halfway through the early afternoon, as neighbours gathered to offer their condolences and whatever assistance was required with errands and other matters, something strange happened. As the handlers were arriving to prepare Ugi'ọmọ's body for the short journey back to her mother's house, a bystander noticed what appeared to be Ugi'ọmọ's arm moving. Closer attention revealed that the dead woman had opened her eyes. She seemed to be attempting to speak. No sound came out between her dry lips which were still closed tightly.

'She seems to be stirring, mother,' panted Adesuwa. The old lady rushed forward to take a good look.

'You're right, my child,' she said to Adesuwa. Imasuen screamed even louder from her grandmother's back.

As they watched in astonishment, Ugi'ọmọ opened her eyes wider and attempted to rise to a sitting position. Her strength failed her and she stayed on her back.

'Ugi'ọmọ, my child,' said the old lady, 'speak to me. I don't know what to do with your screaming baby. Can you hear her?'

Ugi'ọmọ indicated with nods of her head that she could hear Imasuen's screams. She held out her arms to the old lady.

'I think she wants the baby, mother,' prompted Adesuwa.

'I don't know whether it is safe, my child,' sorrowed the old lady.

'We are all here, mother,' reassured Adesuwa, unsure herself.

The baby was taken off her grandmother's back and hesi-tatingly placed in its mother's outstretched arms. The baby lay on its mother's chest and fell silent. The women looked from one to the other.

Ogieva stood at the door, shifting his weight from one foot to the other, obviously bemused by it all. 'Is she alive?' he asked.

'We think so,' answered Adesuwa.

Cases of the dead returning to life were few and far apart. Such an event never failed to arouse dread among the living. For, as the saying went, *ai miose no ye'rinmwin* (witnesses to the spirit world are rare). Such a witness as Ugi'omo was approached with caution.

Then Ugi'omo spoke in a mere whisper. 'So, Imasuen has been screaming still?' she asked. She addressed her query to no one in particular.

'Yes, my child,' answered the old lady. 'No one could stop her. Look at her now,' the old lady added plaintively. 'It is as if she's caused no trouble of any kind.'

At that moment, Imasuen was seen resting her head on her mother's chest, fast asleep.

'That child,' said Adesuwa, 'has not slept a wink since yesterday. Look at her now. There's nothing like a mother,' she sighed.

Ugi'omo asked for water. She sat up on her bed and drank it. She passed a wet tongue over her dry lips. She looked around the room. Then she put her nipple into the baby's mouth. Imasuen sucked rapidly and contentedly.

Ugi'omo looked up from the baby at the old lady and transferred her gaze to Adesuwa and then returned it to the baby at her breast.

'She called me back,' Ugi'omo said in a whisper.

'Who called you back, Ugi'omo?' asked the old lady.

'Imasuen,' replied Ugi'omo without looking up. 'It was her screaming that brought me back.'

Together, Adesuwa and the old lady each drew a deep breath.

'My father,' she said as if talking to herself in a trance, 'he wanted to give me food over there. He said I looked as if I was hungry,' reported Ugi'omo. 'But I couldn't stop to eat. Imasuen's screams would not let me stop to eat.'

'You're lucky, my child,' said the old lady with a knowing

look in her eyes. 'You would never have returned if you had
eaten that food your father offered you. They say that once one
eats over there, one cannot return over here.'

'I ran all the way back,' said Ugi'ọmọ. Those who stood by
spellbound, listened to her words in amazement. Could it be
true, they must have wondered. The crowd began to thin out as
everyone withdrew discreetly from the scene, carrying their
respective versions of the story with them to be gossiped about
later at their leisure.

'And grandfather was angry with me. He said, "Can't you
hear your baby screaming? Return to that child at once. Your
time has not yet come." So, I came running back.'

'Oh, my dear husband,' enthused the old lady, clasping her
hands together reverentially. Tears welled up quickly in her eyes
and streamed down her thin haggard face.

'Ogieva,' she called over her shoulder, 'did you hear that, my
son? Did you hear what Ugi'ọmọ has just said?'

'My father!' panted Ogieva from his position by the door.
'You actually saw my father . . .?'

Ugi'ọmọ interrupted without looking at her husband. 'He
drove me back,' she repeated. If there was any doubt in anyone's mind about her veracity, it certainly was not in the minds
of Adesuwa, her mother-in-law and her husband.

'You were his favourite here on earth,' recalled her mother-
in-law with deep conviction and satisfaction.

The crowd had dwindled to just one or two stragglers who
would never be satisfied until they had drunk the cup of other
people's experience to the dregs. There were sighs in every
corner as if there had been a consensus of approbation. A few
admired Ugi'ọmọ while others just marvelled at her.

Ugi'ọmọ slowly sat erect on her sick-bed and, turning to
Adesuwa, asked for food. Adesuwa sprang to her feet in
response and rushed out into the kitchen, nearly knocking over
her husband by the door.

'Watch where you're going, you . . . you . . .' he said under his
breath, and turned his attention to Ugi'ọmọ.

Ugi'ọmọ looked steadily at her mother-in-law and lowered
her voice as if wanting to confide some secret to the old lady.

The old lady inclined her ear close to Ugi'ọmọ's mouth. 'Grandfather took Imade by the wrist and led her away.'

'Imade!' panted the old lady. Ogieva heard the name and he suddenly came to life.

'What's she saying about Imade?' queried Ogieva. 'Can't you stop being jealous of her? I've warned you time without number. You don't listen.' Ogieva was getting het up.

His mother turned full circle and looked her son in the eye. 'Where has Imade been all this time, Ogieva, my son?' She was in deadly earnest.

'I left her in bed. She was still asleep.' Something seemed suddenly to propel him round on his heel and he hurried back towards his bedroom. Then his voice burst through the sombre air and ran through the house. The sound brought Adesuwa dashing out of the kitchen towards the sick-room.

'Help me,' Ogieva was bawling. 'Mother come quickly. Run.'

The two older women ran to him. 'What's wrong?' they asked simultaneously.

Ogieva was beating his head and his chest with his open hands and pulling at his hair, running agitated fingers down his face and across his forehead. He looked completely demented with eyes bulging out of his head and his nose twitching violently.

'She wasn't ill,' he screamed. 'I . . . I . . . we slept here together last night. She was . . . she was . . . everything . . . and . . .'

He was so inarticulate and incoherent that no one could decipher what he was blubbering about.

'What happened to her, my son?' asked his mother.

'Go in there and look, mother,' screamed Ogieva. 'She's dead.'

'Dead?' repeated the old lady. 'Òsánóbuá help us. Evil has hit my home, my son, Ogieva. Something must be done.'

'Too late, mother,' Ogieva moaned, 'too late.'

11

Dusk

By self alone is evil done
By self is one disgraced;
By self is evil undone.
By self alone is he purified;
Purity and impurity belong to one;
No one can purify another.

(*The Dhammapada*)

DUSK ARRIVED, fast and furious, over a large body of water, in the grey mist of a hazy yellow twilight. It hung in the horizon like Òsánóbuá's distress for long enough to become uncomfortable. Portents could have been missed in the cloud of unknowing; and there was no silver lining for a guide.

There was a breeze, too, although not a tornado. Not at first. Not until the breeze met with the uncertain home-grown cyclone whirling in a reluctant swirl that forgot even to threaten anyone, except perhaps the king himself – principal actor in *destiny*'s melodrama.

'Something big and heavy is about to fall,' said his majesty, in a pensive mood that seemed to have taken hold of him recently. He might have been talking to himself in a trance. His eyelids flickered irregularly as he spoke in a dry-throated voice.

'Òsánóbuá will protect Your Majesty,' said Itohan, attempting to console her husband. She was the most favoured wife in the harem. She held the enviable harem title of Ẹhiọba and was consequently the human embodiment of the king's *destiny* and could be worshipped as a deity. She never expected the title because she didn't think she had earned it. But there she was –

she was the king's Ẹ̀hì (his *destiny*) and she must do the best she could to play the part.

An attack on Ẹ̀hì, whether physical or mental, was a direct attack on the king's *Divinity* and must be carefully and meticulously avoided by all those who wished to live to see another day.

When he ascended the throne with the title of Ovọnramwẹn Nọgbaisi.[1] his majesty had earnestly hoped to carry on all the rich traditions inherited from fifty generations of unshaken and unbroken dynastic monarchy and handed to him intact by his father, king (*Ọba*) Adọlọ.[2] Even if he could not improve on what already existed, he thought, he must maintain it and hand it down intact to his own successor. But the king had not read 'the handwriting on the wall'.

No one else around him made any attempt to decipher it. Or if any one did, he did it for his own private interest and not the king's benefit.

Four hundred years earlier, another king, Ẹwuare the Awesome, predicted that the city and kingdom which he loved so much and did all he could to fortify and protect, would face a storm from across a large body of water, on a hazy day in the distant future. The storm, he prophesied, would be followed by a huge conflagration which would wipe out the city after three days. Then, his majesty said, a new *Dawn* would begin.

The legend of the Tortoise, however, persisted. And Ovọnramwẹn was to be the victim of a fate which brought home to him what Tortoise once claimed, namely: '*Egbemwẹn ẹra na lobi, egbemwẹn ẹra na sịẹre*' (on my body was the poison cooked; on my body was it lifted from the fire). To him was to be revealed the meaning of the portents concealed in the womb of time by centuries of evolutionary processes which began at the first *Dawn*.

The events in the reign of king Akẹnkpaye, two hundred years

[1] Ovọnramwẹn Nọgbaisi was the title taken by the king at his coronation in 1888. Every new king takes a title at his coronation. A breakdown of the title is as follows: 'Ovọnramwẹn' translates as 'The Rising Sun', and 'Nọgbaisi' means 'which spreads over all'.

[2] Adọlọ was the title taken by the previous king, the father of Ovọnramwẹn and it translates as 'The Mender', that is one who sets affairs to rights.

before, had been a mere warning about worse things to come. Akęnkpaye did not survive. Neither did Ovọnramwẹn. But whereas it was his own chiefs and city elders who plotted the deposition of Akęnkpaye in 1684, the deposition of Ovọnramwẹn in 1897 was the combined work of the chiefs and city elders and a foreign force from across the seas.

Ovọnramwẹn was more concerned with Ẹwuare's predictions than with the portents that lay hidden in the events of Akęnkpaye's reign. That prophesy hung over his majesty like a dark shadow, stalking every thought and frequently freezing every spontaneous joyful action in the king's palace. Would the prophesy come true? If so, when and how? What could be done to prevent it? And it was the absence of joyful playfulness that pushed the king's most favoured wife, Ẹhiọba, to seek urgent audience with her husband. The fear hung like a pall on every soul; it was a haunting premonition, a foreboding of a great downfall, foretelling a *Dusk* that would prelude a very, very dark night in the history of the ancient kingdom.

The ghost of a smile touched the corners of his majesty's mouth as he turned to look at Ẹhiọba. She was on her knees before her husband, her hands clasped together and held before her face.

'You are only a woman, after all,' he sighed mournfully. Not that he thought there was anything wrong in being a woman, but simply that there was a great deal that had had to be hidden from women. 'An Ẹdó woman must be protected at all costs', Ẹwuare the Awesome had decreed.

'Yes, my lord,' she replied, 'and one whom Your Majesty has made with your own royal hands.'

'Ẹwuare made many predictions,' his majesty recalled. That far-away sound was still in his voice as he spoke, in the manner of a frightened child seeking both enlightenment and reassurance about the way to safety. Frequently, Ẹhiọba realised, the king was like a baby seeking from his wives the comfort of the mother he had never been allowed to have and could not find among his treacherous chiefs and city elders. There were many foes, and his majesty could never tell how friendships were concealed enmities. But he knew by instinct that a friendly enemy within was much more dangerous than an open antagonist from without. For the latter one could see while the former was invisible.

His majesty looked down on the magnificent figure of Ẹhiọba kneeling at his feet. 'Ẹwuare,' he recalled, 'made many predictions and they have all come true.'

'Yes, my lord,' confirmed Ẹhiọba confidently. She was in the presence of one who knew the truth about everything. 'All of Ẹwuare's predictions have indeed been fulfilled, my lord. We all know that and we are joyful about it.' Past kings, she had been taught, must always be praised in the presence of reigning ones but never in their dispraise. To praise a past king in obvious dispraise of a living one, was to suggest that the living king was in some way deficient. But kings, as far as she knew, could never be deficient in any way because, by divine endowment, Ẹdó kings could do no wrong.

'I think Ẹwuare's predictions were fulfilled by Akẹnkpaye,' said his majesty, 'otherwise, the treacherous Ẹdó chiefs and city elders would never have succeeded in deposing an Ẹdó king.'

'You are right, my mighty lord,' confirmed Ẹhiọba. 'You are right as always. Who can deny that?'

'No one can deny that,' answered his majesty, stirring uncomfortably in his chair. His fingers drummed on his thighs. His back was slightly hunched and his shoulders drooped somewhat. It was as if the weight of kingship was heavy. He couldn't possibly be in any distress, said Ẹhiọba to herself. Kings, she felt, communed directly with Òsánóbuá at times of stress. So, she believed, a king could never be in distress.

'If Ẹwuare's predictions have been fulfilled by Akẹnkpaye,' his majesty reasoned aloud, 'then the deposition of a king cannot happen again in Ẹdó history?' He sighed heavily as if relieved. But if Ẹdó kings were capable of questioning their own judgments, his majesty would probably have wondered why he so desperately needed reassurance about his own fate.

'You are right, my lord,' Ẹhiọba reassured him. She was ever ready to support her royal master in every way. 'Òsánóbuá n'oghodua, no gi'uwẹ agbọn (God Almighty who sent you into the world) forbid a repeat of that long-ago sad event.'

But the king was not fully convinced. There was still something lurking behind his unease. He began to recall that one of Ẹwuare's predictions was that an Èdó king would, in the distant future, be betrayed by his own people to a foreigner who would depose him. The foreigner would come from far away across a huge body of water. At that point in his majesty's memory, he recalled the huge mass of water from which the creator-king once rose to create the world. The memory of that momentous occasion stirred in him a degree of pride and reassurance.

'In any case,' he reflected almost joyfully in his heart, 'numerous foreigners have always come to us from across huge masses of water. None of them has ever posed a threat to the king of his kingdom.'

The past flooded back like a tidal wave into his royal head. He recalled the arrival of 'Ikpotokin'[3] long, long before his own reign, during the reign of the illustrous Ọzọlua,[4] known to all Èdó as 'The Conqueror'. In his mind, he recalled the story as told him by his father, Adọlọ.

'Kie n'ukọ'ba,'[5] a distant but strident voice blared from a palace chamber next to the one where the king was sitting and talking with his Èhì.[6] She had specifically sought the audience in order to discuss the important issues of his majesty's fears and worries. The audience was now in jeopardy, with many unfinished issues to discuss.

'Your Majesty,' called a male voice from the other side of the door, 'uk'ọba,'[7] seeks an urgent audience.'

His majesty rose quickly from his chair. Ẹhiọba wondered whether he had been expecting any message from the city all along; but she did not dare voice her wondering. She bowed her head instead and waited to be dismissed. Then she touched the

[3] Ikpotokin was the Èdó corruption of the word Portuguese and the reference is to the visit of the likes of Jaoa Affoso d'Aveiro in 1485. The Portuguese first made contact with the kingdom of Benin in 1472.

[4] Ọzọlua was the title taken by an earlier king at his coronation around 1481. He expanded the kingdom by conquests.

[5] 'Kie n'uko'ba' is the call from behind the door of a palace chamber when a king's messenger seeks an audience. It translates onto 'Open [the door] for the king's messenger.'

[6] 'Èhì' means destiny.

[7] 'Uk'ọba' is the 'king's messenger.'

floor with her forehead at the king's feet. 'May the message be peaceful and propitious, my lord,' she said prayerfully.

His majesty walked towards the door and gave the next order. 'Let the messenger into the king's presence.'

The door opened from outside. Èdó kings, according to one of the decrees of king Ehẹngbuda N'Ọbo, after his majesty's middle finger was stung by a caterpillar, were forbidden to open doors by themselves. The caterpillar had been sent from the land of the spirits to summon the king 'home', when Ehẹngbuda was being requested from above to return to heaven, was his permanent home, and he had bluntly refused to honour the request. 'If I tell heaven that I'm not returning,' Ehẹngbuda said, 'what can they do about it?' He then drew a dagger and cut off the injured finger. From that moment all future Èdó kings inherited the additional title of 'Ikpihiẹn abọ kpuru nọ gb'oduma', meaning 'the shortened finger that killed the lion.'

The door of the chamber opened and his majesty walked through into an adjoining chamber to receive the messenger. The message was from Osodin, a member of *Uzama* (the seven kingmakers who crown a new king at his coronation). Osodin was the only male person, except for the king himself and the eunuchs who served the king, permitted to enter the king's harem and to touch any of the king's wives. Any other male who touched the king's wife committed an abomination for which he paid with his life. The only exception to that law were the princes, of course. Osodin's special responsibility was to oversee the events in the harem, keep order there and settle minor disputes among the women.

'Long live Your Majesty,' greeted the messenger from a kneeling position. 'Osodin is at the door, praying for entry.'

'Tell them to let Osodin in,' ordered the king over his shoulder, as he walked past the messenger towards the chamber ceremonially called *Iwebo*[8], to be dressed for a public appearance. The messenger watched until the king had dis-

[8] *Iwebo* is the area of the palace reserved for the ritual of dressing the king. There is a palace society called *Iwebo*. The main duties of its members include dressing the king, especially for ceremonial occasions, and taking care of all the beads and other paraphernalia.

appeared behind another door. Then he rose from his knees, relaxed as if relieved of a very heavy burden, and smiled in satisfaction at a mission accomplished. His hopes were for a better day. It was a privilege to serve a king. But it was glory to serve him well. If one did one's job well, one lived. Otherwise, one's head went up on a spike at the palace gate and all passers-by spat at it, calling its previous owner '*Oghiọ'ba*'[9]

Osodin was accompanied by Ẹro, who was another of the seven kingmakers but without any special responsibilities, except those connected with court rituals in which only the most senior chiefs participated in great secrecy. The two chiefs sat side by side in silence awaiting the king's arrival. Eventually, the silence became oppressive and had to be broken.

'I hope his majesty is in a lighter mood,' ventured Osodin.

'I hope so, too,' replied Ẹro. 'I can't forget the events of yesterday.'

'Who can!' sighed Osodin. 'That was dreadful. I tried to hide my face but was nowhere to hide.' He sighed heavily and pulled a white sheet of cloth from his waist and wiped his face and neck. 'I hardly slept last night.'

Ẹro folded his arms across his chest, winced and sniffed the air.

'I don't know how to begin this talk with his majesty when he comes in,' Osodin observed mournfully. He tucked away the white piece of cloth under his belt and folded his arms across his chest.

'When did you last visit the harem?' inquired Ẹro in a hoarse voice, looking straight at his companion. He cleared his throat and waited for an answer, even though he was fully aware that he was dabbling in matters that did not concern him.

'This evening,' Osodin answered frankly, 'Why?'

'Did you see *Ẹhiọba*?' returned Ẹro, disregarding Osodin's anxious look.

'No,' replied Osodin, 'she was said to be with the king. Why did you ask'

'I thought,' replied Ẹro, 'you might open the discussion with a report about your visit to the harem. That might ease us in.'

[9] *Oghion Ọba* translates as 'Enemy of the king' – a traitor.

'Sounds like a good idea,' conceded Osodin. He pulled out his white piece of cloth again and mopped his brow.

'I still suspect Iyaṣẹ's[10] complicity in this matter', confided Ẹro. 'It is not as though we have not been warned.'

'I know we were warned, Ẹro,' returned Osodin with a heavy sigh, 'but his majesty . . .'

A door opened and the king strode in, preceded by the Ọmada,[11] bearing the Ada,[12] and flanked on either side by two of his stalwart personal attendants, each of whom supported one bead-bedecked arm. Behind his majesty followed a dozen other household attendants, all stark naked.

Osodin and Ẹro promptly fell on their knees, held their hands together in front of their faces and chorused the well-known greeting. 'Ọba ghatọ, òkpẹ́rè.'[13]

'Isẹ-ẹ!' ('so be it!') sang the king's retinue in spontaneous unison.

Osodin and Ẹro remained on their knees while his majesty mounted the throne and carefully settled himself on it. The royal attendants ranged themselves reverentially around their lord and master.

'Rise, Osodin,' ordered the king in a gentle and fatherly voice. 'Rise, Ẹro.'

'Long live Your Majesty,' Osodin and Ẹro said and rose to their feet.

'Resume your seats,' the king ordered politely. Osodin and Ẹro resumed their seats solemnly. Looking directly at Osodin, the king said, 'Osodin, your messenger didn't say you were accompanied. We thought you were alone at the palace gate.' It was partially a statement of fact and partially a direct accusation.

[10] Iyaṣẹ is the title of Benin's prime minister and head of the city chiefs. He belongs to none of the palace societies whose members perform all the rituals connected with the king's own person.

[11] Ọmada is the man who carries the king's sword of authority and walks directly in front of the king. The king never goes anywhere without him.

[12] Ada is the name of the king's sword of authority. It is fashioned from burnished brass and is supposed to possess magical powers of its own.

[13] Ọba ghatọ òkpẹ́rè. This greeting means 'Long may the king live and prosper'. When offered, every one in the audience must react to it with the words 'Isẹ – ẹ' which mean, 'so be it'.

Osodin fell on his knees again. 'Long may you live and prosper, my lord,' said Osodin beseechingly. 'We . . . er . . . I . . .' he stammered to a halt and swallowed hard. '*Dọmọ*' (hail), resumed Osodin after a brief pause to recover his normal speech.

Ẹro knelt down beside his companion and held his hands together before his face. 'Long may you live and prosper, Your Majesty,' he prayed, 'Osodin brought me along as a witness to confirm his story.'

The king adjusted himself on the throne and made as if he was ready to listen to Osodin's story. Royal patience is proverbial and is as daunting and volatile as royal patronage, and both must be handled with the greatest care. Osodin and Ẹro glanced briefly at each other.

'Iyasẹ is at the bottom of the present crisis, Your Majesty,' reported Osodin.

The king nodded a knowing head. If his majesty was surprised, he displayed no sign of it.

'That is the truth, Your Majesty,' added Ẹro.

'Iyasẹ's personal interest in the new foreigner can no longer be concealed,' Osodin went on.

'He secretly aids and abets Ẹdoghọ,' added Ẹro.

'Ẹdoghọ' repeated the king. There was a clear indication of distaste as he spoke the hated name. 'That's the Isẹkiri chief who is disputing our rights to trade with the new foreigner.'[14]

'Yes, Your Majesty, long may you live and prosper,' answered Osodin, 'that's the one.'

'We know,' said Ẹro, 'that Iyasẹ is still harbouring his Isẹkiri servant, my lord.'

'The servant whom they say speaks the language of the new foreigner?' asked the king with some interest.

'Yes, my lord,' answered Osodin, 'and the one who was brought in to interpret when I put my mark on the new foreigner's book. It was Your Majesty,' he added quickly in self-

[14] The Isẹkiri were a riverine tribe inhabiting the Niger Delta, south-east of Benin City. Their founder-king was popularly said to have been a Benin prince who had been sent there to keep order and organise good governance. For hundreds of years, they paid tributes to the Èdó kings, whose manners, rituals and dress they happily emulated.

defence, 'who personally ordered me, Your Majesty's trusted servant and personal representative on that particular occasion, to put my mark on the book on Your Majesty's behalf. And I did it proudly, Your Majesty.'

'I remember,' confirmed the king.

'And now the new foreigner is demanding that the embargo on all trade be removed. They want to trade freely, Your Majesty.'

The 'book' to which Osodin put his mark on behalf of the king was the Treaty of 1892, which stated that '[t]he subjects and citizens of all countries may freely carry on trade in every part of the territories of the [*Èdó*] king . . .' It had been written in the language of the new foreigner and not all its implications were fully understood by the king. But the treaty had been 'signed' and the king was expected, on pain of serious reprisal, to keep all its terms to the letter. By ordering an embargo on free trade, therefore, his majesty was said to have 'broken the terms of the treaty'. For that he was expected to answer to the leaders of the new foreigner.

'We can't permit free trade, Your Majesty,' said Ẹro, 'certainly not if it is secretly controlled by Ẹdoghọ and the Isekiris.'

'The impudence!' exclaimed the king, looking away from the prostrate figures of Osodin and Ẹro on their knees before him.

'The *Ikpotokin* [the Portuguese] never behaved in this outrageous manner, my lord,' pleaded Ẹro, with nostalgia evident in every word.

'No, never!' added Osodin. 'My own grandfather told my father, who later told me, that for all those years the *Ikpotokin* knew what respect was due to the *Èdó* monarch and never once did they renege on their oaths and duties and reverence. King Ẹsigie[15] of blessed memory was held in the highest esteem by *Ikpotokin*. And they never asked his majesty to put any mark in any book.'

'I know,' said the king reflectively. 'My father told me the story of how *Ikpotokin* accompanied Ẹsigie to the war against Ida.'[16]

---

[15] *Ẹsigie* was the name of the king who reigned from about the year 1504. He, too, extended the boundaries of the Benin Kingdom by conquest.

[16] The *Ida* were a tribe beyond the Niger river. They were conquered by the *Èdó* during the reign of Ẹsigie.

'Their king was a manly man, Your Majesty. A king of great honour,' recalled Osodin. 'But they say that the king of the new foreigner is a woman!'

'A woman!' repeated the king incredulously. 'Horror of horrors! Is that what makes the new foreigner so intransigent?'

'Perhaps, Your Majesty,' interjected Ẹro. 'A mere woman, Your Majesty!'

'A woman ordering the great Èdó king to . . . to . . .' Deprived of words by internal rage, Osodin failed to complete his statement but swallowed the lump that was rising in his throat and threatening to choke him.

'My grandfather used to say,' reminisced Ẹro, 'that the very first *Ipkotokin* who came here always said that their king respected the Èdó monarch very highly.'

'And so they did,' sighed Osodin, looking somewhat bewildered. The kingdom's worries were obviously weighing heavily on his drooping shoulders.

'And,' pursued the king, 'the foreigner who came after *Ikpotokin*. What was his name?'

'*Guala'yọn da*'[17] recalled Osodin.

'Yes,' added Ẹro, 'that was his name, *guala'yọn da*.' At the repeat of the strange name, Osodin and Ẹro stole sidelong glances at each other and smiled as if something in the very name amused them.

'He was extremely courteous and friendly, Your Majesty,' said Osodin, 'I will never forget . . .'

Ẹro cut in, still smiling but his eyes downcast. 'And after that there was *Ezamani*.[18] He brought friendly messages from his king.'

'I know,' sighed the king.

'But this latest foreigner,' hissed Osodin, 'he is foul-mouthed,

[17] *Guala'yọn da* was the Èdó chiefs' corruption of the name of the Dutch trader, Nyendael, who was in constant contact with the Benin court around 1702 and was very popular among the king's agents, This rendition of his name raised smiles because it means 'look for some alcohol and drink'.

[18] *Ezamani* was the Èdó chiefs' corruption of the word, 'German'. In Benin City, no one distinguished one white man from another. No one knew precisely where they came from. Nor did it matter. They were all called *Ebo* (European), regardless of their origins.

irresponsible and vile in every way. That's what happens when they are ruled by a mere woman.'

The new foreigner was *British* and no one understood him. He was conceited to the point of nausea. He would rather be heard than hear. He would rather speak than be spoken to.

'Your Majesty's agents say that he lies and cheats and even steals,' continued Osodin. 'No one knows exactly how to approach or deal with him.'

'We can tell him to leave, Your Majesty' volunteered Ẹro, 'if he can't stay in peace and respect our laws.'

'Now,' cautioned the king in an avuncular tone, 'don't rush into it. Tread warily [*ai tua gboghiọn mwan, na ghẹ wu lelẹ –*].'[19]

'At the assembly of chiefs and people tomorrow morning, Osodin,' instructed the king, 'raise the Iyasẹ issue. Everybody must be made to know about this intrigue and treachery.'

'Treason, Your Majesty,' elaborated Ẹro.

'Yes,' said Osodin, 'long may Your Majesty live and prosper; this is high treason and heads must roll for it.'

'I know,' replied the king and rose to his feet. He walked thoughtfully out of the audience chamber, leaving Osodin and Ẹro on their knees, his attendants trailing him in silent reverence.

It was a huge assembly that gathered in the palace courtyard the next day. All the chiefs were there in their resplendent regalia. It was like a festival. *Eghaẹvbo N'ore*[20] and *Eghaẹvbo n'ogbe*[21] ranged themselves in their respective groups in order of seniority. The air was thick with expectation.

'Send for Iyasẹ,' shouted the senior chief, Esọn, 'and warn him not to keep the king waiting,' he said and added ominously,

---

[19] This was an ancient Ẹdó saying dating back to Ewuare The Awesome and it means 'one must not seek to destroy an enemy in haste, least one destroys oneself in the process'. (See Part Two: the Proverbs.)

[20] *Eghaẹvbo N'ore* were the chiefs who lived in the city. They had no palace functions. They were responsible to the king for the effective administration of the kingdom's outlying districts. Their leader was Iyasẹ, the prime minister.

[21] *Eghaẹvbo N'ogbe* were the chiefs who lived in the immediate neighbourhood of the palace and formed the palace societies and carried out the ritual ceremonies connected with the king's person. They included the seven kingmakers.

'He doubles his treason if he keeps his majesty waiting, even though he has only one head with which to pay.'

An unspoken mixture of approval and disapprobation greeted the chief's words in a rumble that swept through the assembly. But there were many there who knew that Esọn had not issued an empty threat.

An important palace functionary called Iseghurẹ stepped forward. 'Hail, Esọn,' he saluted, 'my messenger returned from Iyasẹ's palace a short while before I came here. He brought me a disturbing message.'

'And what was the message?'

'The message, my lord, was that Iyasẹ was ill and could not attend this meeting.'

More waves of both approval and disapprobation coursed through the assembled crowd of nobility.

'May he never recover,' cursed Esọn in as loud a voice as he could summon.

'Isẹ – ẹ,' (So be it) echoed through the assembly.

When the king eventually appeared and was given Iyasẹ's message, he was furious. He looked majestic in his scarlet dress and the mass of beads that adorned his person from head to foot. Lending awe to his figure was the anger that could be seen on his divine face. His arms were supported on both sides by dutiful attendants and he was preceded as usual by his *Ọmada*, bearing the *Ada* – the sword of authority. His majesty seated himself on the throne and faced his subjects. In his anger he looked more like a god than a mortal. Every word that issued from his divine mouth, with teeth lightly clenched, meant either life or death.

'Esọn,' commanded his majesty, 'arrest Iyasẹ and bring him here in chains.'

'Long may you live, Your Majesty,' responded Esọn apologetically on his knees, hands clasped together before his face, 'I have ordered Iyasẹ's arrest, Your Majesty, but the arresting party returned empty-handed.'

'How so?' queried the king, almost rising but quickly resuming his seat. 'What did your arresting party say?'

'Hail, my king and master,' replied Esǫn, obviously troubled, 'they said that Iyasę has disappeared.'

'Disappeared?' echoed many astonished voices, taking the word out of the king's mouth.

'He has dematerialised,' sighed the king, 'but we shall see which is the more potent, Iyasę's magical powers or the king's divine strength. Find him and bring him to justice,' he ordered.

'Yes!' yelled the crowd in approbation.

As the sound died down, Ovbivbi[22] who had travelled all the way from the village of Okhunmwun, five days' march from the city, to take part in the day's meeting, inched his way forward, led by the hand by a child. He was bent almost double by the burden of age and care.

'Long may you live and prosper, my royal lord and master,' saluted the blind seer.

'*Be quiet*, all of you,' shouted Esǫn, 'Ovbivbi wants to address the king.' Silence descended on the assembly.

'Speak up, Ovbivbi,' ordered the king, but with deep respect which amounted almost to veneration. Because of his age and his invaluable contribution to the welfare of the kingdom and the overall well-being of the king, Ovbivbi enjoyed the privilege of not kneeling before the king. His supernatural powers prevented him from such obeisance, even in a private audience with the king.

'The foe at the city gate, Your Majesty,' ventured Ovbivbi in a shrill voice, 'has conspired with the enemy within the city wall. The omens are ugly.'

The assembly was stunned into deeper silence. There were some in the crowd who could hardly breathe. Two of the minor chiefs among the ranks of *Eghaęvbo N'ore* pitched forward in a deadly faint. They were carried off into an outer chamber of the palace to be resuscitated and later interrogated.

'What can we do, Ovbivbi?' inquired Esǫn, speaking for the king. Tears were running freely down his haggard face.

---

[22] Ovbivbi was the name of an old blind seer. He was born blind but was given the gift of inner sight and of prophesy by the spirits. He served the king and was summoned to the palace in Benin City from time to time, especially at times of national crises.

'That,' replied Ovbivbi, 'I dare not say'. He sighed heavily and withdrew slowly, gently led away by the child.

When he rose from the throne to return to the palace, the king was accompanied closely by Eson, Ero and Osodin, together with the rest of the kingmakers. They followed his majesty into a private chamber and ranged themselves in order of seniority before him. He had not yet fully recovered from the shock of Ovbivbi's statement. And he was still very angry about Iyase's disappearance.

'I have had Iyase's Isekiri servant arrested, my lord,' reported Eson. He knew that it was no real consolation to the king. But at a time of such crisis and stress, Eson thought, anything was better than nothing. 'He is in chains in the palace prison.'[23]

'The prisoner,' added Eson, 'is awaiting Your Majesty's pleasure; but he can be tried by us, if that is what Your Majesty would wish.'

'Good, Eson,' replied the king, 'tomorrow he will be sacrificed to my head.'

The chiefs readily assented, arms folded across chests.

'As for the recalcitrant foreigner,' warned his majesty in his usual conciliatory manner, 'you must treat him with the kindness and hospitality for which my kingdom and people are now famous all over the world. He must be protected according to Ewuare's decree.'

Ero and Osodin nodded assent respectfully.

'Care must be exercised,' said the king, 'in killing the mouse that has fallen into your pot of water, lest you kill the mouse and break the pot as well.' (That was another ancient Èdó proverb dating back to the time of Ewuare.)

'Long may you live and prosper, my lord,' said Osodin. 'As my father told me, all those foreigners who have ever come to your kingdom from far away places have, without a single exception, expressed their admiration for our government, our laws, our tolerance, our hospitality our care of strangers and our independence.' The chief exhibited clear signs of pride in

---

[23] The palace prison had existed for hundreds of years. It was founded by an Èdó king, Ewedo, after whom it was named and who is said to have reigned from around the year 1255.

his historical memories. Obviously, his memory of his father was evergreen and full of pride. To be the son of a great and illustrious Èdó and to inherit one's father's title and reputation was not to be taken lightly. 'And come to think of it,' the chief continued, 'my illustrious father used to tell us when we were only children, that *Ikpotokin* and those who came later, always praised our wealth and industry and held us up to their own people as so well governed by our kings and nobility that theft was unknown among us. And indeed, we live in such security that we have no need to bolt our doors, even at night.'

'I know that,' said the king quietly. And offering his own reminiscence, he spoke about what he had learnt from his own father. 'My late father,' he recalled, 'peace be his in his resting-place above . . .

'*Isẹ - ẹ*' ('So be it'), interrupted the attentive listeners.

'He used to tell us when we just young princes that all the foreigners who have ever come to trade in Benin City swear to it that the Èdó have good laws and a well-organised judicial system; and, that we live on good terms with all the foreigners who come to trade here and to whom we show great friend-ship.'

'True, Your Majesty,' confirmed both Ẹro and Osodin.

'But why,' grumbled Ẹro, 'why this new foreigner can't see what his forerunners have experienced and enjoyed baffles me.'

The king looked kindly down on his devoted chiefs. There was an air of pity around his majesty's eyes. He cleared his royal throat and the chiefs knew there were more words of wisdom to come. They listened carefully.

'Before you go,' said the king, 'let me ask you a question, both of you, Osodin and Ẹro.'

Arms folded across their chests, eyes downcast, they waited attentively.

'Ẹro,' said the king, 'let us say that you are about to take your bath.'

'Hail, Mighty king,' interjected Ẹro, 'let us say that I am about to take my bath,' he repeated to show that he had listened carefully to his king.

127

'You are standing naked beside your bowl of bath-water and your clothes are in a neat pile nearby.'

'Long live Your Majesty,' rejoined Ẹro after repeating the king's suggestions.

'Now,' said the king, relishing his position, 'let us say that a naked madman comes along, picks up your clothes and runs away with them under his arms. What would you do?'

Ẹro and Osodin stole side-long glances at each other.

'Here is a puzzle,' said Ẹro in a mild understatement. 'What could one do in a case like that? I . . . I . . .' stammered Ẹro. He swallowed in his usual manner. 'I would run after the madman, Your Majesty,' said Ẹro, apparently under pressure to say something. 'I would try to get my clothes back from the madman,' he concluded somewhat lamely.

'You would run naked behind a naked madman, would you?' asked the king, 'in broad daylight, just to get your clothes from him?' The king was grinning but without any malice.

'Then,' said Osodin, 'whoever saw you like that would say, "I saw two madmen chasing each other down the street".'

'Quite right, Osodin,' commented his majesty with a broad smile. 'That's how it should be in your dealings with the new foreigner,' advised the king.

'Long may you live and prosper, Your Majesty,' intoned both chiefs.

'I understand,' said Ẹro, bowing his head.

Slowly, almost reluctantly, the chamber emptied, the king having retired deeper into the palace, still brooding over Ovbivbi's ominous warning. Was this, he wondered, what Ewuare had predicted? Would there be another deposition of an Èdó king after Akẹnpaye of blessed memory, his majesty wondered fretfully? If there was, how could it be prevented? That was the most vexing question to which he wanted to seek an effective answer.

When the Isẹkiri servant was brought out of Ẹwẹdọ the next morning, he had no doubt about what fate awaited him. Ovọnramwẹn sat in all his awesome majesty on his throne. The Isẹkiri prisoner, his wrists and ankles shackled, was thrown in the dust before the king. Standing firmly to one side of the throne was Ehondo whose specialist duty in the palace was to slaughter the sacrificial victims. The knife he used in the performance of his duties was called *Abiẹzẹ*, a term which described the sharpness of the knife and was as old as any other term associated with palace events in Benin City. Other human sacrificial victims, earmarked for slaughter that same morning, were close by. Whatever sacrifices could be offered to save the kingdom from any impending catastrophe would be offered, said the king. Human sacrifice was the highest sacrifice that could be performed; and the king alone could order it.

'I know I am about to die,' announced the Isẹkiri victim. His voice rang above the excitement that rumbled through the shrine. The victim, during his service under Iyasẹ, had learnt to speak the *Ẹ̀dó* language quite fluently.

'Silence before the king,' yelled the chief, Isekhurẹ, whose part in the ritual was to say the prayers that preceded the slaughtering of the victims.

'Let him speak,' ordered the king. 'These are his very last words on this earth. I will hear them.'

'Before I die,' said the victim without any remorse, 'I must tell you something I know. The new foreigner is coming to get you. He will depose you, burn down your palace, lay waste your kingdom and carry you off into exile from which you will never return.'

The king blinked. It was as if the victim had memorised the very words of Ẹwuare's 400-year prophecy. This had been the king's secret dread in recent months. Would it really happen, he wondered. It was a thought that engendered panic.

In spite of all the stories which their fathers and grandfathers had told the king and his chiefs, there were huge gaps in their knowledge of the older foreigners, whom they all seemed to admire a great deal. Looking back over the years since the *Dusk* that overshadowed the ancient kingdom in 1897, it is not clear if it would have made any difference had any one told Ovọnramwẹn that, in 1255, when Ewedo built the palace prison as part of his law-enforcement policies, the new foreigner and his arrogant forebears had only just established their Magna Carta, as a guide to order among civilised and cultured people. On the other hand, one wonders if it would have made any difference to the woman-monarch who ruled the land of the new foreigner, had anyone told her of the world-wide reputation of the Benin kingdom which she sought so mindlessly to take over and dominate; had she known that long before she even existed the Èdó king had an army of 20,000 stalwarts in his command and that, if needs be, he could increase that number to 100,000 by simply snapping his finger.

Ovọnramwẹn was reduced to fretting and frenetically making human sacrifices to protect his kingdom, which had also been seriously undermined by domestic intrigues. When the Isẹkiri victim pronounced what sounded like a death sentence on the king, the Èdó stood still, shocked beyond description. How, they wondered, did the Isẹkiri victim know what he said he knew? Was his knowledge reliable?

Hearing the victim's threatening prophesy inflamed the king. He nodded in Ehondo's direction and that official, taking the king's attention as signal for action, stepped gingerly forward, seized the cantankerous victim by the hair and slashed his throat with a single stroke of *abieze*. Blood fountained up and hit his majesty, like a bullet, straight between the eyes. Had he not been dressed in scarlet battle attire, his white wrapper would have been stained with the hated victim's blood.

'Isẹ – ẹ,' called Esọn. 'The position of the blood, Your Majesty, tells us that your Head has accepted this sacrifice.'

The remaining victims were quickly despatched with the same dexterity by Ehondo and the crowd that had gathered to witness the event dispersed in various directions, feeling reassured by their unquestioned belief in the efficacy of what they had just witnessed. They were convinced that their king was taking the right and necessary steps to protect them.

What followed the sacrifice was an unmitigated blood-bath in Benin City. More and more human sacrifices were called for. The need became desperate in order to appease the various gods who must be persuaded to check the threat hanging over the king and his kingdom. The widespread knowledge that, some 400 years earlier, Ẹwuare-the-Awesome had spared no pain to reinforce and strengthen the defences of the realm against external aggression, played little or no part in the people's thought. And, had Ovọnramwẹn tried to raise an army, the Iyasẹ and his co-conspirators had so divided the city and the kingdom that his majesty would not have been able to raise an army of even 100 able-bodied, willing and loyal fighting men against the imminent threat to his authority.

If there was to be war against the new foreigner, Iyasẹ was determined to take no part in it. He was still hiding, but he had behind him more than half the fighting force that could be mustered by the war lord, the senior chief, *Esọgban*, and the other military leaders of the realm.

'You will not be obliged to fight for the king,' Iyasẹ had informed his followers. 'But you are not obliged to fight against him, either. *Òsánóbuá N'ọyan agbọn* (The Supreme God who owns and rules the world) forbid I should renege on my oaths of allegiance and loyalty,' he said, 'but *erhẹn gha tọn ọmọ tin iye, edọmwan d'uhunmwun ẹrẹn ẹrọ sinmwin*' (when a child and his mother are trapped by fire, it is each one who seeks safety individually). 'So,' concluded Iyasẹ, 'you must all be prepared to defend and protect your own lives.'

When the message arrived in the palace that the new foreigner was seeking an urgent audience with the king, the fatal plot thickened. It was the wrong time for a foreigner to seek such an audience. For it was *Aguẹ*[24] and that time of the year the king could see no strangers of any description, however urgent or important the request might be.

'Tell him to wait until after the *Aguẹ* Festival,' ordered the king, 'then I will grant him an audience and treat him to the legendary Èdó hospitality.' His majesty meant it, too. But, realising that his political and military position had been seriously undermined by Iyasẹ and his co-conspirators, he knew he had to play for time.

Regardless of the mild and friendly nature of the king's message, the new foreigner insisted on imposing his visit on Benin City.

[24] The *Aguẹ* Festival in Benin lasted three months. It was a fasting period and in those three months people did not eat, bathe themselves, drink alcohol or engage in any merry-making. Foreigners were banned from the City. It was similar to the Moslem Ramadan, although much older.

'Tell your king,' he replied haughtily, 'that I can't wait. Tell him that the heavy rains are approaching and I want to get the visit over with before they come down.'

His majesty was at the point of succumbing to the new foreigner's demands. But there remained among his chiefs and warriors some who still so revered their customs and traditions that they were prepared to lay down their lives to defend and preserve them. They, of course, could not openly disobey their king in defence of the customs and traditions of which he was the human embodiment. Their choice was between the wrath of the Èdó gods and the anger of the king who, they were convinced, would be easy to placate once he had been fully briefed on what they had done on his behalf.

They ambushed the new foreigner, perpetrating what was later to be widely described as 'The Benin Massacre' which took place in February 1897. Its immediate consequence was the so-called 'Punitive Expedition' which brought the ancient kingdom and its king to their knees on 17 February 1897.

With Iyasẹ in hiding with half the city's defence forces, the king's defences had become fragmented and heavily dependent on the arrival of forces of the few powerful nobles who remained loyal to the very end. Leading them were men with ancient titles and unimpeachable honesty. Theirs were the hereditary titles in the kingdom. What held them together and cemented them to the royal cause was their ancient oaths of office. Theirs was the responsibility of holding the principal entrances into the city in case of an invasion from outside. Since no one, except perhaps Iyasẹ, knew whether or not there would be an invasion, it was impossible to plan any sustainable and reliable defence of the citadel.

The news of the 'massacre' reached Esọn in the palace. He could answer none of the questions put to him by his majesty. He was innocent of any collusion and the king believed him. But some answers were required which the senior chief could not provide. He, of course, got the sharp end of the king's verbal stick. He was also well aware of the hopelessness of the city's defences.

Esọn returned to his own palace a beaten and depressed man.

He dismissed all of his servants and sent for his senior wife and head of his harem, a stolid Èdó woman called Ẹdugie. She must have been born on the day of a memorable national festival to have been given that name by her father who had been a high-ranking chief in the time of a previous king of Benin. Broken down to its constituents Ẹd'ugie means Ẹdẹ, which is the Èdó word for day and Ugie, which is the Èdó word for festival. Thus the combination, Ẹd'ugie, means 'The Day of Festival'.

Ẹdu'gie appeared before her husband in a hurry, only half dressed. She, no doubt, expected to be despatched on an urgent errand. But she was wrong.

'Stay here with me,' Esọn ordered. 'I . . . I . . .' Esọn could find no words to express what he was thinking. Ẹdu'gie was bewildered and began to worry about her husband's state of mind.

'Whatever you ask, my lord,' she said, 'will be done.'

She stroked his aching feet. She massaged his back, taking great care to ensure that the left-hand fingers did not stray to his head. The head of the highest chief in the kingdom, like that of the king, was forbidden, on pain of death, to be touched with the left hand of a woman – any woman! The left hand, as all Èdó men and women know, is a 'dirty' and 'evil' hand. Nothing good can ever be done with the left hand; and, among the Èdó even until very recently, one gave something away with the left hand only to someone whom one despised or even hated. The right hand is the hand of friendship and respect and honour.

Esọn's senior wife, kneeling beside her prostrate husband, did all she could do to comfort the old kingmaker. She made no headway and eventually she fell asleep at his feet, her head resting on one of his outstretched legs. Meanwhile, Esọn dreamt. Had his wife been awake to see the way her husband rolled his head from side to side, she would have known that he was having a bad dream.

In his nightmare, Esọn was defending his king. A woman in the nightmare was bearing down on his majesty. Her left hand was poised to rest on the king's head from behind. Esọn struggled frenetically forward, shouting, at the top of his voice, which was rapidly cracking.

'No,' he was shouting, 'never. Never will a woman touch the king's head with her left hand. Never will a woman rule my king or his kingdom. No. No. No.' He rolled over, grabbed the little dagger that he wore on his belt and plunged it into the throat of the nightmare woman. He jumped to his feet. Horrified, he saw his Edu'gie lying in a pool of blood, a dagger in her throat.

Not a cry was heard. Not a struggle offered. Devastated, Eson felt that his own end was at hand.

That same night, as the palace courtyard cleared to *Akaeromwon*'s strident cry, the king saw visions of the ancient *Èdó* past. The image of the creator-king flooded his Majesty's vision. Then followed the images of the numerous earliest kings, known collectively as *'Ogiso'* ('Kings From The Sky') with their famous Tortoise and other creatures floating before *Òsánóbuá* who had appeared among them to sort out some difficult problem. Then came the vision of the first Éwéká, the founder of the present dynasty, followed by Ozolua, Ewuare, Esigie, Ehengbuda – all of whom were his forebears. None of them, however, was offering Ovonrawmen any help. Adolo, his own father, had brought up the rear in the procession of kings through the vision.

Rather, he sat alone with his chin cupped in his hand, staring into empty space.

'My father,' pondered the king, speaking aloud to himself. 'Why is he alone and deserted? That couldn't be,' he thought, 'special sacrifices were offered at his shrine.' He wondered whether or not the spirit of his father actually accepted the sacrifices that were offered to him. And if he did not accept them, then why? Lastly came the image of Aiguobasinmwin, his eldest son, the crown prince who would succeed him in later years to the ancient throne. The name of the prince, broken down means 'kingship is indisputable.' In the vision, the prince was alone, facing what looked like a gigantic wall. The prince's back was turned to the outer palace wall. A cudgel was in his right hand and in his left hand the prince held the *Ada*, the king's sword of authority. He seemed to be fearlessly and determinedly challenging his enemies to dare to advance. In the enemy camp, facing the prince, his majesty thought he had seen the image of Iyasẹ. Then the light went out somewhere deep down inside him and the vision faded out completely.

'Long may you live and prosper, Your Majesty,' a quiet voice spoke at his elbow. He snapped into immediate consciousness. The speaker was Asuẹn, one of his chiefs who still remained faithful and loyal to him. He had an urgent message from Esọn's palace to the effect that the impetuous new foreigner was already on his way to the city. What was to be done?

Esọn was never to be seen in the palace again after that night. He pined away and died short after accidentally murdering his wife, whom he had mistaken for Queen Victoria in his nightmare.

The news of the massacre of the new foreigner and his followers was kept from Ovọnramwẹn until well after the *Aguẹ* Festival, although he inquired about the new foreigner.

'He is nowhere to be found, Your Majesty,' reported Esọn's son and successor. When his father had died suddenly, at night, the son, as of right, had immediately stepped into the old man's shoes and assumed the palace duties which his illustrious father had once performed. The king lamented the death of his best ally and friend.

'The new foreigner did not arrive in *Iwebo*,[25] Your Majesty,' reported the young statesman. (His whereabouts remained a mystery until a short while before the British 'Expeditionary Force' marched on Benin City.)

His majesty began to worry about the fate of the new foreigner. He really didn't want his blood on his hands. But he knew the mentality of many of his over-zealous followers who would never hesitate to take a mile when given only a single inch. The king was fully aware that if the new foreigner had been murdered, it was he who would be asked for an explanation. He didn't like the look of things. And that same night, Esọgban sought the safety of Iyase's hide-out and joined the traitor's forces.

---

[25] *Iwebo* is the name of the section of the palace reserved for the king's regalia. It was also said to be the area where the white foreigners were accommodated during their stay in Benin City.

Reprisals for the massacre arrived swiftly from across the waters. Ẹro and his troops were to defend the city at the Ọvia entrance. His army was formidable and well drilled. Ezọmọ, another of the old faithfuls and one of the kingmakers, was to defend the Ughọtọn entrance. Ezọmọ was capable, loyal and willing to lay down his life for his king and kingdom. He and his army were quite indomitable, as the Portuguese must have discovered from their contact with his great-great grandfather. Uso, yet another of the stalwarts, despite his youth and inexperience and feminine looks, was to defend the Agbọ approach. He was trustworthy and his troops were disciplined and willing to defend their king and kingdom. It was the duty of every Èdó male citizen to take up arms for his land of birth. And it was the proud duty of every Èdó female citizen to support her man in every possible way during the war, short of taking up arms herself.

The only entrance that was left virtually unmanned was the Ologbo route. The swamp on that route was, itself, a sufficient natural defence. At least, so it was decided at the meeting of the War Council. Nothing, the king and his advisers were assured, could enter the city from that direction. The chief called Ogiamiẹn, leader of that portion of the ancient city, was therefore left virtually alone to mind his private family affairs.

Sadly, however, everyone concerned was wrong about the Ologbo route. For it was the route that the invading army chose to enter the city. The invader, guided and ably supported by the swamp-dwelling Uhobo and the water-loving Isẹkiri, under the pay of the Isẹkiri chief, Ẹdoghọ, traversed the supposedly impenetrable swamp and invaded the city from the most unexpected quarters. Esọn's troops defending the palace were mown down by the invaders' guns. The young Esọn himself perished in the great onslaught, which seemed to last an eternity. Yet victory was not that easy for the invading army. For, unknown initially to both armies in that quarter, the greatest hero of the war stationed himself there. His name was Asoro, which is also the name by which the Èdó describe a spear.

Almost single-handedly, Asoro held the invader at bay for

136

five days, defying blazing guns and ploughing maniacally into
the enemies' midst to deal out death and mutilation among
them. Steeped to his back teeth in magic, Asoro would not fall
to gun or sabre. His deadly poisoned arrows and his huge
broad-sword hit their marks with devastating accuracy all
around. When he fought in the midst of any of the enemy
groups, he never left until every man in it bit the dust. Then he
moved on. There was only one condition he had to obey in
order to stay alive. It was that he should never look back over
his shoulder.

Asoro fought and fought and fought. Then suddenly the
quiver of arrows that hung from his left shoulder seemed to
have been snatched away. He looked right and left but could
not find it. The pressure was on him from all directions.
Inadvertently, he looked back over his shoulder and saw
Ofoe. He fell down on one of his own arrows which pierced
him to the heart and expired on the spot. An enemy soldier cut
off his head and carried it into the city on the tip of a bayonet.
But even after Asoro's head had been severed from his body on
the battle-ground, it was said that his torso rose from the dust
and carried on fighting. He finally dropped just inside the inner
city-wall, at a point directly opposite the present-day Church
Missionary Society (CMS) church (known as St Matthew's
Cathedral on Sokponba Road). There is no plaque to mark
Asoro's final resting-place. Yet, in the jungle, some ten miles or
so south-west of the city, lies a concrete monument raised to the
new foreigner who, with his followers, was massacred there.

The city fell to the invader and so did the ancient kingdom.
The date was 17 February 1897. The palace was put to the
torch and so was the city. The burning city recalled the fire lit by
Ewuare's incantation half a millennium earlier. Except that
Ewuare burned the city in order to re-create it, while the new
foreigner burned it in order to destroy it.

The king had been smuggled into hiding by his supporters.
And it was Asuẹn, the last of the king's men to defect to Iyasẹ's
side, who finally betrayed his majesty to the invader by revealing his hiding-place. In fact, the king did not realise that he was
'hiding'. In spite of the death and destruction that surrounded

him, he still wanted to see the new foreigner, in order to make peace and tender his apology for the misdeeds of his chiefs. But his mis-advisers deceived him into believing that the new foreigner had promised to seek friendly audience in due course.

'Let things cool down, Your Majesty,' they pleaded, deceitfully. 'Then Your Majesty can see the new foreigner and talk to him.'

His majesty accepted this ill-advice and waited, and while he waited the enemy sneaked in through the back-door and took him. He was arrested and taken out with manacled wrists and ankles, paraded before his subjects and publicly humiliated. His sacred head was, at last, touched by the left hand of the woman who ruled a long, long away across the waters. And the daylight went out for ever over the ancient kingdom.

On his way to the boat which took him into the exile from which he was never to return, accompanied by his Ẹhiọba and only a handful of his personal attendants, he pronounced the now famous lamentation, crying,

> I appeal to the Almighty and the spirits of the departed Ọbas of Benin, my fathers, to judge between me and the Binis who ill-advised me and cunningly sold me into the hands of the foreign troops in search of their own liberty and benefit. Oh! Benin, merciless and wicked! Farewell! Farewell!

Secretly, though, deep down in his heart, the exiled king envied and admired the 'magic' which had taken from him his ancient throne and kingdom. And, as Ẹhiọba was later to reveal, his majesty's Ùhímwẹ̀n[26] while still alive was that, in his next incarnation, he would learn the secret of the invader's 'magic' and be able to beat him at his own game. In so doing, he set the tone of the life he would live on his return to the world.

---

[26] Ùhímwẹ̀n is the choice one makes about one's life before being born.

PART TWO

12

xᑬᑯᑬx

Selected È̩dó Proverbs

Introduction

THESE PROVERBS have been selected from a large number of sayings that have been handed down from one generation to another since time immemorial. They represent only the tip of an iceberg. It is hoped that the handful recorded in this book may provide a clear enough picture of the general attitude of the È̩dó to human life.

From such a picture, it should not be too difficult to see Mallory Wober's 'structure of cognitive development patterned differently than in Western cultures' (*Psychology in Africa,* 1972). Such cognitive development must be seen as based upon what Jung called 'presuppositions', which distinguish the African (in the present case È̩dó) from the non-African, without in any way suggesting that the former is either more or less 'logical' than the latter. More importantly, the images that lie beneath the proverbs should provide the necessary building blocks to recognise, as stated above, the structure of cognitive development ...

The proverbs are arranged according to themes although the themes tend to overlap. They are all extracted from real, practical human experiences, spread over millennia, in the daily lives of the people (the È̩dó) who have invented them.

1. The General Human Condition

A young man was faced with a dilemma: he had either to stay at home and live like the rest of his family or to go abroad and learn a new way of life. To his aged father he complained that home was too crowded; but, at the same time, living among complete strangers would be too dangerous an adventure. His father answered: 'If the world is bad and heaven is not good, where is the alternative?'

The various statements selected here demonstrate the general attitude of the Ẹ̀dó to the whole of the human condition. They, of course, do not exhaust the store of such proverbs but they are representative of the overall character.

The general attitude of the Ẹ̀dó to life may be criticised as stoical in some respects and fatalistic in others. While, however, there may be nothing particularly good or bad in either stoicism or fatalism, it needs to be remembered that both outlooks are produced by practical human experience of life as it is actually lived by individuals. Thus, the Ẹ̀dó do not first construct some theory about how things should be and then go out to find evidence in support of such a theory. On the contrary, they start with the realities that surround them in everyday life and, perhaps, construct theories based upon their experiences later.

1. *Òsọ́nmwūnkpọn ẹ́imwẹ̀n ẹ́du'wū.*
   (A rag has no day earmarked for its death.)

2. *Ọ̀mwan n̄'ohanmwẹ̄n gbe, ẹ́i mina miọ́fumwē 'gbē.*
   (The hungry person cannot dream of peace.)

3. *Ọ̀b~ayọ̀n wé ná lé 'mãkhẹ̀ írẹ̀n; ẹ́imwẹ̄n ọmá mi~emwin y'ēma r̃u: ọ̀gha mi~uhuñmwun ȳa rhé, ọ́ghi r̃i'ema; ọ́ma mi~uhumwun ȳa rhē, á ghì ye~ma ruẹ̀ró wẹ̄.*
   (The palm-wine tapper who orders pounded yam against his return home from tapping will always find a use for it because, if he returns safely, he will eat the pounded yam; but if he breaks his neck in a fall from the palm tree, the pounded yam will become the funeral feast in his honour.)

4. *Ámá k'ẹ̀zẹ̀ r̃he nẽ, ãi khá m'ōkhuo ghe aghā mu~ehẹn n~ọkpọlọ nẽ.*
   (Until one returns from a fishing trip, one does not promise a woman a big fish for dinner.)

142

5. *Ái gu'ẹ̃hiọmwan vẹ̃n.*
(One does not challenge one's alter ego to a wrestling match.)

6. *Ọ̀vbókhãn mã kpo~bọ, ẹ́i guẽ n'ọ̃wanrẹn rhĩ̃'evbãre.*
(Without first washing his hands, a child cannot eat with his elders.)

7. *Ènághẽde, ẹr~ana mwẹn obọ vbo~wẹ.*
(It is to avoid falling that we possess arms and legs.)[1]

8. *Íranmwẹn s'óvbia'zẹn, òdazẹ́n eḡbe; Àzẹ́n má yẽ ivbi erhẹ-e n'ĩrẹn gbẽle rẽ: yà rõ egbe ghe ẹ̃ra yá bu~ohiẹn n'Ẹ̀dò. Èmũin náirúẹ̃ rè, ghẹ ̃ru ọmũan r̃e.*
(The witch is upset because an ant has stung her child; but she forgets the numerous other people's children whose blood she sucks every night. Putting yourself in another person's position is the way to settle disagreements among the Ẹ̀dó. Never do to another what you do not want done to you.)

9. *Àghà gbì'kían, àgbé'gbe am̃a gbí'kìan àgbé'gbẹ.*
(Whether or not one kills the fly that alights on one's body, it is on one's body that the blow aimed at the fly must land.)

10. *Àghà gb ó'bòdò gâ ègbé ígbá ùrí, ígbá ọ́gbàn, ísétù ẹ̀rọ́kô'díyèkè.*
(Even if we spin around 130 times, it is our buttocks that remain behind.)

11. *Ámá rúkhộ, ái wú khộ.*
(If one doesn't live an evil life, one cannot die an evil death.)

---

[1] In Edo the concept of 'hands and feet' used in this proverb is complex. Included in 'hands and feet' are (a) one's children; (b) one's other immediate relations; (c) one's friends. The concept of 'the extended family' applies in this respect and the importance of that concept is exemplified in this proverb. All those involved exist for the purpose of supporting the individual at difficult times, thus protecting the individual from 'falling', especially falling in the metaphorical sense. Hence, in the true sense, one's children, relatives and friends are one's props and supports when disaster threatens, even if such disaster is the consequence of one's own mistakes. In another proverb, the Edo would say, *'ai khu'omo dan n'ekpen gbere'*, meaning, 'one does not chase even a bad child into the jaws of a tiger.'

12. *Èrúnmwùnd'ówînâ ní họmwan ẹ̀rá ná kâ èrhánsê;*
    áimîemwin nâ rû nô'gbôi nẹ́ yọ̀rê.
    (It is on account of fellow craftsmen that one must exhib-
    it high skill in wood carving. For the novice will admire
    whatever is offered him.)

13. *Ènọ̀ wọ̀'vbókhân mî òfẹ́n, ẹ̀rọ́ zí ghô èvbákhûẹ nẹ̀ yâ*
    kpó'bọ̀.
    (Whoever encourages a child to handle a mouse must pro-
    vide the soap for washing the child's hands.)

14. *Èmwín n'ọ̀má, ẹ̀i mó bọ̀ tộ.*
    (The good thing [in life] usually never lasts.)

15. *Àwá ghà mú'vẹ́, ọ́ghî làhîẹgbẹe rhê.*
    (When a dog grabs a bone, it foresakes its family.)[2]

16. *Èmwîn'ọ̀bâ-â ghá khían súnù, èkọ́nkhọ́kkhọ̀ ghà dègbè*
    òkútá ộghî vá rê.
    (When disaster is in the offing, even an egg will break a
    stone.)

17. *Ọ̀khọ́khọ̀ î wân vb'ọ̀kâ.*
    (A fowl is never wise in matters regarding corn.)

18. *Èvbí bíọ̀'mwân ẹ̀rá khộ.*
    (We always resemble those who have produced us.)

19. *Èní ghà gbèrhá, èbè vbí'rûnmwûn ghi lòvbiẹ̀.*
    (When an elephant passes by, grasses and leaves must lie
    down.)

20. *Ìkù n'ọ̀ghámâ vbó'tá, òwíe ẹ̀rá yá mù'ègbè ẹ́rè.*
    (The celebration that will be successful in the evening
    must be prepared for in the morning.)

21. *Èvbéná rẹ̀n ọ̀mwân sẹ̀, èrhiá gi'ọmwan sẹ́.*
    (It is the extent to which one is known that one is
    described.)

---

[2] This proverb is commonly used to depict a selfish person who, on achieving a
measure of success, turns his back on those with whom he once associated.

22. *Òhànmwẹ̀n ghà làhín ùsẹ́ rhè, èkhèhe ẹ̀r'ọ́kẹ̀vbọ̀.*
(When hunger is removed from suffering, there is little suffering left.)

23. *Ènọ́rẹ̀nrẹ̀n íghírẹ̀n ghá lò'dẹ̀, ẹ́i nẹ̀ yó'dẹ̀.*
(One who knows he will go along a path does not defecate on it.)

24. *Ẹ̀dẹ́ ná búohiẹn gb'óghíọ nmwàn, ẹ̀rá buóhẹ̀n gbè'gbè ọmwan; àghà mù ìhọ́'mwan yó'tọ̀, ègbè ọmwan ẹ̀rá mú yó'tọ̀.*
(The day we pass judgment on our enemy is the day we pass judgment on ourselves; when we bury contemporaries, we bury ourselves.)

25. *Úgbé ná dẹ̀ghè, ẹ́i rhú ọmwàn áró.*
(The stone which we see flying towards us cannot blind.)

26. *Òvẹ̀n – î – kó'wiẹ́ bálé'gbẹ́.*
(The sun does not overheat itself early in the morning.)

27. *Ádéghè òwá – î – mà, ái muegb'ùgbò.*
(When domestic life is poor, one does not prepare for work on the farm.)

28. *Ádéghè òwá má gbọ̀'mwàn, òrè – î – sẹ̀tìn.*
(If one's own home does not destroy one, the world outside cannot.)

29. *Èghẹ́ kàzẹ̀ khẹ̀mwẹ̀n ẹ̀rá miẹn, ái míe'ghézẹ̀ lèlè mwẹ̀n.*
('Don't choose before me' is natural and understandable, not 'don't choose after me'.)

30. *Àghà fúẹrè, éi gbá óbọ̀ .*
(In a frenzied scramble, some will go without.)

31. *Emwín nó'má gíọ'díọn wán, ọghá sọ̀'vbòkhàn ègbè.*
(That which prevents the adult from developing will also affect the youth.)

32. *Àghá hô nâ rẹ̀n vbén'úwótọ̀ yéhẹ̀, ághì n'ọ̀fíontọ̀.*
(If we want to know what things are like under the earth, we must enquire from a rodent.)

145

33. *Ẹdú'wú – î – mwẹ̀n ẹ̀bô.*
    (The day of death has no medicine.)

34. *Áhiánmwẹ̀n nọ́ múohú òtọ̀ tínyân ùlèlèfè; ùlèlèfè nọ́ tínyân, òtọ̀e ẹ̀rọ́ ké zọ̀rhè.*
    (A bird, hating the earth, perches on an ant-hill; but the ant-hill itself has grown out of the earth.)

35. *Ẹ̀dẹ́gbè, ọ̀vbókhán ghọ̀ghọ̀ ọmárẹ́n îghẹ̀'dẹ̀hì ẹ̀rọ́ fẹ̀kô gbá khîan.*
    (A child is glad that a new day has dawned; he doesn't realise that it is the end of life (his final destiny) that is gradually approaching.)

36. *Àkhián mìe'gbè ẹ̀rọ́ ghọ̀ yè.*
    (Mutual respect can be sustained only if encounters are restricted to occasional meetings.)

37. *Àghá guálé'fé, tú'hùnmwùn gú'rórámẹ̀n; àghà mìọn nẹ̀, ùhúnmwún îghí gú'onúrhò.*
    (When searching for wealth, the head will pass through the eye of a needle; but once it is found, the head will become too big to pass through a doorway.)

38. *Àkò'tà ẹ̀ráyá rẹ̀n vbe ná hí hẹ̀.*
    (It is only in the evening [of life] that we know what destiny has awaited us.)

39. *Ènọ̀khúọmwán má múdià, ènákhú – î – múdiá.*
    (If the pursuer does not stop, the pursued cannot stop.)

40. *Ìbalè'gbè ẹ̀rọ́ gbú'dián.*
    (It is impatience that leads to the tsetse fly's [premature] death.)

41. *Àghà mié'nọ́wú, à mié'ñorhá'gbọ́n nẹ̀, òhán èkpò îghî muọ̀'mwàn.*
    (Once we've seen both the dead and the living, we stop being scared of a masquerade.)

42. *Èmwín nọ̀ kpè'mà ní'dù, úwó'tọ̀ – ọ̀ – yè.*
    (The dove's drummer lies underground beneath the dove's feet.)

43. *Òwẹ̀ ọ́kpókpà ẹ̀razẹ̀ vbòkọ̀ ẹ̀dín.*
(It is one step at a time that is taken when mashing boiled palm nuts [in the processing of extracting palm oil].)

44. *Àghà khìrhì fiúzô, ághì hàrè fúà.*
(If you rush into shooting at an antelope, you will scare it off.)

45. *Ọ̀kàfì ẹ̀rọ̀ fí'ènèkhèrhè.*
(Who strikes first strikes the weaker blow.)

46. *Ùkhúnmwún ghá fí, ẹ̀rá nárẹ̀n ọmwàn nè mwẹ́n ákháẹn.*
(It is in a time of famine that the world discovers the self-less person.)

47. *Ẹ̀hiẹ́ndò kànmwàn, ùzà ẹ̀rọ́ zẹ̀.*
(Small though the alligator pepper is, it carries lethal strength.)

48. *N'òwẹ̀ ghẹ́ mù òmwàn ùhúnmwún fúà; n'ùnú ghẹ́ mì'ùbì gì'ọmwàn èhọ́, ẹ̀rọ́ rè èrhùnmwùn nà nà.*
(That the feet may not lead one into danger; that the mouth may not bring a blow to one's ear – that is the prayer one should say.)

49. *Tá'kọ̀n vb'áránmwẹ́n yè gúì vbù'nù.*
(Even the tongue and the teeth disagree within the mouth.)

50. *Ènọ́ ghùghẹ́rhè ghá gh'onísẹ́nrhẹ̀-e, ọ́ – z'ọ́ghé obọ́ n'àg-bọ̀n ghè.*
(He who bends down to peer at another's anus exposes his own to others' gaze.)

51. *Órhúnmwọ́nkpá ẹ̀rọ́ gbá'wá, ẹ̀rá ná ghí tíẹrè idúnmwùn igbà'wà.*
(It is the killing of a dog by one person that has earned the entire street the nickname of 'dog-killing' street.)

52. *Àghà zìn ègbè nà'zẹ́n zènú'nú ẹ̀rẹ̀n, tá rié ọ́mọ̀ vbéhé nẹ́ gbèrè.*
(If a witch is permitted to explain her actions, it is likely she will be offered another child to be eaten.)

53. *Tá kpó'bọ̀ ná yá muí isàn, ái fían fúa.*
(The hand that has touched excrement is never to be cut off but only to be washed.)

54. *Ẹ̀wáẹ̀n ẹ̀ráyá gbó'fẹ́n nọ̀rúwá'khè, na ghẹ́ gbà'khè gb'òfẹ̀n.*
(It is with care that one must kill the rat that has hidden inside an earthen pot, lest one kills the rat and break the pot in the process.)

55. *Ẹ́hún Òvbìogùe ẹ̀rọ́ wià vbì'kò.*
(It is the 'fart' of the poor that smells in a crowd.)

56. *Tọ́ yiẹ̀ Ọ́ba ẹ̀rọ́ nà giẹ̀, ẹ́re n'Ẹ̀do bà ga-e.*
(A king smiles only out of courtesy, not to please his subjects.)

57. *Nọ̀ mwẹ̀n ọ̀nà, ẹ́i mwén ọ́ní.*
(He who possesses *this* does not (necessarily) possess *that*.)

58. *Àghà mié'námásê, ùwú – î – giá wù.*
(When we encounter one whose condition is worse than ours, we no longer have the urge to die.)

59. *Àrànmwẹ̀n nẹ́ mwẹ́n ákọ̀n, ẹ̀rọ́ ká sì ísíógûi.*
(It is the toothless animal that is the first to arrive for fruit gathering.)

60. *Òhuẹ́ ghà dẹ̀ghè àrànmwẹ̀n nọ́ lóvbiẹ̀, ọ́ghì bà khuẹ́-e ghè: ọ̀má rẹ́n déghè òwẹ́ khiárè.*
(When a hunter encounters a beast lying down, he approaches it just in case it has a bad leg [and therefore cannot escape].)

61. *Nọ́ hóẹ̀n 'mù mẹ̀', ẹ́i họn sîemwẹ̀n.*
(One who hears 'help me put this load on my head' usually never hears 'help me take the load from my head'.)

62. *Àlúe n'ómò, ái rhíeghọ́ n'ọ̀mọ̀.*
(One may chew food for a baby, but one cannot swallow it for the baby.)

63. *Ézẹ̀ ẹ̀ró 'yà khìn. Ọ̀ghà s'ọ̀mwàn ẹ̀kún ámá kiẹ̀rè, ọ̀ghà s'ọ̀mwàn ẹ̀hó ọ̀ghì gbọ̀ 'mwàn.*
(Insult is like a river: if one does not get out of it when it rises to one's waist, it will drown one when it rises to one's neck.)

2. On Human Courage

64. *'Èmwàn ẹ̀ráná gbẹ́rúà' ẹ̀rọ́ má sẹ̀ 'èmwàn ẹ̀rọ́ nà sàn fi'òhà'.*
('Here is where he was killed' is preferable to 'Here is where he escaped into the bush.')

65. *Ènọ́zín ègbè nà gbẹ̀rúà ẹ̀rọ́dín sẹ̀ ẹ̀mwàn hià.*
(He who submits himself to be killed is the bravest of all men.)

66. *Òkpia nọ́ yó'bọ́ mù ẹ̀yẹ̀n n'òkhùo ghẹ̀bà tiẹ̀rè àvbiẹ̀rẹ̀, ẹ̀rọ́ gbé'gbẹ́ rè.*
(The man who picks up a snake with his bare hands, to avoid a woman calling him a coward, is a self-destroyer.)

67. *Àdéghẹ̀ ọ́ká máfó, àgbànwèn – î – rọ̀.*
(Until the corn-cob is bare of seeds, the jaw can take no rest from chewing.)

68. *Ámá wè'gbé, âi mwẹ̀ mwẹ̀n.*
(Without courage, no one can be a madman.)

69. *Àghà tàlọ̀gbè, ághí tàlọ̀ mà óghí'ọmwàn.*
(He who grumbles too loudly too often is bound to reveal his weakness to his enemy.)

70. *Ọ̀mwàn nọ́tú yò'bọ́ gbẹ̀'wẹ́-e, ẹ̀rọ́ wénẹ̀ ẹ̀rínmwín rèn èke nù'dùẹrè yè.*
(He who cries and beats his chest in agony reveals to evil spirits where his heart lies.)

71. *Èmwín nàhó ná támaẹ̀rímwìn, ékhọ̀e ẹ̀rá táiyì.*
(What is to be told to the gods must be told to / or in the mind.)

72. *Òdẹ́ – î – lẹ́ né ẹ̀rhẹ́n ẹ́gbò.*
(The bush path never runs away from a bush fire.)

73. *Ọ̀mwàn nọ̀ yù'nuẹ̀rẹ̀n tè'mwín ní'rẹ̀n rùkhọ̀, ẹ̀rọ́ wé nẹ̀'rhẹ́-e ghẹ́ fà irẹ̀n.*
(He who publicly confesses his own misdeeds avoids embarrassment by anyone else.)

3. On Caution and/or Moderation

74. *Ái fi˜ugbé fiẹ́kì nàghẹ̀ yá fìgbì'yọ̀mwàn.*
(One does not throw a stone into the market, lest one hits one's mother.)

75. *Ùwọ̀nmwẹ̀n ghá riẹ̀nriẹ̀n, tá mwẹ̀n ẹ̀waẹ́n nághẹ́ fín íkpínhíanbọ̀ rè.*
(When soup is very sweet one must be careful not to bite off the fingers with which one eats it.)

76. *Àghá yè vbé né'gbé yátọ̀lọ́mwàn tọ̀lọ́e, ègbè ghì bòlò.*
(If you scratch your skin as fiercely as it itches, you will tear it to pieces.)

77. *Ọ̀kpà ghạ̀ sẹ̀'vbò ọgbọ́n, ọwẹ̀ ọ́kpá ẹ̀rọ́yá múdiá: ọmárẹ̀n déghè ivbi ẹ̀vbò ní yò'wẹ̀ èvèvà mùdià.*
(When a cock arrives in a strange country, he stands on a single foot because he is not yet sure whether the native inhabitants stand on both feet.)

78. *Èní ghá khọ́n, èní ẹ̀rọ́vbê mû ígbínà.*
(When elephants fight, it is elephants that can intervene.)

79. *Ọ̀mọ̀ nọ̀ fín íyẹ́-e èwẹ́n rè, ẹ̀rọ́ wé ná yóhànmwẹ̀n gbì'ren.*
(The baby who bites its mother's nipple is asking to be starved.)

80. *Àghà rhùnmwùn d'óghiọ̀mwàn rhúa'ró, ái mièn aro yà dèghè ọ̀ si'ọ̀mwàn.*
(If you put out your eyes so as never to see your enemies, you will have no eyes with which to see your friends.)

150

81. *Àghà tuá gbó'ghiọ́nmwàn, ághí wù lèlẹ́-e.*
(He who attempts in a hurry to kill his enemy is certain to die alongside the enemy.)

82. *Èrhẹ̀n yè gbè'gùi nọ̀ yẹ́'mátọ̀n sẹ́wù àmáwé ọ́khọ́khọ́ nọ̀ yígán há-àn.*
(If the iron-clad tortoise succumbs to fire, what chance has the chicken dressed in flimsy feathers?)

83. *Ẹ̀mwẹ̀n rhé 'ghádè dó rió'vbímwẹ̀n'.*
(There is bound to be a hidden motive behind [the words] 'come and marry my child'.)

84. *Èno suá'bẹ́-e ókhókhó eságiẹ̀n ẹ̀rọ́ yá hárè ósá.*
(Whoever strikes a knife's blade with his bare knuckle must expect to pay with his own blood.)

85. *Ẹ́i rèvbé ná yá mú ẹ̀rá yá sọ̀e.*
(It is not necessarily how one starts that one must end.)

86. *Ái hín èrhẹ́nhiẹ́n kọ́lọ́ ẹ̀hiẹ̀n, tá khián lẹ́gá rè.*
(You harvest pepper fruit by walking round the pepper tree, not by climbing it.)[3]

87. *T'ẹ́rhuẹ̀ rhié'bé nẹ́ghairè ẹ̀rhú ẹ̀rè ná tàn.*
(It is because the deer ate the leaves it should never have eaten that its neck became elongated.)

88. *Ọ̀vbókhàn nọ́ muósísí dèdè ẹ̀rọ́ gbé egbẹ̀'rè.*
(The child who dares kiss the cannon asks to be blown to pieces.)[4]

89. *Ùnú ẹ̀rọ́ sì'ọmwàn fí ẹ́tìn.*
(It is [word of] mouth that drags one into trouble.)

90. *Ẹ̀mwẹ̀n dán ẹ̀rọ́ miú'bí giẹ́'họ̀.*
(It is careless talk that earns a blow to the [speaker's] ear.)

---

[3] Anyone who knows what a pepper tree looks like knows that it cannot support even the weight of a child. It cannot therefore be climbed by an adult. To climb the tree in order to pick the pepper fruit is to destroy it, thus destroying a valuable commodity.

[4] When the Edo tell one how to handle 'joy' and 'happiness', etc. they are not necessarily playing the 'kill-joy', but they believe that 'human joy has a slender body which breaks easily.' Human joy is never permanent; it is made, it breaks and has to be remade only to break again.

151

91. *Ámá gbíná fó nè, ái rèn vbé nó'tò mósè hè.*
(It is only after fighting that one realises how beautiful the [battle] ground is.)

92. *Tá nò èhò áté ghá fièrú'bì.*
(Before slapping an ear, it must first be consulted.)[5]

4. On Pride and Prejudice

93. *Èmwìn nà mwèn èráyá ghághà. Oní èró zè – e nè èlédé ná sù'hèrè raè nà'gbòn ghá ghè.*
(It is what one has that one shows off. Hence the pig leaves its anus open for the world to look at.)[6]

94. *Èkò nó gúe'vbàrè, éi gúe'míamwèn.*
(A stomach that is filled with food has no room for illness.)

95. *Èké nó gúe'má, èró vbê guè nò kpè'rè.*
(Where there is room for the drum, there must also be room for the drummer.)

96. *Omó èró r'ôyénmwínyè, vbé no'bí r'òyénmwén ìvbièkpò, vbé n'ókhuò r'ò yénmwén òdòrè.*
(A child is the joy of his mother just as poison is the joy of the rattlesnake and a wife is the joy of her husband.)

97. *Aí mí'yó bá ná yá gbí'yó mwá-àn.*
(Having seen the mother of a king, one doesn't go home and murder one's own [mother].)

---

[5] A woman carelessly throws out water from her cooking-pot, little realising that something will germinate on the spot on which the water has been thrown. Forethought is the mother of caution, which is the mother of moderation and to possess the one is to possess the other – all to human benefit. Thus caution demands that before any action is taken one must consider its possible consequences. But, since 'what is said too frequently loses its value', it is well to remember that 'If life is a game, it must be played according to governing rules.'

[6] If one accepts and cherishes what one possesses, one is unlikely to become envious of what others possess. If one is hard up enough to wander into the forest in search of snails and if, during a leisurely walk, one finds a snail on the wayside, one will pick it up, counting one's blessings for an unexpected bonanza.

98. *Aí mú èní yán ùhúnmwùn nà vbè yó'wẹ ghá tọnọ̀ àsẹ́lẹ́.*
    (No one carries a dead elephant on his head and still digs
    for a cricket with his toe.)[7]

99. *Ònì - î - gbà'ghè àmẹ̀.*
    (The cold-water pot does not feel any cold.)

100. *Ènọ́ mí ùhé rù ẹ̀rọ́ mié'nètó - î - yè.*
     (It is only the man who has access to coitus who may com-
     plain about the absence of pubic hair.)

101. DIALOGUE BETWEEN A MOTHER AND HER IMMATURE SON.

A little boy once ran home to complain to his mother.

Little boy: Mother, I will never again go out to play.
Mother: Why so, my son?
Little boy: Because my playmates laugh at me for not
being able to run as fast as a hare.
Mother: If *Òsánóbuá* intended that you should run as
fast as a hare, *Òsánóbuá* would have created
you a hare, not a human being.
Little boy: Then, *Òsánóbuá* hasn't made a mistake?
Mother: No, my son. *Òsánóbuá* never makes mistakes.
Little boy: So, I'm okay as I am?
Mother: Yes, my darling, you are perfectly okay as you
are.
Little boy: But what should I tell my friends when they
laugh at me next time?
Mother: Next time they laugh at you, ask them what
they would do to a cripple who cannot even
walk as you do, let alone run.
Little boy: Because a cripple cannot even walk, let alone
run.
Mother: That is correct. And what is more: tell them
that

---

[7] It is greed that leads to discontentment in life. A dead elephant is big enough
to supply plenty of meat. Yet, having secured a dead elephant, the greedy person,
on carrying it home, still stops on the way to dig for a mere cricket with his
toe. The cricket, presumably, is meant to supply additional meat to that of the
elephant.

102. *Àghà miènámásè̩, ùwú – î – gia wu.*
(When we encounter someone who is worse off than we are, we are forced to abandon the thought of committing suicide.)

Little boy: There's always someone worse-off than we are?
Mother: Of course, darling. After all

103. *Ái mièno̩ fó nà.*
(No one is perfect.)

Little boy: Even my friends who can run as fast as a hare are not perfect?
Mother: No, my dear, they are not perfect.
Little boy: But they will still laugh at me.
Mother: Let them laugh because

104. *Èno̩ wénà ghé̩ gí'rè̩n, è̩ro̩ wé ná ví'rè̩n.*
(He who does not want to be laughed at has asked to be wept over.)

Little boy: So, I must just stay as I am?
Mother: Just stay as you are. That is the way *Òsánóbuá:* meant you to be. And

105. *Vbé nò'rìnmwìn yè èriá fín ídíe̩n rè̩n.*
(A grave is dug only according to the size of the corpse.)

106. *Àgbò̩n – î – mà, è̩rínmwín – î – mà, íhè ógièhà – î – rho̩.*
(The world is bad, heaven is not good, but we have no third choice.)

107. *Èkhèrhèkèrhè è̩rá'me̩ yá lá òkpàn ná'má fián.*
(It is by slow degrees that water seeps into an uncut gourd.)

108. *Déghá'má múfuá, ái mìe̩n rhie.*
(If one doesn't lose, one cannot expect to win.)

109. *Ewin'Òsà khàrè è̩ro̩ rò'de̩.*
(*Òsánóbuá*'s will is the only correct way.)

110. *Ái múa ẹ̀mwẹ́n Òsà.*
   (There's no disputing God's word.)

111. *Úwọ́nmwèn íy'ọ́mọ̀ ẹi khọ̀ mọ̀ ùnú.*
   (A mother's soup is never tasteless in her child's mouth.)

The Ẹ̀dó's contentment, illustrated by the above proverbs, is the product of a deep-seated and all-embracing belief and faith in Òsánóbuá (the 'God Almighty' to whose existence 'Europeans' tend to put claims of ownership). The Ẹ̀dó firmly believe that Òsánóbuá is the creator of everything and everybody, and that Òsánóbuá is the father of all, regardless of place or condition of birth, status in life, creed or whatever. Their faith in Òsánóbuá is such that they actually thank him for evil as well as for good. They know that if they are grateful for good fortune, they must also be grateful for misfortune – both of which they believe to be controlled by Òsánóbuá. Thus, they can 'meet with Triumph and Disaster', as Kipling would have it in his poem 'If', 'And treat those two impostors just the same.' Indeed, faced with misfortune, the Ẹ̀dó believe that it has been sent for the purpose of preventing the affected person from greater danger or even death.

Perhaps the clearest evidence of their belief and faith in Òsánóbuá lies in the names that they give to their newborn babies. Any Ẹ̀dó name that begins with Òsà is directly linked to Òsánóbuá. The Ẹ̀dó concept of Òsánóbuá, furthermore, is closely bound to their concept of Ẹ̀hì (the so-called alter ego, for want of a better term). Their story of creation, which is told in Chapter 2, explains that Òsánóbuá creates human beings individually, which accounts for individual differences in the world. That story contains the details of the link between Òsánóbuá and Ẹ̀hì, and that link is vital to the attitude of the Ẹ̀dó to human beings and their destinies, from which God is never excluded. Thus, it makes sense to say that:

112. *Ẹ̀hì ẹ̀rọ́ z'ógié.*
   (It is destiny that decides prosperity.)

113. *Ẹ̀hì má mi'éghó, éi gi'ọ̀bó gbè.*
(Unless destiny permits it, no magical power can hurt /
harm one.)

114. *Vbé ná hí, èrhiá dè.*
(We all end up exactly according to the dictates of our
destinies.)

5. On the Self and Others: the Concept of Fairness

Among the Ẹ̀dó, *Ùhúnmwùn* (literally 'head') and *Ẹ̀hì* ('destiny') are somewhat synonymous, indeed coeval. This makes
some 'scientific' sense, since all the *thinking* that affects human
life goes on in the head. On the other hand, both *Ẹ̀hì* and
Ùhúnmwùn are closely linked with what is generally referred to
as 'luck'. Thus when a person is 'lucky' he is said to possess a
'good head' or a 'good *Ẹ̀hì*'.

Ẹ̀hì / Ùhúnmwùn has an enormous influence on the Ẹ̀dó
concept of fairness in relationships between an individual and
others. Since every person is endowed with an *Ẹ̀hì* (is *destined*),
the Ẹ̀dó believe in the action of 'live and let live'.

115. *Aí z'ẹ̀hí n'ọ́mọ́.*
(No one chooses his child's destiny.)

Everyone chooses his / her own *Ẹ̀hì* independently of everyone
else. The chooser is bound to live according to his / her own
choice and nobody and nothing on earth can alter that. Such
rigid *fatalism* points, in fact, towards various forms of permis-
siveness. At the same time, fairness that is lived rather than
preached is of great importance. Fairness is as integral to daily
life as that life is integral to religion in those who live religious-
ly. As such,

116. *Èmwín nái ruẹ́rè, ghẹ́ rú ọmwàn rè.*
(Never do to anyone what you would not like done to
you.)

117. *Ènáìká vẹ́n, ẹ́i ká vọ́n ọmwàn.*
(One who would not be cursed should never curse.)

Although every individual has the right to be him / herself, the

distinction between a right and a privilege is well established
and is a sure guide to the relationship between one person and
another. Thus when the Ẹ̀dó say

118. Èmwìn nẹ́igiá fiàn, ẹ̀rẹ́ giá gháè.
(The only thing that cannot be cut up or divided is the
thing that cannot be shared.)

they are actually demonstrating the concept of 'live and let live'.
It expresses their personal contentment, among other things,
and establishes the basis of interpersonal relationships. It also
sets the stage for the fight against selfishness and greed, For,

119. Ínú ẹ̀vbò ọ̀rhé Òkẹ́kpẹ̀n, ná ná gbẹ̀'wè ẹ̀và nọ̀ má gbà
òbọ́.
(What is the population of Okekpen [a village] such that
two slaughtered stags cannot go round?)

It is selfishness and greed that will prevent a group of people
from sharing and sharing alike. But, for the Ẹ̀dó, 'sharing alike'
is based upon *seniority*, which is highly respected: the older
person takes a larger share than the younger person and is
always the first to receive his / her portion. The youngest person
in every group, therefore, looks forward to becoming old – that
hope is itself a strong motivator, although it does not lead to
any inordinate ambition. The Ẹ̀dó have a great deal of respect,
bordering on reverence, for old age. As they say

120. Ùhúnmùvun ọ̀diọ́n – î – mà vbó'khókhó.
(The head of an elderly person is not meant for knocks.)

Plato could not have failed to realize that death and birth are
the two phenomena that, together, restore balance to Nature. In
this respect, the ancient Greeks (of Plato's day) and the ancient
Ẹ̀dó (at least until their 'dusk') 'spoke the same language' (and
'science' ignores that language at its peril).

   In the *Republic*, Plato relates the during-death and after-
death story of *Er* who died in battle but was not buried for 12
days. His body was eventually placed on a funeral pyre; but,
just as the pyre was about to be set alight, *Er* returned to life
and sat up (the story of the woman, *Ùgi'ọ́mọ̀* in Chapter 10),

probably looking rather bewildered. He then proceeded to report as follows:

> Each soul, as it arrived (in the other world) wore a travel-stained appearance . . . and those who had descended from heaven were questioned by those who had risen out of the earth; while the latter were questioned by the former about earth. The souls about to enter earth life were thus addressed: 'A new generation of men shall here begin the cycle of its mortal existence. Your destiny shall not be allotted to you, but you shall choose it for yourself . . .' It was truly a wonderful sight to watch how each soul selected its life. The experience of their former life guided their choice . . . It so happened that the soul of Odysseus had drawn the last lot of all. The memory of his former suffering had so abated his ambition that he went about a long time looking for a quiet, retired life, which [had been] thrown contemptuously aside by others. He chose it gladly . . . Now, when all the souls had chosen their lives . . . they took up their quarters by the bank of the River-of-Indifference . . . each as he drinks forgets everything . . . In a moment, the souls were carried up to their birth, this way and that, like shooting stars. (see *The Probability of the Impossible*)

There is a remarkable similarity between this narrative and the Èdó story about reincarnation. For a start, Plato's 'River-of-Indifference' is what the Èdó call Èzè ní mìmìkpọ́, which occupies the boundary between heaven and earth. Then there is the issue of 'destiny', which is chosen by oneself, not allotted. The dialogue between the newcomer in heaven and those who are already resident has already been compared to the story of Ùgi' ọ́mọ̀. Finally, the Èdó also believe that souls are 'carried up to their birth, this way and that, like shooting stars'. And when a great man dies, his passing is marked by the appearance of shooting stars in the night sky; the greater he is, the more numerous and the brighter and larger are such stars.

Once Èzè nímìmìkpọ́ has been crossed, we forget what choice we have made, which has been sanctioned by Òsánóbuá and can never be altered on earth. This belief is called fatalism, and it is present at the core of all religions and in all faiths.

One of the vexing questions raised by the belief in fatalism is this: would any rational person deliberately choose a life of hardship, pain and suffering in preference to its opposite? The answer offered by the Ẹdó is that at the point of choosing one's destiny, such value-judgments as 'good' or 'bad / evil', 'beautiful' or 'ugly', 'sweet' or 'bitter' do not exist. One's choice, in other words, is not based on any judgmental or ethical system. Like babies, we are not guided by any standards. On the contrary, we choose, as children do, as our immediate fancies dictate. It is only those who have been through a previous life, like Odysseus in Plato's story about *Er*, who are guided by their previous experiences. And this is where the so-called alter-ego (the Èhì) plays its correcting part.

This is where any mortal errs when s/he prays for this, that and the other. It is a prayer that no one hears because there is no one to hear it. Someone, therefore, who is not *destined* to be wealthy in life may pray for wealth until doomsday without becoming wealthy in life. And here the ancient Greeks, like the ancient Romans and the ancient Ẹdó, found little justification for the institution of slavery, for example, and for their ideas about social stratification: slaves, they believed, were *born*, not made. It was on this ground that John Knox justified his so-called 'Doctrine of the Calling', which counselled that one should accept one's station in life, regardless of what that station may be. That attitude may be said to inhibit ambition; but ambition, it has been claimed, is the sin by which the angels fell. The evidence of that surrounds us all today.

Among the Ẹdó, therefore, fairness towards one's neighbours is based upon a deep psychological orientation which is the direct product of the racial memory of the people. In modern times, the biologist, Jacques Mond, has articulated this point in an insightful manner:

> Everything comes from experience; yet not from actual current experience, reiterated by each individual new generation, but instead from the experience accumulated

by the entire ancestry of the species in the course of its evolution . . . In systematically confronting logic with experience, according to the scientific methods, we are, in fact, confronting all the experience of our ancestors with our own . . . Every living being is also a fossil. Within it, all the way down to the microscopic structure of its proteins, it bears the traces if not the stigmata of its ancestry. (see *Chance and Necessity – an Essay on the Natural Philosophy of Modern Biology*, 1972))

Thus, in the concept of fairness, as the Ẹ̀dó see it, 'one cannot defecate on the path as one passes along it and yet not expect to be mobbed by flies on one's return journey along the same path'. The only solution to that problem is that one does not return by the same path, if one returns at all. And, as the Ẹ̀dó would say, one who wishes to return to the world must ensure that he / she does not defecate on the path that leads to heaven.

The call to be fair to others is connected with the acceptance of poetic justice, which in Hinduism and Buddhism is referred to as the Law of Karma. The Ẹ̀dó say that one who does not wish to step on water should never pour water on his own doorstep. And one who does not wish to be born maimed must never maim anyone during his / her lifetime. It is based on a rationality that looks both ways – to the before and after. In other words, the Ẹ̀dó, whether acting or merely reacting, are constantly conscious of consequences – consequences to themselves as well as to others. Hence, as they frequently say,

121. Àmẹ̀ ghà sí'híọn tọ́ghá sè'gbè.
(Once bath-water reaches the sponge, it is bound to reach the [bather's] body.)

6. On The Self and Others: the Family and Child-rearing

Anthropologists (ethnographers, in particular) over the last hundred years or more, have been misled by the so-called scientific pronouncements of universal psychology into typologies that aim at distinguishing between superior and inferior child-rearing practices. With perhaps the single exception of Margaret Mead, they have assumed that the child-rearing practices of the 'civilized' European are superior to those of the 'primitive' African, including the Ẹdó. Consequently, the former must undertake to 'educate' the latter, that education being based on the presumption that all human societies are psychologically the same. To use a single, perhaps inadequate, instance, it has been presumed that Freud's concept of the Oedipus Complex is a universal human problem. However, even if that concept is valid among the pre- and post-Freudian Europeans, it is unknown and non-existent among the Ẹdó.

Given the Ẹdó creation myth, the relationship between the child and its parents is grounded in a psychology of a type that is totally different from European psychology. First, Ẹdó parents do not claim to own their children. The Almighty (Òsánóbuá) alone owns the child, making the parents nothing more than custodians of their children. There is a logical and psychological validity to this situation, and it is as follows: it is the child, at its creation, who chooses its parents. To that choice, the Almighty gives assent, witnessed by the Ẹhì. Therefore, second, the chosen parents are grateful to the child (directly) and to the Almighty (indirectly) for choosing them as parents. Third, the 'love' of the parents for the child is expressed through the *feeling of responsibility* that the parents must bear for the child and to the Almighty. And fourth, the child, being the chooser rather than the chosen, is duty-bound to respect and honour the chosen parents. By choosing them, the child has committed him / herself to take care of them when it becomes necessary to do so (in old age, for example). For at the parents own time of choosing, they chose to be parents to children who would, in time, take care of them. Otherwise, they would have chosen to live childless.

With regard to the structure of the Ẹdó family, much has been said and written about 'the extended family', a great deal of which stands up to no examination. The traditional Ẹdó family is polygamous. And contrary to European speculations about the reasons behind the practice of polygamy, it is not because the traditional Ẹdó needs many wives for the purpose

161

of cheap labour on the farm or in the household. It is the man, and his male children and his neighbours who work on the farm while the wives and daughters stay at home to cook, wash, clean and care for the children. In this regard, there is a rigid division of labour between men and women and that division is sanctioned by the traditional law.

However, the structure of the family is analogous to the natural ordering of the heliocentric universe: the man (father) is the sun around which revolve the women (other 'planets'), around which revolve the children ('moons'). Each mother in the Ẹ̀dó polygamous family is immediately surrounded by her brood of children with whom she is directly in contact. All children born to the same mother are naturally expected to be closer to one another than to their half-brothers / sisters. Hence,

122. Òbví'erhá wé gí'ẹdẹ́ gbè; òvbí'yé wé'ké nọ́ sẹ́ ìrèn lèlẹ̀-e
    sẹ́.
    (Whereas the half-brother / sister may wish to wait until daybreak [for action to be taken], the full brother / sister insists on going the whole way, regardless of weariness.)

The woman is more directly in touch with her children's father than the children can ever aspire to be. She is a conduit by which the children reach their father. Hence, in many cases, the children of the favourite wife receive, usually indirectly, greater attention from their father than many of their siblings. Indeed, it is said that

123. Òhàmwẹ̀n – î – gbè n'íyẹ́-e rú'kònì.
    (One whose mother is in the kitchen never feels the pangs of hunger.)

Cooking for the entire family is shared among the women in the harem. The women take turns in the family kitchen although, when not so engaged, each woman may feed her own children from her private cooking-pot. The raw material for the family kitchen is provided in cash or in kind by the father. Thus it is inevitable that the favourite wife, having easier and greater access to the husband's available resources, is in a position to secure a greater supply of food and money than those who are less favoured. Here, surely, one sees the analogy with the helio-centric universe: the planets that are closer to the sun receive greater amounts of light and heat from the sun, and the 'moons' depend largely on the planets around which they revolve for the sun's light and heat.

Given the above description of the structure of the traditional Ẹdó family, it is possible to understand more clearly the 'psychology' that informs the relationship between children and their parents. As the following saying reveals,

124. Ẹ̀kó ẹ̀yẹ̀n ẹ̀r'ẹ̀yẹ̀n ná rí'obí.
(It is from a snake's womb that its offspring acquires its poison.)

The family is, metaphorically at least, a womb to all the children in it. But in the traditional Ẹdó family, the mother is generally held responsible for the behaviour of her children; when that behaviour is acceptable to the neighbours, the child is the pride of both his / her parents. On the other hand, if the behaviour is unacceptable to the neighbours it is largely the mother who takes the blame.

The child's behaviour reflects on the family of his / her origin and is also a strong indicator in assessing the nature of that family itself. A 'bad' child is the image of a 'bad' family. And this is a deciding factor in young people's choice of husbands or wives. One is known by the company one keeps; and one's first-ever 'company' is one's family.

125. Ẹkpẹ́kpẹ́yẹ́ î – mà ovbìẹrè àkhuẹ̀.
(The duck, like the drake, does not need to teach its duckling how to swim.)

The mother, in particular, and the family, in general, represent the 'duck' while the child is the 'duckling'.

126. Èkhuè – Î – mù òyì vbè nọ̀ mùọ 'ti'ọ́nrẹ̀n.
(The thief caught in the act is never as ashamed as the members of his / her family.)

127. Ọ́gh'ọ́mwàn ẹ̀rá ghè vb'ùghè.
(It is one's own dancer that one admires in a collective dancing occasion.)

128. *Àrèn ègbè ẹ̀rọ́ má giá tòn òfẹ́n òwá rè.*
(It is familiarity that prevents one from eating a house-mouse.)

It is practically impossible to be more familiar with anyone than a member of one's family. It is to that familiarity that the traditional *Ẹ̀dó* owe their legendary family solidarity. One may privately chastise an erring member of one's family; but never in public.

129. *Ái wè ùhé òmwàn fíẹrú'bì.*
(No one openly exposes his / her buttocks in order to slap them.)

130. *Ọmwàn nọ́ w'írẹ̀n – î – khúan nọ̀ 'ọ̀mọ̀ òvbìogùe ẹ̀rọ́ wú yí.*
(Anyone who refuses to provide for his / her children, will die in poverty.)

131. *Ùkpọ́'khọ́khkọ́ – î – gbò'vbìẹrè.*
(The beak of a mother hen does not kill the chick.)

Early in life, the child in the *Ẹ̀dó* family begins to receive verbal and non-verbal teaching from its mother that is to last through its lifetime. Punishing children, whatever the age, for misbehaviour is a common practice in the traditional *Ẹ̀dó* family, where the child is never spoilt and the rod is never spared. Yet punishment is never indiscriminate, mindless or malicious.

132. *Ái khú ọ̀mọ̀dán nẹ̀'kpẹn gbèrè.*
(One does not chase a naughty child into the jaws of a tiger.)

133. *Òbọ́ náyá gb'òvbí ọ̀mwàn, ẹ̀rá yạ sìẹ̀kẹ̀ ègbè.*
(It is the hand with which one smacks one's child that one employs in petting him / her.)

134. *Gbo'vbimwẹ̀n mẹ̀, òkpú'nù – ọ̀ – yè; ghẹ́ gbèmwẹ̀n ruà, ọ̀ró tọ́ íbíẹ.*
('Beat my child for me' is a request from the lips only; 'don't kill my child' is a cry from the heart.)

The care and attention with which parents (especially mothers) treat their children must be reciprocated by the children. Thus, for example,

135. *Úwónmwèn ìy'òmò –êi – kh̀ọmò ùnù.*
(A mother's soup is never tasteless in a child's mouth.)

136. *Ìsán érhá – î – wía sù òmò.*
(The child does not turn up his / her nose at his / her father's excrement.)

Among the traditional Èdó the 'good' child never runs into the street when being chastised indoors.

137. *Aí yà'góbò giè òwé'rhó mwàn.*
(One does not point out one's father's house with one's left hand.)

Among the traditional Èdó, there are taboos attached to the use of limbs. There is, for example, a big difference between the right hand and the left. The left hand is identified with dirt and evil and is never permitted to be placed on anyone's head, the latter being considered as sacred. Thus, as in the above saying, to point the left hand at one's father's house is an abomination: it indicates great disrespect to one's father. It is the left hand that is used to handle things such as women's menstrual flow and human excrement, and anything that is despised and rejected. On the other hand, the right hand is the hand of friendship. It is the hand used to put food into the mouth. It is the hand that is used to pet and soothe. It is the hand that is placed on the head of another person for whom one has respect and affection. What is true of hands is also true of feet. In a culture in which people carry their shrines on their persons, the right toe, for example, represents the mother's shrine on which libation may be poured anywhere at any time; while the left toe represents the father's shrine for the same purpose.

Interestingly – and perhaps understandably – the right hand is referred to as 'Ób'íyé' (mother's hand) while the left hand is referred to as 'Ób'érhá' (father's hand); the left foot is referred to as 'Ów'érhá' (father's foot) while the right foot is referred to as 'Ów'íyé' (mother's foot).

Afterword

The Origins of the Name 'Benin'

I cannot tell you my AGE if all you wish to know is
the number of years I carry on my back from the moment
I screamed forth from my mother's womb without any account
taken of the period I spent inside the amniotic ocean.

(Iro Eweka, *Black Boy in Search of Life*)

THIS FINAL STORY in this book straddles the very old and the very modern in Ẹdó history. Ẹdó has not always been called Ẹdó, nor has it always been known as *Benin*. Its oldest name was, apparently, Igodomigodo, a name which no one, not even my own parents, knows the meaning of the origin.

The first dynasty was dominated by kings known, individually, as Ògìsó ('sky king'), a title that sought to give credence to the divinity of the king. Each Ògìsó had his own personal (given) name, but when he became king he became known as Ògìsó. Thus the title existed rather like the title of Pharaoh by which a succession of ancient Egyptian kings were known. No one knows exactly how many Ògìsó there were. But it is claimed that there were between nine and twelve of them (J.U. Agharevba places the number at eleven[1]) altogether. What is known is that the last Ògìsó in that dynasty was Ówódó.

Ówódó had one son, Prince Ekaladerhan. He was a handsome and high-spirited young man, well liked by all the people

[1] Jacob U. Egharevba, *A Short History of Benin* (Ibadan: Ibadan University Press, 1934, new edition, 1968).

166

and the apple of his father's eye. Ekaladerhan was strong and athletic, wayward without being offensive or disrespectful to his father or his father's chiefs and attendants. He would join his father's cattle-men and chase cows all over the backyards in the harem. He could jump and run as well as the next person; and given half a chance, he would outswear any trooper. He was kind and gentle, too, especially to the elderly, the poor and the children, all of whom were beneficiaries of his generosity. Ekaladerhan was easily the toast of the entire kingdom and women pined secretly and often openly for him. But he remained a virtuous, celibate bachelor.

However, it was during a cattle-chase through the backyards in his father's harem that something happened that changed his whole life and the history of the kingdom. This, of course, was the fulfilment of his destiny.

The prince was loudly urging his companions to follow him. He was enjoying the fun of the chase when, suddenly, he stopped dead in his tracks. He was transfixed by what he saw. It was a woman, standing naked behind her own house in the harem, taking a bath. Prince Ekaladerhan was completely dazed by her shimmering beauty and heavenly comeliness, exaggerated by the water gently flowing over her frame and sending out sparkles of silver and gold and rich rubies all around her. Unable to resist his impulse, he rushed forward like a hurricane, swept the naked woman off her feet and carried her, kicking and screaming, to his own section of the palace where he ravished her and kept her prisoner. He did not even stop to ask who or what she was. But, as it turned out, she was his father's newest and most favoured bride.

Sensational reports soon reached Ówódó. The king was so enraged and racked with jealousy and bitterness that he ordered the immediate arrest of his only son and successor to the throne. Had the prince been any other man, his head would have been struck off his trunk without the slightest argument. What he had done was an abomination, according to the laws of the kingdom. But, being the king's son, it would also have been an abomination to put him to death. Ówódó, in consultation with his horrified court, did the next best thing that could be thought

167

of. He banished the prince, not only from the palace but from the kingdom. Then he made the law, which was still in force until recent years, that never again were princes to be allowed access to the king's harem.

The day Ekaladerhan left the ancient city was a sad and depressing day. There was neither rain nor sunshine. To this day, such a day is called Ekaladerhan's Day (*ẹd'ékáládèrhàn*). The city was thrown into gloom. He was sorely missed.

The exiled prince entered the jungle and headed south. He travelled for months until he emerged among the Yorubas in a city called *Ìfẹ̀*, which the *Ẹ̀dó* later corrupted to *Ùhẹ̀*. The Yorubas showed him tremendous kindness and hospitality. They took him to their own king who treated him with great generosity. It was strictly up to him to keep his penis under control in a foreign country and he did just that. He lived peacefully and happily among the Yorubas and learned their language and their ways. (Later his relationship with the Yoruba king was to be like that of Joseph and the Egyptian Pharoah.) The Yorubas called the exiled prince from Igodomigodo, Oranyan (probably 'The Gorgeous' or 'The Magnificence') which was later corrupted by the *Ẹ̀dó* to Oranmiyan. And on that happy note the story might have ended. But destiny decreed otherwise.

For who should turn up through the jungle at *Ọ̀ràn(mi)yàn*'s court but Tortoise. Tortoise was extremely well received by *Ọ̀ràn(mi)yàn*'s servants and was soon presented to their master who displayed great courtesy and bestowed great generosity on his visitor. But although, after so many moons, the prince did not recognise Tortoise, the inimitable Tortoise did recognise the prince, despite showing no sign of that recognition.

After a long stay, Tortoise returned home. His journey just happened to coincide with the demise of *Ówódó*, leaving no heir to the throne. This threw the elders into chaos and confusion. And it was at that precise moment of crisis that Tortoise made his appearance from the jungle. Tortoise counselled the elders to go south where they would find the successor they sought.

When the elders arrived in *Ìfẹ̀* / *Ùhẹ̀* and consulted the

Yoruba king, His Majesty reluctantly returned Ọ̀ràn(mí)yàn to them, and they took him back home and crowned him. But he didn't know their language and he found their manners irritating and their customs incomprehensible to an annoying degree. Having done the best he could, he succumbed to anger and decided to return to the Yoruba land. He renamed Igodomigodo, calling it Ilẹ-Ibinu (land of vexation), later corrupted to Ubini and further corrupted to Bini and later still to Benin. In fact, until recently, the Ẹdó were otherwise called the Binis. Ọ̀ràn(mí)yàn returned to Yoruba land but not before fathering a child by the beautiful daughter of the chief of Use. The birth of a boy gladdened the hearts of the elders of Ubini / Bini / Benin because now they had a successor to the throne that Ọ̀ràn(mí)yàn had vacated in anger. But, to their horror, they found that the successor could not speak. How could they crown a dumb king? They rushed back to Ìfẹ̀ / Ùhẹ̀ to consult the boy's father. He gave them the now-famous ákhúẹ. They returned home with a bag full of the charmed seeds with which they managed to persuade the boy-king to play.

It was during one of the ákhúẹ games that the child spoke his first word, ọwọ̀míká, which was his father's (Yoruba) word for 'my hand has grabbed everything'. Indeed, his hand had grabbed the throne vacated by his father. It was with the title, Ówọ̀ míká that the Ẹdó kingmakers crowned him, later corrupting it to Ẹ̀wẹ̀ká. He was the founder of the second dynasty which has remained unbroken to this day and of which the present king, Érédiáuwà, is the thirty-eighth king in the same line of succession. Ùbíní / Bíní / Benin remained the name of the city and kingdom until Ẹwuare the Awesome ascended the throne some 300 years later. It was Ẹwuare who changed the name of the city and kingdom to Ẹdó (see the story in Chapter 8, above).

A Personal Note

What follows is purely speculative and should be viewed separately from the rest of the book.

If we allow an average of 50 years per generation of Ẹ̀dó kings, the Second Dynasty came into existence about 1900 years ago. In other words, Ẹ̀wẹ́ká became king in or around the year 95 AD. And if we allow the same 50 years for nine rather than 12 Ògìsós of the First Dynasty, we reach 450 years. That would mean that Igodomigodo was a flourishing place with a well-defined order of kingship, some 2,350 years ago, i.e., since 355 BC. The Ògìsós, then, were contemporaries of the likes of Alexander the Great (356–323 BC) and Archimedes (297–212 BC). Further, if the Second Dynasty was inaugarated around 95 AD, Ẹ̀wẹ́ká I reigned 201 years before Athanasius and lived 455 years before Mohammed, the founder of Islam.

There is some argument in my own mind about the British takeover of the Ẹ̀dó, not just the kingdom. The latter was historically inevitable. The British fought the Ẹ̀dó and won in 1897. I can never forget that fact. But what I do not remember is how the British also took the Ẹ̀dó man, woman and child, and squeezed out of them their natural integrity, their cultural pride and their innate humanism. How, I ask myself, did the British do that? Why did the Ẹ̀dó let the British do that? If you knock me down in physical combat, it may mean that you are physically stronger than I am, but it will not necessarily follow that you have won my heart and my soul.

At the end of *Dawn to Dusk*, we see that Ovọnramwẹn secretly envied and admired the 'magic' that had caused his downfall. We also see what his Majesty's Ùhímwẹ̀n was, as reported by the closest person to him in his last years, Ẹ́hiọ́bá herself. And we see that, on his reincarnation, he hoped to learn the white man's magic, in order to beat him at his own game. If His Majesty has since reincarnated, he must be frustrated and disillusioned, because he must have found out by now that the British had no 'magical powers' other than greed, lies and hypocrisy, which enabled them to trick the foolish Ẹ̀dó elders and chiefs who were only interested, as the king himself realised too late, in their own 'liberty' and interests. The freedom to trade with the foreigner already existed. But, as far back as 1688, Olfert Dapper (a Dutchman) wrote that, 'Not everybody [in Benin] is allowed to bargain with the Dutch but only certain people whom the king (Ọba) licenses.' He went on to describe the behaviour of the *'fiadors'* in the warehouse at the trading-port. What emerges clearly is that trade was a royal monopoly, and the 'liberty' for which the Ẹdó elders and chiefs sold their king and, in the process, their ancient kingdom, was motivated by greed and ambition – to trade on their own terms with the foreigners. It was not, however, as though the Ẹdó elders and chiefs were restricted in this respect. Indeed, every city chief was sole governor of a section of the kingdom. He only had to report to the king as a matter of routine, and the king took the chief's word as final. The chiefs and elders prospered by this system.

Let us look now at a little of what various foreigners have written about Benin. In 1968, Alan Ryder wrote that,

> Ọba Ewedo showed his authority by several changes in ceremonies, such as making all chiefs stand in his presence. Other important changes were the building of a new palace apart from the chiefs' compounds and the organisation of chiefs to serve the palace. This became a compli-cated system of men and women devoted to the service of the Ọba. Although many new titles and small changes were introduced into the palace organisation over the centuries, the way it was in the nineteenth century seems very similar to the pattern established by Ewedo.

Here we find some useful insights into the close relationship of the Ẹdó king to his chief as early as 1255 AD. That closeness was maintained for several centuries before the arrival of the British. Ten years after Alan Ryder, Basil Davidson wrote in *Africa Revisited*:

> The coast of Benin was first discovered in the 1470s, but not until 1486 did a Portuguese man, Joao Affonso d'Aveiro, get inland. D'Aveiro attempted to set up friendly relations and trading ties, and in the same year samples of pepper from Benin was 'presently . . . sent to Flanders (Holland) and to other parts, and soon it fetched a great price and was held in high esteem'. Many things about their African business partners surprised the Europeans.

They were astonished at the quality and variety of the goods they had to offer, and at their good business sense. They respected the majesty of the kingdom and city of Benin.

That respect was well earned and remained intact until the arrival of the British, who lacked the decency even to understand the people whose trade they coveted. They had not come to make friends. They had come to bully and to rob, to cheat and to steal. And they succeeded through the connivance of the Ẹ̀dó elders and chiefs. Selling one's 'birthright for a mess of potage' may have some precedence elsewhere, but to do so first and then, later moan that,

Ìmẹ̀ té yàn ụghé
Ìmẹ̀ té yàn ụghé
Ìmẹ̀ té yàn ụghé ní'guọ́bó dẹ̀.

I used to own this boulevard
I used to own this boulevard
Oh! I used to own this boulevard
which I bought from the supernatural!

It is quite astonishing, to put it mildly, and seems peculiar to the Ẹ̀dó. Perhaps more importantly, why are the Ẹ̀dó, long after the dusk of their ancient birthright, continuing to sell what remained of it? The Ẹ̀dó of today is so much less an Ẹ̀dó than the Ẹ̀dó of even 50 years ago. What 'poison' did the British administer to them and how was it administered?

As recently as 1994, a British television team, searching for Ẹ̀dó history, wrote that,

> Benin was a great kingdom, prosperous and sophisticated, which flourished in the forest of what is now Southern Nigeria, during the Middle Ages of Europe and beyond. Its 800-year history lasted from its development in the eleventh and twelfth centuries, through its height from the 1400s to 1600s, to its decline and ultimate seizure by the British in 1897.[2]

[2] Cathy Midwinter, Benin: an African Kingdom (World Wide Fund for Nature, 1994).

172

'Seizure' may be a concept of which the British are proud. But is it also one about which the Èdó should be proud? Can any human being be proud that what naturally belongs to him / her has been seized by someone else? By what 'magic' did the British succeed in 'seizing' not only the Èdó's land and its wealth, but also their minds and their souls and their spirits, so that today, one hundred years after the 'seizure', the Èdó no longer have even a language of their own? True, the British seized Benin kingdom and burned down Benin City. What they took away with them was the material wealth of the land; they also took the Èdó language, there is no evidence that they had any use for it. But perhaps they 'burned' down that as well, along with the mode of dress, the food, the integrity, in short Èdó customs – tradition – culture in the broadest sense of the word. The ancient gods that sustained emotional and spiritual stability and guaranteed moral probity, were also 'burned down' in 1897, or were surrendered shortly afterwards, leaving a vacuum in which every man, woman and child now flounders in search of life's meaning. One looks back, without a touch of nostalgia, and all that one can think of is the mournful song,

> Èrhá – ô
> Ìyé – ô
> rhín rhín
> Ọwà nù'wá wá bọ̀
> Ọwè'gbè mi'úwa'rè . . .

> Father – o
> Mother – o
> long, long ago,
> The house you ordered built
> Has been seized by a strong hand . . .

Nowadays, there are a great many post-mortem compliments about Benin from the grandchildren of those who 'seized' Benin; they inform their contemporaries of Benin's 'vast system of defensive earthworks and moats, the longest in the world',[3] while the Èdó themselves do not (they probably no longer dare)

---

[3] Ibid.

acknowledge the existence of this marvel of human ingenuity, let alone be proud of it, for fear of being classified as 'primitive' and 'superstitious'.

Long ago, in 1702, the Dutch trader, Van Nyendael, wrote that, 'Around Benin City the soil at some distance from the river is extraordinarily fertile; and whatever is planted or sown there grows very well and yields a rich crop . . .'[4]

But, today, the Ẹ̀dó cannot feed himself or his family. He has to depend on every conceivable type of imported and packaged food (some of which has been banned by law from use in the country of its origin). When Van Nyendael wrote that 'Benin is admired for its government, laws and tolerance, for its hospitality, care of visitors, independence and well-organised security,' he should have waited 200 years before singing such praises of a city in which daylight robbery, murder and every vice known to British and American cinema, are now the order of the day. And, again, when Olfert Dapper wrote in 1688 that the Ẹ̀dó 'are people who have good laws and a well-organised judicial system. They live on good terms with the Dutch and other foreigners who come to trade with them and to whom they show a thousand marks of friendship,' he had certainly not yet heard of the British.

Obviously, the Ẹ̀dó that Ovonramwen knew – or thought he knew – was a totally different Ẹ̀dó from the one that now bears the same name. What brought about the change is yet to be carefully and thoroughly investigated. But who is better equipped to carry out such an investigation, the British or the Ẹ̀dó? Long before there was a people called the British, the Ẹ̀dó had evolved a civilization that compared well in every respect with the ancient Egyptian, Greek and Roman civilizations, from which the British begged, borrowed and stole what the Victorians chose to call their own. After a hundred years of imperialist thraldom, it is about time the Ẹ̀dó re-evaluated their position vis-à-vis the 'Europeans'.

Meanwhile, in the words of Alan Ryder, one of those few voices in the wilderness now leading the attempt at that re-evaluation, I want to hope that 'night does not irrevocably fall

[4] Ibid.

upon the world' portrayed in this book. That world is filled to
the brim with personal tragedy and grief. It was not the deposed
Ovọnramwẹn alone who grieved. Everyone in Benin grieved the
loss of a king, a kingdom and an entire way of life that had
existed for centuries.

Expressing this grief, many years after Ovọnramwẹn's arrival
in Calabar, his place of exile, a song was written. It went as
follows:

Èvbákhávbókùnmwẹ̀n, nó Óvbi'Óvọ́nrámwẹ̀n,
érhá wẹ́ dò.
Vbọ́ dó nù dó
Vbọ́'rhìọ́ vbè mién mwún úké gbè,
Vbọ́ 'dó nù dó!
Ákhúankhúan mwẹ̀n ùkpọ̀n ọ́kpá
Nọ́ yá kín'úrhù
Ìmẹ̀ ghá mwẹ́n ọ́ghó mwẹ́n
Tí tètẹ̀-e khián
N'àgbọ̀n gùn mwẹ̀n yìn.

My Evbakhavbokun, daughter of Ovọnramwẹn,
greetings from your father.
Greet me no greetings
For a foreigner has stolen
the dance from beneath my feet,
Greet me no greetings!

The vulture has only one piece of cloth
which he winds round his neck;
When I get my own [piece of cloth]
I shall take good care of it
So that I may live in the world.

Such a dirge transcends the merely sentimental. It is a lament for
the loss of something much greater than the self. And, today,
looking back over the past hundred years, that 'something' is
greater than it was the day the kingdom of Benin fell, with its
king, into foreign hands.

Index

Page references followed by "p" denote a proverb

For Product Safety Concerns and Information please contact our EU
representative GPSR@taylorandfrancis.com
Taylor & Francis Verlag GmbH, Kaufingerstraße 24, 80331 München, Germany